MEN FROM THE BOYS

Tony Parsons is the author of *Man and Boy*, winner of the Book of the Year prize. His subsequent novels – *One For My Baby*, *Man and Wife*, *The Family Way*, *Stories We Could Tell*, *My Favourite Wife* and *Starting Over* were all bestsellers. His first non-fiction title, *Tony Parsons on Life, Death and Breakfast* is out now, in hardback. He lives in London.

Praise for *Men From the Boys*:

'Parsons manages to astutely cut right to the heart of family life' *Woman and Home*

'An accomplished piece of work' *Mail on Sunday*

'It's a remarkable novel, compellingly told' *Mirror*

'The novel's key strength . . . is its basic questioning of assumptions and prejudices which, even 11 years on, has a freshness and daring of its own' *Time Out*

'A fab read giving a man's take on love, relationships and what it really means to be a father' *Grazia*

'As usual life gets worse before it gets better, making for exactly the sort of cathartic emotional rollercoaster read we've come to expect from Parsons' *Glamour*

'Parsons' storytelling is superb and in his depiction of the complex father/son relationship makes this a funny, insightful and unforgettable book' *She*

MEN FROM THE BOYS

Tony Parsons

HARPER

Harper
An imprint of HarperCollins*Publishers*
77–85 Fulham Palace Road,
Hammersmith, London W6 8JB

www.harpercollins.co.uk

Special Waterstone's edition 2010
1

First published in Great Britain by
HarperCollins*Publishers* 2010

Copyright © Tony Parsons 2010

Tony Parsons asserts the moral right to
be identified as the author of this work

ISBN: 978 0 00 741568 7

Set in Garamond 3 by Palimpsest Book Production Limited,
Falkirk, Stirlingshire

Printed and bound in Great Britain by
Clays Ltd, St Ives plc

Mixed Sources
Product group from well-managed
forests and other controlled sources
www.fsc.org Cert no. SW-COC-001806
© 1996 Forest Stewardship Council

FSC is a non-profit international organisation established
to promote the responsible management of the world's forests.
Products carrying the FSC label are independently certified
to assure consumers that they come from forests that are managed
to meet the social, economic and ecological needs
of present and future generations.

Find out more about HarperCollins and the environment at
www.harpercollins.co.uk/green

For my son.
And for my daughter, too.

'I remember everything!' cried Pinocchio. 'Tell me quickly, dear snail, where did you leave my good fairy? What is she doing? Has she pardoned me? Does she still remember me? Does she love me still?'

Carlo Collodi, Pinocchio

part one: *autumn term — the secret language of girls*

one

September. The first day of school. New blue blazers everywhere, leaves and conkers underfoot, but an untouched sky and summer clinging on. And now I thought I understood why my son had been so quiet and preoccupied all through the long holiday. I should have guessed, shouldn't I? Sooner or later, there was going to be a girl.

I had wanted to believe it was just because he was almost fifteen.

I watched my son watching the girl. His face got red just looking at her.

'You could talk to her,' I said. 'You could just walk right up to her and – you know. Talk to her.'

Pat laughed. He watched the girl dawdling by the school gates. Black haired, brown eyed. Laughing, swinging a rucksack stuffed with books. Tall for her age. Radiant in the blue blazer of Ramsay MacDonald Comprehensive School. Surrounded by admirers.

'Talk to her?' he muttered, all polite disbelief, as though I had said, *Levitate, why don't you? The ladies love a bit of levitation. The chicks go crazy when they see a lad who can levitate.* 'Probably not,' he said.

'Is she in your year?' I said.

He shook his head, and a matted veil of blond hair fell over his eyes. He pushed it away with a sigh, the love-sick Hamlet of the local comp.

'No, she's in the year above me.'

So she was fifteen. Or maybe already sixteen. An older woman. I should have guessed he would fall for an older woman.

I watched him fumbling nervously with the Predator football boots that were resting on his lap.

'Do you know her name?' I asked. He took a breath. He swallowed. He brushed some flakes of dried mud from his Ramsay Mac blazer. He did not look at me. He kept looking at her. He was afraid he might miss something.

'Elizabeth Montgomery,' he said.

The eight syllables tripped off his tongue. The way he said them, it was infinitely more than a name. It was a sigh, a prayer, a kiss, a love song. He slumped back in the passenger seat, weak with exhaustion. It had taken a lot out of him, saying Elizabeth Montgomery's name.

'Just talk to her,' I said, and his face burned again at the very thought of it.

He looked at me. 'But what would I say?'

'What do you want to say?'

'I want to tell her . . .' He shook his head, struck dumb, but then it came in a barely audible torrent. 'I want to tell her that she is the most beautiful girl I've ever seen. That her eyes – they shine. They just shine, that's all. Like . . . black fire or something.'

I shifted uneasily in my seat.

'Well, Pat, some of that stuff you might want to save for the second date.'

He was that age where he still believed in the secret language of girls.

The age where you believe that girls speak in an Esperanto that is alien to you – a mere boy, consumed with longing and unworthiness, tongue-tied by youth and yearning.

And I wanted to help him. I really did. I wanted to be the Yoda of love he could turn to. And even if it did not work out with him and Elizabeth Montgomery – if they never fell in love, if he was not the millionaire who shared her wedding day, if she never became the one the angels asked him to recall – then at least I thought I might be able to

4

help him have a conversation with the girl. That did not seem too much to ask.

A distant bell began to ring. Elizabeth Montgomery moved off, the centre of attention in a blue-blazered crowd of boys and girls. It was not just Pat. Everybody loved Elizabeth Montgomery.

I drove him to school every morning. Although by the time they are pushing fifteen you no longer really drive them to school. You drive them close to school and let them walk the rest of the way before you have a chance to embarrass them with kisses, hugs or words of sage advice on the mysteries of attraction. He opened the passenger door.

'You around tonight?' I said.

He pushed his hair out of his eyes. It had grown long over the summer. 'I've got my Lateral Thinking Club after school and then I'm around,' he said. 'What about you?'

'I'm around,' I said. 'But late – there's some black-tie thing. The show's up for an award. Lateral Thinking?'

'You know. Thinking outside the box. Creative thinking. Edward de Bono.'

'Oh right – Edward de Bono. Used to be married to Cher. No, that was Sonny Bono. Before your time.'

'Everybody was before my time,' he laughed, getting out of the car. 'I haven't had my time yet.'

He slammed the door shut and looked at me through the window.

'Enjoy your Lateral Thinking,' I said. 'And talk to her, kiddo. Talk to Elizabeth Montgomery.'

He waved and went. That was my son. Some kids his age were out mugging old ladies for their iPods. But he had his Lateral Thinking Club and his one-way love for Elizabeth Montgomery. I watched him go as the bell faded away.

Parents were still milling around, so I did not look twice at the woman parked directly across from the school gates. In fact, I didn't really look at her once. But then she got out of her car and I saw that she was watching Pat too.

And now I looked.

She was tall, blonde, and a little too thin. Dressed for serious exercise — a dark tracksuit, proper trainers — and a raincoat thrown over the top of her running clothes. Looking a touch unkempt and exhausted, but who doesn't in the aftermath of the school run? Despite the blue September sky, the morning was cold enough for me to see her breath.

I stared straight at her, and straight through her and then we both watched Pat go through the gates, the tail of his white shirt already coming out of his trousers, unfurling like a flag of surrender.

And then I looked at her again and something deep inside me fell away.

Because I always think that it is bizarre — no, I always think that it is unbelievable — that you can love someone, really and truly love someone, and then one day you do not recognise their face.

If you have loved someone, you would think that you would know that face always and forever — wouldn't you? Shouldn't every line of that face be stamped on your heart?

But it is not. Your heart forgets.

Especially after — what? Seven years? Could it really be seven years since I had seen her? Where did seven years go?

She got into her car and as she pulled away she looked at me with a kind of wary interest.

So she felt it too. Who is this stranger?

And by then it was all coming back to me. All of it. Oh yes. She had changed — older, thinner and many miles travelled in worlds that had nothing to do with me — but I remembered Gina.

I remembered loving her more than I had ever loved anyone, and I remembered our marriage and the birth of our son, and I remembered how it felt to sleep by her side. And I remembered how all that was good had gone bad, and how it had hurt so much that I truly believed nothing could ever be good again.

So, yes, now that I came to think of it, she did look vaguely familiar.

*   *   *

We envied families who had had a good divorce.

Families where the love was still intact, despite everything. Families where they remembered every birthday – on the actual day. Families that did not let entire years slip by, entire years just wasted. Families where the absent parent turned up at the weekend on time, stone-cold sober and eager to prove the wise old saying, 'You don't divorce your children.'

But some people do.

So we – my son and I – looked longingly on the families that had had a good divorce.

To us, they were like the family in a commercial for breakfast cereal, an impossible ideal that we could never truly aspire to, a wonderful dream that we could only gawp at with our noses pressed up against the windowpane.

Families that had had a good divorce – they were the Waltons to us. They were the Jacksons. They were the Little Broken Home on the Prairie. They were what we would have loved to have been and what we would never be.

Families that had had a good divorce – we could hardly stand to look at them. Because it was nothing like that for us. Me and my boy.

It never felt like much to ask. A life like other lives. A divorce that could hold its head up high. Some love to remain after the love had flown.

Dream on, kiddo.

Home at midnight. And in a bit of a state.

I had not really touched dinner – rubber chicken for five hundred – so now my stomach was growling and my head was reeling and I was a shade drunker than I had planned to be. My bow tie was coming undone. There was a smear of crème brûlée on the black satin collar of my dinner jacket. Now how the hell did that happen?

It was a school night and Pat should have been tucked up in bed like the rest of the family. But he was sitting at the dining-room table, Japanese homework scattered around him, pushing a fistful of hair out of his eyes as I came into the room with the exaggerated care of the accidental drunk.

He was always mad at me if he thought I had drunk more than I could take.

'Celebrating, are you?' he said, tapping an impatient biro.

I suddenly realised that I was carrying a bag containing a magnum of champagne and – something else. I looked inside. The something else was a shiny gold ear set on a base of glass and chrome. My award. The show's award. I placed both the bottle and the award on the table, careful to avoid Pat's homework.

'Congratulations,' he said, softening a little. 'The show won. You won.' But then he scowled again when he saw me fumbling with the foil on the bottle. Just a nightcap, I thought.

'No show tomorrow?' he said. 'I thought you had a show tomorrow.'

'I'll be all right.'

'And I thought recovering from hangovers became harder as you got older.'

I had removed the foil and now I was easing off the wire. 'So they say.'

'They must be getting really hard for you then,' he said. 'Now you're forty.'

I stopped and looked at him. He had this infuriating smirk on his face. 'But I'm not forty, am I?' I said. 'I'm only thirty-nine and three-quarters.'

He got up from the table. 'You're almost forty,' he said, and exhaled the endlessly exasperated sigh that only a teenager can make. He went off to the kitchen and I put the champagne unopened on the table. It was true. We were on air tomorrow. Opening a bottle at midnight was possibly not the best idea I ever had.

Pat came back with a pint glass of water and gave it to me.

'Dehydration,' I said, trying to worm my way back into his good books. 'My body's dehydrated.'

'And your brain,' he said dryly, and he began collecting

8

his books. I saw that he had been waiting up for me. Then he thought of something. 'Someone called. He wanted you. An old man. He didn't leave a message.'

'That's strange,' I said. 'We don't know any old people, do we?'

'Apart from you, you mean?'

I chugged down some water and followed him as he went around turning off lights, and checking locked doors.

I watched him making sure we were safe, and with my wife and our daughters sound asleep upstairs, for a few moments it felt as though the family had once again boiled down to just the two of us. The last light went out.

I did not mention his mother.

The next day, when he was back from school, we walked to the large expanse of grass at the end of our street.

The recreation ground, it was called with no apparent irony. There was a patch of concrete where some lost civilisation had once built an adventure playground, brimming with swings and slides and seesaws and all manner of wonders. But that was all long gone, destroyed by vandals and health and safety officers, and now the recreation ground was just a place to boot your ball, or take your dog for a dump, or get your head kicked in after dark.

'Three and in?' I said, balancing the football on my forehead, feeling some flakes of dried mud fall away.

Pat was sitting on the grass, lacing his Predator boots. 'Just take shots at me,' he said.

We took off our tracksuit tops, threw them down for goalposts and I smiled as Pat went through some stretching exercises. He was tall for his age, all long-limbed awkwardness, and he always seemed surprised at how far and how fast he had grown. But he looked like what he wanted to be. He looked like a goalkeeper. And I really thought he would make the school team this year but I knew better than to mention it.

Some things are too big to talk about.

I curled a shot at him and he leapt up and snatched it from the air. There was a round of mocking applause and we turned and saw a group of teenagers who had annexed the two benches that were the highlight of the recreation ground. They were maybe a bit older than Pat. Or perhaps just wilder. A couple of girls among a group of boys. One of them was a lot bigger than the rest, built more like a man than a boy, and the shadow of his beard looked all wrong above his Ramsay Mac blazer. They leered at us, roosting on the back of the benches with their feet where their baggy-arsed trousers were meant to go.

Pat rolled the ball out to me and I drove it back at him, low and hard. He got down quickly, his body behind the ball. More applause, and I turned to look at them again. In the fading light, their cigarettes glowed like fireflies.

'That's William Fly,' he said. 'The big one.'

'Just ignore them,' I said. 'Come on.'

Pat threw the ball out to me and I trapped it, took another touch, and banged it back. Pat skipped across his goalmouth and hugged the ball to his midriff. No applause this time, and I looked up to see the little group had wandered off to the knackered strip of shops that lay beyond the recreation ground.

'William Fly,' Pat said. 'He nearly got expelled for putting something down the toilet.'

'What did he put down the toilet?'

'The physics teacher,' he said, bouncing the ball at his feet. 'William Fly is famous.'

He kicked the ball back to me.

'No,' I said, watching it coming. 'Winston Churchill is famous. Dickens. Beckham. David Frost. Justin Timberlake is famous. This guy is not famous. He's just a hard nut.'

'Same thing,' Pat said. 'Same thing when you're at school.'

He was on the balls of his feet, springing around the goalmouth because he saw me flicking up the ball, getting ready to unload my legendary volley. I laughed, happy to be here, and happy to be alone with my son.

The ball came off my instep with a crisp smack. Pat threw himself sideways, stretched at his full length, but he couldn't get to it.

Then he went to get the ball while I ran round in circles in the fading light, trying to avoid what irresponsible dog owners had left behind, my arms held aloft in triumph.

Cyd went to the foot of the stairs and called their names. All three of them. Pat. Peggy. Joni. My kid. Her kid. Our kid. Although after ten years we thought of them all as our kids.

From the kitchen I heard chairs being shoved back from computers, doors slamming, laughter. A high, tiny voice struggling to make its point amid two bigger voices. And then a small herd of elephants – our mob coming down for dinner. Cyd came back and watched me trying to chop up parsley without removing a few fingers.

'Did you tell him yet?' Cyd said.

I shook my head. 'Not yet,' I said. 'The time wasn't right.'

'He has to see her,' she said. 'He has to know she's back. He has to see his mother.'

I nodded. I wanted him to see her. I wanted it to be great.

Cyd poured the pasta into a colander and looked at me through the steam.

'Are you afraid of him getting hurt, Harry? Or are you afraid of losing him?'

'Can't I be afraid of both?'

Our mob came into the dining room. Pat. Peggy. Joni. This was a bit of an event because we rarely ate dinner together.

My radio show, *Marty Mann's Clip Round the Ear*, went on air at ten, four nights a week, so I was usually around for dinner. But at seven Joni had the social life of Paris Hilton, a constant round of playdates and dance lessons. Peggy had a best friend – the kind of giddy, isolationist, all-consuming friendship you have at fifteen – and was often at the friend's house, which wasn't a problem just as long as she observed the curfew. Pat had Lateral Thinking and football. And Cyd's catering business, Food Glorious Food, meant she was sometimes going out to work when everyone else was coming home.

So often, only bits and pieces of the family sat down for dinner together. But not tonight. Tonight we were eating together, and Cyd had made spaghetti meatballs, because it always felt like celebration food. So I naturally felt a spike of irritation when the doorbell rang just as I was about to take off my apron.

Here's one for the show, I thought, as my family began without me. Reasons to be angry, number ninety-three. *Someone ringing your doorbell when you never asked them to.*

There was an old man on my doorstep, eyes bright behind his glasses.

He was short but too broad in the shoulder to be thought of as small. And immaculate – everything about him was smart, in an old-fashioned, Sunday-best sort of way. He was wearing a shirt and tie with a dark blazer and lighter trousers. Clean-shaven and smelling of things that I thought that they had stopped making years ago. Old Spice and Old Holborn.

The neatness of this old man – that's what I noticed most of all. Even at that first moment of seeing him, that was what I saw above everything – that military bearing, tidy and trim and ship-shape to the point of fanaticism.

As though he was on parade, and he would always be on parade.

He blinked at me through his glasses.

'Good evening,' he said, his voice thick with formality and old London, and I wondered what he could possibly be selling that I could conceivably wish to buy. 'I'm looking for Mr Silver.'

'You found him,' I said coldly. I could hear my family eating dinner behind me.

And then the old man laughed at me.

He took me in – the white Ted Baker shoes that I wore to stave off the black day that I bought a pair of slippers, the frayed black jeans from Boss Homme, the floral Cath Kidston apron – and the cheeky old git looked at me as if I was some kind of transsexual.

12

I felt like saying, It's an apron, not a frilly pink dress. What do you wear when you're chopping parsley? But he probably never chopped parsley in his life.

'But you're not Pat Silver,' he said, bristling slightly, and despite the effort to be polite, I could see he had a temper on him. It happens as you get older. You just get grumpier and grumpier. By the time that Marty Mann is that age, he will probably be on the roof of some public building with a high-velocity rifle.

'Pat's my son,' I said, and I could see no connection that this belligerent old hobbit could possibly have to my boy. And then I got it. 'And my dad,' I said, as the ship came out of the mist. 'You're looking for my father, aren't you?' We stared at each other. 'You better come inside,' I said.

'Kenneth Grimwood,' he said, and we shook hands. 'I was in the same mob as your dad.'

He called their outfit his *mob* – the same word I used to describe my family, and I remembered that they were as close as a family, that diminishing band of brothers, those old men who had been Royal Naval Commandos before they were out of their teens.

'We served together,' Ken Grimwood said, as we came down the hall. My family looked up at us from their pasta, as I wondered – do people do that any more? Talk about serving? These days everyone wants to be served.

He stared at them and gave no sign of embarrassment, no sense that he even saw them. 'Your dad and me were in Italy together,' he said. 'Sicily. Salerno. Anzio. Monte Cassino.'

And suddenly I felt a mounting excitement. Because this old man must have been with my father at Elba. Where he won his medal. Where he nearly died.

I remembered my dad taking his shirt off on summer days on English beaches and in our back garden, and people who did not know him staring with horror at the starburst of scar tissue that completely covered his torso. That was from Elba.

I wanted to know all about it. So much had been lost, so

13

much that I would never know. Here was my last link to the past.

'And Operation Brassard,' I said. Oh, I knew all about it. I had read books. I knew everything apart from what had actually happened. What it was like. 'The raid on Elba. You must have been with him at Elba.'

But the old man shook his head. 'No, I didn't make it as far as Elba,' he said, and he stared at my youngest daughter. She had a loose front tooth and was working it with her tongue as she stared back at the old man.

I felt the disappointment flood me. He wasn't at Elba? Then I would never know.

Cyd was on her feet and smiling. She came over to us and shook his hand. Introductions were made. She pointed at our children, told him their names.

'You're having your tea,' Ken said, and I hadn't heard that for years. It was a word from my childhood – when your lunch was your dinner and your dinner was your tea.

Cyd asked him to join us and he took one look at what we were eating and recoiled. For a moment I thought he was going to say something about, 'Foreign muck,' which I also had not heard for a while. But instead he looked at Pat – really looked at him – with a sly smile.

'You're the grandson,' Ken said. 'You're the apple of his eye.' The old man nodded emphatically. 'Named after him, you are. He thinks the sun shines out of your arse.'

A silence settled across the dining room. Not total silence – I realised that Bach's 'Sheep May Safely Graze' was playing on the Bose. Joni covered her face with her hands.

'Arse,' she guffawed. 'The man said arse.'

'No need for you to repeat it, young lady,' Cyd snapped, and our daughter looked at her plate of pasta with wry raised eyebrows.

Ken Grimwood looked at me appraisingly. I was still wearing my Cath Kidston. I quickly pulled it off and tossed it aside. I did not want him to see me in an apron. Even if he wasn't at Elba.

'Our mob are marching,' he said, 'that's why I'm here.'

Then I watched in horror as he took out a pack of cigarettes with a death's head covering most of the packet. Perhaps I imagined it, but I think I heard Cyd's intake of breath.

'Didn't have any Old Holborn in your newsagent,' he told me, as if I was personally to blame. 'The geezer didn't seem to know what I was talking about. Foreign chap.'

The children were all staring at him, their dinner forgotten. They had never seen someone taking out a pack of fags in our house – or any house – before. That twenty-pack of Silk Cuts had the exotic danger of an Uzi, or a gram of crack cocaine, or a ton of bootleg plutonium.

'You know,' Ken said. 'At the Cenotaph. The eleventh hour of the eleventh month of the eleventh day.' He stuck a Silk Cut in his mouth. 'Nearest Sunday, anyway,' he said, fumbling in his blazer for a light. 'What did I do with those Swan Vestas?' he muttered.

My wife looked at me as if she would tear out my heart and liver if I did not stop him immediately. So I took his arm and gently steered him to the back garden.

I sat him down at the little table at the back, just beyond the Wendy House. Through the glass I could see my family eating their dinner. Joni was still laughing at the hilarity of someone saying 'arse' and thinking they could smoke in our house.

And I realised that Ken Grimwood talked about my father in the present tense.

'But he died ten years ago,' I said, afraid he might unravel. 'More than ten years. Lung cancer.'

Ken just looked thoughtful. Then he struck a match, lit up and sucked hungrily on his Silk Cut. I had brought a saucer out with me – we hadn't owned an ashtray since the last century – and I pushed it towards him.

'I'm sorry,' I said. 'Someone should have told you.'

He took it surprisingly well. Perhaps he had seen enough death – as a young man, as an old man – to vaccinate him against the shock. I had seen a few of them over the years – those old men from my dad's mob. I remembered their green berets at the funeral of my father, and later my mother, although there were less of them by then. But Ken Grimwood was new to me.

'You lose touch over the years,' he said, by way of explanation. 'Some of our mob – well, they liked the reunions, the marching, putting on the old medals.' He considered his Silk Cut and coughed for a bit. 'That wasn't for me.' He looked at me shrewdly. 'Or your old man.'

It was true. For most of his life, my father never gave me the impression that he wanted to remember the war. Forgetting seemed like more his thing. It was only towards the end, when the time was running out, that he talked about going back to Elba, and seeing the graves of boys that he had known and loved and lost before they were twenty. But he never got around to it. No time.

And it turned out that Ken Grimwood's time was running out too.

'Lung cancer,' he said casually. 'Yeah, that's what I've got.'

He stubbed out his Silk Cut, lit up another and saw me looking at him, and his cigarette, and his fag packet with a skull. 'You've got to go sometime, son,' he chuckled, dry-eyed and enjoying my shock. 'I reckon I've had a good innings.'

And we sat there in the twilight until he could not force any more smoke into his dying lungs, and my meatballs had gone stone cold.

I walked him to the bus stop at the end of our road.

It took some time. I had not noticed until we were out on the street that he had a slow, strange walk – this laborious, rolling gait. When we finally got there I shook his hand and went back home.

Cyd was watching the bus stop from the window. She's a kind person, and I knew she would not approve of me abandoning him on the mean streets of Holloway.

'But you can't just leave him out there, Harry,' she said. 'It's dangerous.'

'He's a former Commando,' I said. 'If he's anything like my dad, he's probably killed dozens of Nazis and he's probably had bits of old shrapnel worming its way out of his body for the last sixty years. He can catch a bus by himself. He's only going to the Angel.'

She started to follow me into the kitchen. And then she stopped. And I heard it too.

A smack of air, then breaking glass, and then laughter. And again. The crack of air, the breaking glass, and laughter. We went back to the window and saw the two men standing in front of the house across the street.

No, not men – boys.

A security light came on – the kind of blinding floodlight that was becoming increasingly popular on our street – and illuminated William Fly and his mate, a spud-faced youth who cackled by his side, every inch the bully's apprentice.

Fly lifted his hand, pointing it at the light, and I heard my wife gasp beside me as the air pistol fired.

The security light went dark in a tinkle of glass and a ripple of laughter.

They moved on down the street, letting the next security light come on, and I was glad that we had decided against getting one. Fly shot out that light too, and they sauntered on, down to the bus stop where the old man was sitting.

My wife looked at me, but I just kept staring out the window, willing the bloody bus to come.

The two boys looked down at the old man.

He stared at them curiously. They were saying something to him. He shook his head. I saw the air pistol being brandished in the right hand of William Fly.

Then my wife said my name.

And we both saw the glint of the blade.

I was out of the house and running down the street, a diminished number of the security lights coming on as I went past them, and I was almost upon them when I realised that the knife was in the hand of the old man.

And they were laughing at him.

And as I watched, Ken Grimwood jammed the blade deep into his left leg.

As hard as he could, just below the knee, half of the blade disappearing into those neatly pressed trousers and the flesh beneath. And he did not even flinch.

There was a long moment when we stood and stared at the knife sticking out of the old man's leg.

Me. And the boys. And then William Fly and Spud Face were gone, and I was approaching Ken Grimwood as if in a dream.

Still sitting at the bus stop, still showing no sign of pain, he pulled out his knife and rolled up his trousers.

His prosthetic leg was pink and hairless – that's what struck me, the lack of hair – and it was like a photograph of a limb rather than the thing of flesh and blood and nerves that it had replaced.

And all at once I understood why this old man had not been at Elba with my father.

two

By the time I came down the dishes from last night were clean and drying, and there was tea and juice on the table.

Pat was shuffling about the kitchen. I could smell toast. I went to pull the newspaper from the letterbox and when I came back he was putting breakfast on the table.

The girls were still upstairs. Pat was Mister Breakfast. He had been Mister Breakfast since the time he had been old enough to boil a kettle. That was the thing about the pair of us – it worked. And it had always worked.

The thing that used to get on my nerves was when people said to me, 'Oh, so you're his mother as well as his father?' I could never work that one out.

I was his father. And if his mother wasn't around, then I could still only be his father. If you lose your right arm, does your left arm become both your right and left arm? No, it doesn't. It's still just your left arm. And you get on with it. Both his mother and his father? Hardly. It took everything I had to pull off being his dad.

'You all right?' he said, wiping his hands on the dishcloth, looking at me sideways.

'Fine,' I said. 'All good.'

And still I did not mention his mother.

Joni appeared. At seven, her footsteps were so light that, if she was not rushing somewhere, or talking, or singing, you often did not hear her coming. You turned around and she was just there. She shuffled slowly towards the table, dressed for school but still more asleep than awake.

She yawned widely. 'I don't want to eat anything today,' she said.

'You have to eat something,' I said.

She cocked a leg and hauled herself up on her chair, like a cowboy getting on his horse.

'But look,' she said.

She opened her mouth and as Pat and I bent to peer inside, she began to manoeuvre one of her front teeth with her tongue. It was so loose that she could get it horizontal.

She closed her mouth. Her eyes shone with tears. Her chin wobbled.

Pat went off to the kitchen and I sat down at the table. 'Joni,' I said, but she held up her hands, cutting me off, pleading for understanding.

'Cereal hurts my gums,' she said, waving her hands. 'Not just Cookie Crisps. All of them.'

I touched her arm. Upstairs I could hear Cyd and Peggy laughing outside the bathroom door. I groped for the correct parental soundbite.

'Breakfast is, er, the most important meal of the morning,' I reminded her, but my daughter looked away with frosty contempt, furiously worrying at her wonky tooth with the tip of her tongue.

'There you go,' Pat said.

He placed a sandwich in front of Joni. Two slices of lightly toasted white bread with the crusts removed, the chemical yellow of processed cheese sticking out of the sides like a toxic spill. Cut into triangles.

Her favourite.

Pat returned to the kitchen. I picked up the newspaper. Joni lifted the sandwich in both hands and began to eat.

Here's a good one for the Lateral Thinking Club – if a marriage produces a great child, then can that marriage ever be said to have failed?

20

If the marriage produces some girl or boy who just by existing makes this world a better place, then has that marriage failed just because Mum and Dad have split up? Is the only criterion of a successful marriage staying together? Is that really all it takes? Hanging in there? Butching it out?

Does my friend Marty Mann have a successful marriage because it has lasted for years? Does it matter that he likes his Latvian lap dancers two at a time before going home to his wife? Has he got a successful marriage because it remained untouched by the divorce courts?

If a woman and a man abandon their wedding vows and run eagerly through all the usual hateful clichés – saying hurtful things, sleeping with other people, cutting up clothes, running off with the milkman – then is that a failed marriage?

Well, obviously. It's a bloody disaster.

But still – I could not bring myself to call my union with my first wife a failed marriage. Despite everything. Despite crossing the border between love and hate and then going so far into alien territory that we could not even recognise each other.

Gina and I were young and in love. And then we were young and stupid, and getting everything wrong.

First me. Then both of us.

But a failed marriage? Never.

Not while there was the boy.

As the record came to an end, I looked at Marty's eyes through the studio's glass wall.

'Line two,' I said into the microphone, 'Chris from Croydon.'

Marty's fingers flew across the board, as natural as a fish in water, and the light on the mic in front of him went red. Marty adjusted himself in his chair, and leaned into the mic as if he might snog it.

'You're with *Marty Mann's Clip Round the Ear* live here on BBC Radio Two,' Marty said, half-smiling. 'Enjoying good sounds in bad times. Mmmm, I'm enjoying this ginger nut. Chris from Croydon – what's on your mind, mate?'

'I can't go to the pictures any more, Marty. I just get too angry – angry at the sound of some dopey kid munching his lunch, and angry at the silly little gits – can I say gits? – who think they will disappear into a puff of smoke if they turn their Nokias off for ninety minutes, and angry at the yak-yak-yak of gibbering idiots –'

'Know what you mean, mate,' Marty said, cutting him off. 'They should be shot.'

'Whitney Houston,' I said, leaning forward. '"I Will Always Love You".'

'And now a song written by the great Dolly Parton,' Marty said. He knew music. He was from that generation that had music at the centre of its universe. This wasn't just a hit song from a Kevin Costner film to him. 'Before all music started sounding like it was made from monosodium glutamate.'

This was the starting point for our show – nothing was as good as it used to be. You know, stuff like pop music, and the human race.

Whitney's cut-glass yearning began and Marty gave me a thumbs-up as he whipped off his headphones. He barged open the door. 'Four minutes thirty-seconds on Whitney,' I said.

'Great, I can pee slowly,' he said. 'What's next?'

I consulted my notes. 'Let's broaden it out,' I said. 'Non-specific anger. Rap about being angry about everything. Being angry with people who litter. Yet also angry with people who make you recycle. Angry about people who swear in front of children, angry at traffic wardens, angry at drivers who want to kill your kids.'

'Those bastards in Smart cars,' Marty said, as he kept moving.

'People, really,' I said, calling after him. 'Feeling angry at people. Any kind of rudeness, finger wagging or ignorance. And then maybe go to a bit of Spandau Ballet.'

'I can do that,' he said, and then he was gone.

'Two minutes forty on and we're back live,' said Josh, the Oxford graduate who ran our errands – the BBC was full of them, all these Oxbridge double-firsts chasing up wayward mini-cabs – and I could hear the nerves in his voice. But I just nodded. I knew that Marty would be back just as Whitney was disappearing from Kevin Costner's life forever. We were not new to this.

Marty and I were back on radio now – a couple of old radio hams who had taken a beating on telly and crawled back to where we had begun. It happens to guys like us. In fact, I have often thought that it is the only thing that happens to guys like us. One day the telly ends. But we were making a go of it. *A Clip Round the Ear* was doing well – we had that glass ear awarded by our peers to prove it. Ratings were rising for a show that played baby boomer standards and boldly proclaimed that everything was getting worse.

Music. Manners. Mankind.

I watched Marty come out of the gents, clumsily fumbling with the buttons on his jeans – I know he was angry about there never being zips on jeans – and saw a couple of guests for the show next door do a double take. Since his golden years as the presenter of late-night, post-pub TV, he had put on a little weight and lost some of that famous carrot-topped thatch. But people still expected him to look as he did when he was interviewing Kurt Cobain.

'What?' he said.

'Nothing,' I said, and I felt an enormous pang of tenderness for him.

Being on television is a lot like dying young. You stay fixed in the public imagination as that earlier incarnation. Someone who interviews the young and thin Simon Le Bon – they do not grow old as we grow old. But every TV show comes to an end. And, as Marty was always quick to point out, even the true greats – David Frost, Michael Parkinson, Jonathan Ross – have their wilderness years, the time spent working in Australia or getting rat-faced in the Groucho Club, waiting for the call to come again.

Marty settled himself in front of the mic, and pulled on his headphones. I didn't know if Marty – and by extension, his producer: me – would ever get that call. For every great

23

who comes again there are a thousand half-forgotten faces who never do come again. As much as I loved him, I suspected that Marty Mann was more of a Simon Dee than a David Frost.

'You are angry because you know how things should be,' Marty was saying to his constituency, as he teed up Morrissey. 'Anger comes with experience, anger comes with wisdom. This is *A Clip Round the Ear* saying embrace your anger, friends. Love your anger. It is proof that you are alive. And – how about a bit of English seaside melancholia: "Everyday Is Like Sunday".'

Then the two hours were up and we gathered our things and got ready to go home. That was a sign of the times. When we worked on *The Marty Mann Show* – when he was television's Marty Mann – we always hung around for hours when we were off air, working our way through the wine, beer and cheese and onion crisps in our lavish green-room banquet, coming down off of that incredible rush you only get from live TV – even if you are behind the cameras. When we were doing *The Marty Mann Show* ten years ago, we could carouse in the green room until the milkman was on his way. But that was telly then and this was Radio Two now.

Broadcasting House was a bit of a dump when it came to post-gig entertainment. The place did not encourage loitering, or hospitality, or lavish entertaining. There wasn't a sausage roll in sight. You did your gig and then you buggered off. There was nothing there – just a couple of smelly sofas and some tragic vending machines.

The green room. That was another thing that wasn't as good as it used to be.

Gina was waiting for me when I came out of work.

Standing across the street from Broadcasting House, in the shadow of the Langham Hotel, just where the creamy calm of Portland Place curves down to the cheapo bustle of Oxford Circus.

She looked more like herself now – or at least I could

recognise the woman I had loved. Tall, radiant Gina. Loving someone is a bit like being on TV. A face gets locked in a memory vault, and it is a shock to see it has changed when you were not looking. We both took a step towards each other and there were these long awkward moments as the cars whizzed between us. Then I shouldered my bag and made it across.

'I couldn't remember if you were live or not,' she said.

'What?'

'The show,' she said. 'I didn't know if you recorded it earlier. Or if it really was ten till midnight.'

I nodded. 'A bit late for you, isn't it?'

'My body's still on Tokyo time,' she said. 'Or somewhere between there and here.' She attempted a smile. 'I'm not sleeping much.'

We stared at each other.

'Hello, Harry.'

'Gina.'

We didn't kiss. We went for coffee. I knew a Never Too Latte just off Carnaby Street that stayed open until two. She took a seat in the window and I went to the counter and ordered a cappuccino with extra chocolate for her and a double macchiato for myself. Then I had to take it back because she had stopped drinking coffee during her years in Tokyo and only drank tea now.

'How well you know me,' she said after I had persuaded some Lithuanian girl to exchange a coffee for tea. Was she that sharp when we were together? I don't think so. She was another one who had got angrier with the years.

'Sorry,' I said. 'Stupid of me not to read your mind.'

And we took it from there.

'Japan's over,' she said. 'The economy is worse than here.'

'Nowhere is worse than here,' I said. 'Ah, Gina. You could have called.'

'Yes, I could have called. I could have phoned home and had to be polite to your second wife.'

'She's not my second wife,' I said. 'She's my wife.'

My first wife wasn't listening.

'Or I could have phoned your PA at work and asked her if you had a window for me next week. I could have done all of that but I didn't, did I? And why should I?' She leaned forward and smiled. 'Because he's my child just as much as he's your child.'

I stared at her, wondering if there ever came a point where that was simply no longer true.

And I wondered if we had reached that point years ago.

'What's with the keep-fit routine?' I said, changing the subject. She was in terrific shape.

'It's not a routine.' She flexed her arms self-consciously. 'I just want to look after myself as I get older.'

I smiled. 'I can't see you on the yoga mat.'

She didn't smile back. 'I had a scare a couple of years back. A health scare. That was something you missed.'

'Sorry.'

'Please don't apologise.'

'Jesus Christ – why can't you just let me say I'm sorry?'

'And why can't you just drop dead?'

We stared at our drinks.

We had started out with good intentions. Difficult to believe now, I know, but when we divorced back then we were a couple of idealistic young kids. We really thought that we could have a happy break-up. Or at least a divorce that always did the right thing.

But Gina had blown in and out of our lives. And gradually other things got in the way of good intentions. In my experience it is so easy to push good intentions to the back of the queue – or to have them quietly escorted from the building.

Gina wanted to be a good mother. I know she did. I know she loved Pat. I never doubted that. But she was always one step from fulfilment, and life got in the way, and everything let her down. Her second husband. Working abroad. And me, of course. Me first and worst of all.

We sat in silence for a bit.

'Is this the way we are going to do it?' I said.

'What way?'

'You know what way, Gina.'

'What way do you want to do it? Shall we be nice to each other? First time for everything, I guess.'

'I don't want us to be this way,' I said. 'How long are we going to spit poison at each other?'

'I don't know, Harry. Until we get tired of the taste.'

'I was tired years ago.'

We sat in silence as if the people we had once been no longer existed. As if there was nothing between us. And it wasn't true.

'He's my son too,' she said.

'Biologically,' I said.

'What else is there?'

'Are you kidding me? Look, Gina – I think it's great you're back.'

'Liar.'

'But I don't want him hurt.'

'How could he be hurt?'

'I don't know. New man. New job. New country. You tell me.'

'You don't break up with your children.'

'I love it when people say that to me. Because it's just not true. Plenty of people break up with their children, Gina. Mostly, they're men. But not all of them.'

'Do you want me to draw you a diagram, Harry?'

'Hold on – I'll get you a pen.'

I lifted my hand for the waitress. Gina pushed it down. It was the first time we had touched in years and years, and it was like getting an electric shock.

'I broke up with you, Harry – not him. I went off you – not him. I stopped loving *you* – not him. Sorry to break this to you, Harry.'

'I'll get over it.'

'But I never stopped loving him. Even when I was busy. Preoccupied. Absent.' She sipped at her tea and looked at me. 'How is he?'

'Fine. He's fine, Gina.'

'He's so tall. And his face – he has such a lovely face, Harry. He was always a beautiful kid, wasn't he?'

I smiled. It was true. He was always the most beautiful boy in the world. I felt myself softening towards her.

'He's in the Lateral Thinking Club,' I said, warming up to the theme, happy to talk about the wonder of our son, and we both laughed about that.

'Bright boy,' she said. 'I don't even know what Lateral Thinking is – thinking outside the box? Training the mind to work better?'

'Something like that,' I said. 'He can explain it better than me.' I had finished my coffee. I wanted to go home to my family. 'What do you want, Gina?'

'I want my son,' she said. 'I want to know him. I want him to know me. I know we – I – have wasted so much time. That's why I want it now. Before it's too late.'

And I thought it would never be too late. There was a Gina-sized hole in Pat's life, had been for years, but I thought that it could never be too late to fill it. For both of them – I thought that there would always be time to put things right. That's how dumb I am. Already my mind was turning to the practicalities of shipping Pat around town.

'Where you living, Gina?'

'I've got a two-bedroom flat on Old Compton Street,' she said. 'Top floor. Plenty of space. Nice light.' She looked out the window. 'Five minutes from here.'

I was amused. 'Soho?' I said. 'That's an interesting choice. What you trying to do – recapture your youth?'

Her mouth tightened at that.

'I didn't have any youth, Harry,' she said. 'I was married to you.'

Then my phone began to vibrate. I took the call as Gina looked away and a woman with a Jamaican accent told me that they had Ken Grimwood at the hospital.

*   *   *

28

When he was seven years old my son almost drowned. We were in a quiet corner of Crete called Agios Stephanos – years before the island was claimed by the boys in football shirts – and the last thing we were expecting on our mini-break was death and tragedy. We could get all that at home.

These were the years after I split up with Gina, and then my dad died and then my mum got sick – and it felt like every time you turned around someone was either walking out or dying. We were not really in Crete for sun, sea and Retsina. We just wanted to catch our breath.

In my mind I see a windy, rocky beach. And I see Pat – all skinny limbs and tangled blond mop and baggy trunks, splashing out with a float while I settled down with a paperback.

My son at seven.

He made me smile, because he was wearing a pair of sunglasses that were way too big for him, purchased at the airport and proudly worn ever since, even at night. He would squint at his moussaka and chips in the Cretan twilight.

The waves were whipping up, but it did not cross my mind to be worried. He did not go far. But sometimes you do not have to go far to get into more trouble than you can handle. He had settled down on his float, got all dreamy in the sunlight and then he must have drifted. And by the time he noticed, it was more than drifting.

'Dad!'

You know your child's voice. Even on a crowded beach, with small children shouting and calling out on all sides, you know it instantly.

He was trying to stand up, although you couldn't really stand up on that float, and he kept sinking to one knee as it threatened to pitch him into the sea. And he was scared. Face pale with fear behind those oversized sunglasses. Calling for me.

And I was on my feet and running, my heart a hammer as I ran to the water, suddenly aware of the speed of the clouds, suddenly noticing the swell of the waves, suddenly remembering that it can all fall apart at any moment.

He was a good swimmer. Even at seven. Maybe that's why it happened, why I was too relaxed about letting him go out with a float. But suddenly it wasn't enough that he could rescue a plastic brick while wearing his pyjamas.

I crashed through waves that seemed to be at once taking Pat out to open sea and smashing me back to the shore, switching between breaststroke and crawl and back again, getting a sickening gutful of water every time I called his name.

Finally I got to him. One hand on a corner of the float, another wrapped tight round a skinny limb. It was like trying to hold a fish.

And that was when he went into the water.

Flailing white limbs in the foggy depths. Silence, apart from the rushing sound in my ears. And then one of my arms wrapped around his waist as I kicked for the surface. The float was above our heads and somehow I got him on it and I made him lie flat on his belly, while I lumbered back to the beach, telling him that everything was all right. He clung on, somehow still wearing those oversized sunglasses and too numb to cry.

Then finally we were on the beach.

How bad was it? The parental mind has this endless ability to vault to the absolute worst-case scenario. No trouble at all. A parent panics not because of what is happening but because of what might.

But this was bad enough for everyone on the beach to put down their suntan lotion and copies of *Captain Corelli's Mandolin* and stare at us even when it was clear that nobody was going to die, even as we staggered off to our shared hotel room, both salty with tears and regurgitated Aegean. Bad enough for me to remember for the rest of my life.

And what I remember most is the feeling of trying to reach my son as the sea and the wind and tide combined to push me back to the shore while they tried to carry Pat out to the open sea. That's what I remember the most. Because sometimes it felt like that was the story of us, the story of me and my boy. Trying to reach each other, wanting to reach each

30

other, but forever kept apart by forces that were bigger than both of us.

And the funny thing about calling your child's name is that it doesn't do a blind bit of good.

But you do it anyway.

Ken Grimwood sat propped up in his hospital bed in a robe that enveloped his small body like a circus tent, and when he grinned at me he was gummy as a newborn baby. On the bedside table, his false teeth sat in a glass of water.

'They found him at the bus depot,' a Filipina nurse told me. 'He was unconscious. He couldn't breathe. And he had a cigarette in his hand. We found this in his pocket.'

She handed me a BBC business card with my name on, as if I might want it back. And I remembered giving it to him before he left my house only because I wanted to get rid of him. And here he was, bounced back into my life because he had my card.

'I hardly know him,' I said, keeping my voice down. 'He's not actually anything to do with me.'

Ken laughed and we watched him produce a tin of Old Holborn and a packet of Rizlas from somewhere inside his giant robe. He must have been the only person left who wasn't using roll-ups to smoke illegal substances. He flashed his toothless grin and as the nurse advanced towards him he stuck his smoking paraphernalia under the sheet.

'Just pulling your leg, sweetheart,' he said.

She took his blood pressure, shaking her head.

But when she left he produced his baccy tin and his papers. He winked at me slyly.

I walked down to the nurses' station. The Filipina was there with a large Jamaican duty nurse. They looked at me as if I had done something wrong.

'Your father is a very sick man,' the duty nurse said. 'There's fluid on his lungs and I don't know how much longer he can breathe unaided, okay? And of course you are aware that the cancer is at an advanced stage.'

'He's not my father,' I said.

'Friend of the family?' the duty nurse asked.

'I wouldn't go that far,' I said.

It was clear they wanted the bed. They wanted him out of there. But they would not discharge him without someone to take care of him. And I realised that just because I had been dumb enough to give him my business card, the National Health Service were nominating me.

'I hardly know him,' I told them. 'He was a friend of my father's. I've only met him once. I think he has children. Do his children know? Can't his children come?'

The nurse looked at me as though I had suggested putting him in a plastic bag and leaving him on the pavement. But she talked to Ken and got a couple of telephone numbers from the old boy. There was a daughter in Essex and a son in Brighton. I quickly took out my phone and began calling.

I got through to an answer machine. And then another answer machine. I left messages on both – telling them what had happened to their father, telling them to come quick, telling them to call me back. Then I held my phone, expecting it to vibrate at any moment. But it did not stir, as if his children were reluctant to claim him too.

Down the hall I could hear a Jamaican accent telling Ken Grimwood that there was no smoking on hospital premises.

And as I stared at the silent phone in my fist, I could hear the mocking sound of the old man's laughter.

three

Joni grinned at me with her vampire smile.

Her two front teeth were both gone now. The wonky one had come out in her sandwich and the one next to it had quickly come out in sympathy. It must have been looser than she knew when she was focusing all her attention on the wonky one. So now when she smiled the milk teeth that remained at the sides of her mouth appeared like fangs.

'I'll brush my teeth,' she said, and her gummy grin gave her a jaunty air, like a sailor on shore leave. 'You get the book.'

'Okay.'

She had strict bedtime rituals. When she was in her pyjamas and her remaining teeth had been cleaned, she hugged everyone who was in the house and told them she loved them. But she didn't kiss anyone, because kissing was gross this year. Then she trooped up to her room and I read her a story. As she settled herself under the duvet, I looked at her bookcase for something suitable.

Joni was at that awkward age when she was getting too old for princesses and fairies but was still too young for anything to do with having a crush on boys. My wife and I had made half-hearted attempts to interest her in the Hannah Montana industry and the *High School Musical* business but when Joni watched the TV shows, or saw the DVDs, she was unmoved by all those white teeth, all that canned laughter and all those teenage children trying to talk like they were in a Neil Simon play. Joni was never going to go for cheesy American rubbish. So I stuck with the classics.

Terrible curses. Murderous adults. Wicked stepmothers. Beautiful maidens being taken to the woods for slaughter. Girls drugged and placed in glass coffins. All the stuff to give a seven-year-old a good night's sleep.

Tonight it was Aurora.

We settled down. I had just got to the bit where Briar Rose had realised that the nice peasant boy and Prince Philip were – conveniently enough – one and the same when Joni yawned, lay back on her pillow and raised her hand, bidding me stop.

For a long time – years – Joni had been afraid of Maleficent, and at first I thought that she wanted me to stop before I reached the wicked witch losing her rag.

But it wasn't that.

'They all end the same way, don't they?' said my daughter. 'The princess stories. They start off a bit different but they all end the same way. The prince saves them and they get married and they live happily ever after.'

I smiled and closed the book. 'Well, it's true,' I said. 'It's always the same ending.' I felt like kissing her on the cheek but I knew that wasn't allowed. So I just touched her hair. 'You're getting a bit old for these stories now.'

She snuggled down and I pulled the duvet up to her chin.

'It's a load of arse,' said my seven-year-old, and I cursed the day that Ken Grimwood had come to our door.

Elizabeth Montgomery was being dropped off at school.

She was in the car in front of us as I pulled up to let Pat out. And I know he saw her too, because he was perfectly still yet poised for flight, like a rabbit who suddenly realises that he is loitering in the fast lane of a motorway.

Elizabeth Montgomery wasn't being dropped off by her dad. Not unless her dad had a barbed-wire tattoo at the top of his arm, and played the Killers at full volume at eight thirty in the morning in his souped-up BMW. Which I suppose was entirely possible in the lousy modern world.

In the passenger seat, Pat sat petrified.

'Probably her brother,' I said, but before the words were out the driver in front had his tongue in Elizabeth Montgomery's ear, and she was laughing and squirming away. 'More likely a cousin,' I said.

And I felt like saying, Ah, don't care so much, kiddo. Don't be so quick to say, Here's my heart. Why not have a game of five-a-side football with it? Go ahead. And I felt like saying, You will meet a dozen like Elizabeth Montgomery. A hundred.

But I didn't, because I knew it was not true.

My son was almost fifteen years old and there would only ever be one Elizabeth Montgomery.

And I felt it again – I wanted to give him some sage advice. I wanted to say something meaningful about the fleeting nature of desire, or the way the person who cares the most is always the person who gets hurt the most.

I wanted to talk about love. But everything I could have said would have been about forgetting Elizabeth Montgomery. And I knew he could not do that.

So what I said was, 'I saw Gina.'

He started at his mother's name. A physical flinch, as if he had been struck. That is what it had come to.

He turned away from Elizabeth Montgomery in the car in front of us and looked at me. And I saw that his eyes were exactly the same colour as his mother's eyes. This Pacific Ocean blue. The blue you see on a Tiffany catalogue. It is a special blue.

'What do you mean – you saw her?'

'She's back from Japan,' I said.

'A holiday?' he said.

'Back for good. Back in London. She wants to see you.'

I have this theory about divorce. I have this theory that it is never a tragedy for adults and always a tragedy for children. Adults can lose weight, find someone nicer, get their life back. Divorce gives grown-ups a get-out-of-jail-free card. It is the children who pay the price, and pay it for the rest of their lives. But we can't admit that, all us scarred veterans of the divorce court, because it would mean admitting that we have inflicted wounds on our children that they will carry for the rest of their lives.

Pat was looking back at Elizabeth Montgomery. But I don't think he was seeing her any more.

'How long . . .'

'I saw her last week,' I said. 'She's been back for about a month. She wants to see you.'

I watched the fury flush his face. 'And you tell me now? You get round to telling me now?'

The children of divorced parents hold something back. They get so used to shuttling between warring homes when they are little that it stays with them. This restraint, this pragmatic reserve, this need to be a pint-sized Kofi Annan diplomat. So when they lose it, they really lose it.

He was out of the car, hauling out his rucksack, furious with me. I wasn't so naïve that I thought it was just me that he was angry about. It was divorce, separation, the absent parent – it was the whole sorry package that he had been handed without ever asking for it.

'You around tonight?' I said.

'I don't know,' he said, and he slammed the passenger door.

I watched him walk through the school gates, his rucksack slung over his shoulder, his shirt miraculously unfurling from his trousers, the swatch of white cloth that appeared as if from a magician's hat. Then he was gone, but still I sat there, boxed in by the car in front and the car behind.

Watching Elizabeth Montgomery snog the boy with the barbed-wire tattoo, as the bell rang for registration.

Riddle me this, Lateral Thinking Club – she is my daughter but I am not her father: who am I?

I am a step-parent. Ah, but I don't really believe in the term step-parent. I don't think the role exists. Not really. For in the end you are either a child's parent or you are not. And blood does not have a lot to do with it. At least, that is what I would like to believe.

Cyd and I watched Peggy coming down the stairs. She was almost exactly the same age as Pat and yet she seemed to be effortlessly gliding on air to adulthood. Peggy went to stage school, and every day of her life she danced and she sang, and she studied the performing arts and wrestled with the sub-text of difficult plays while other girls her age were snogging older boys with cars and barbed-wire tattoos. While other kids wore blazers, Peggy donned a black leotard and learned to dance jazz, ballet and tap. Above all, she wanted to act, following in the footsteps of Italia Emily Stella Conti, her school's founder, and her father, a TV cop.

Peggy made life look easy.

Now she was all dressed up for going out – a cowboy hat, and cowboy boots, a retro Motorhead-London T-shirt and a skirt that was way too short. She kissed both of us on the cheek and glided off to the mirror in the hall. We could hear her humming a popular tune.

Cyd was looking at me and smiling. 'Don't say it,' she said.

I looked dumb.

'You know,' she said. '"You're not going out dressed like that."'

What women forget is that men know boys. We know what is in their heads and in their hearts. We are all poachers turned gamekeepers. Every single one of us. And I knew that no boy was going to look at Peggy and think, Yeah, Motorhead, Lemmy and all that, yeah, they were a pretty good band. I knew exactly what they would be thinking, the dirty little bastards. And I didn't like it.

'It's only her dad,' Cyd said.

We heard a motorbike outside and Peggy ran to the door with a happy, 'I'll get it!'

Cyd gave me a look and drifted off to the kitchen. I went to the door and looked out at Peggy's dad sitting astride his Harley.

Jim Mason. Ten years ago he was the bad boy. The deserter, the fornicator, the runaway. The absent father. But in recent years I had to admit Jim's stock had risen. After a long, disorderly line of Asian girlfriends in the wake of his marriage to Cyd, he had been married to a nurse from Manila for years – but there had been no more children. And I suspected that must have been a relief for Peggy.

I never really spoke to the guy, beyond platitudes about what the latest weather meant for motorbikes. A couple of years ago, when his TV show was taking off – you might have seen him, he was the divorced, alcoholic detective on *PC Filth: An Unfair Cop* – he had offered to start paying Peggy's school fees. I had brushed him off, told him that Cyd and I had it covered. But I felt that he could teach Gina and me a few lessons about how to conduct yourself after a divorce. Despite his inappropriately long hair, and Lewis Leathers, and past crimes, Peggy's dad was living proof that you could be an absent parent and still be some kind of presence in your child's life.

An absent parent but a parent still.

Peggy pulled on her helmet and climbed on to the pillion. They both raised their hands and I waved as they shot off, the throaty roar of the Harley ringing through the neighbourhood. The group of kids loitering at the end of the road watched them go. Long after they had disappeared, I could hear the growl of the motorbike.

And I felt a dull ache of resentment towards him. I could not help it. Because although the guy did his best to be a good dad to Peggy, there was so much he had missed. She was my daughter although I would never be her dad. We did not have the unbreakable bonds of blood, but we had something else.

I was the one who was there when, aged ten, she split her head open on the ice rink at Somerset House, foolishly attempting a complicated leap. And I was the one who was there when she endured two terms of bullying at her old school before we got her into Italia Conti. And I was there for other stuff – no blood, no tears. But meals shared together, and TV watched together, and holidays, and walking to school, and a good-night hug. Sometimes I think that stuff is more important than the times of high drama, when there is blood on the ice rink and a mad dash to Accident and Emergency.

She was not my daughter but we had been part of the same family for ten years. And I was more of a father to her than her real dad would ever be – wasn't I?

Sometimes I thought so. But when she went off once a week on the Harley, looking so happy on that pillion, with her dad the big-shot actor, well, then I wasn't so sure. And mostly I tried not to think about it at all.

Because it's like someone says in *The Terminator* when cyborgs are coming back in time to murder children yet unborn:

You could go crazy thinking about this stuff.

Marty and I sat in the Pizza Express next to Broadcasting House and nobody looked at him twice.

TV fame is like youth or money. It just runs out when you are not looking. Ten years ago, Marty walked into a room and everybody stared at him. But the years on radio had eroded that recognition factor, and we were left unmolested by the early evening crowd.

Next to us was a table full of ageing lads in business suits. Their banter was of a sexual nature – birds and blow-jobs. Effing and blinding. Taking the front way and the back way. The usual stuff. Little did they know that they were next door to Marty Mann, the presenter formerly known as edgy and controversial.

And even less did they care.

It was the usual crowd. BBC worker bees grabbing some carbs before the evening shift. Office workers dawdling before they caught the train home. And revellers off to frolic in the tawdry lights of the West End.

The demographic skewed to a younger crowd – probably too young to listen to *A Clip Round the Ear* on Radio Two – but looking for a table among the funsters were a pair of old ladies who had big night out written all over them. I wondered what musical they were going to see, and I thought of my mum happily singing along to *Chicago* and *Les Misérables* and *Guys and Dolls*. It seemed like a lifetime ago now.

The old ladies carefully parked themselves two tables away from us. The lads in their suits were next door. And suddenly they seemed louder than ever.

'No, fuck it, this is a true story,' one of them said, holding his hands up at the derisive profanities of his chums. 'Guy goes to a whore and says, "How much for a hand-job? One hundred quid? That's a lot." But the whore says, "Listen, see this Rolex, I bought it by giving hand-jobs."'

Marty looked up at me from his Four Seasons. He glanced quickly at the old ladies and looked away. You would think that a man with Marty's CV would not care about profanity in the pizza parlour. But, like all transgressors, he understood that context is everything.

The old ladies were staring at each other. The suits were in uproar. The comedian took a bite of garlic bread and ploughed on.

'Next day he goes back and says to the whore, "How much for a blow-job?" She says, "Five hundred quid." "Five hundred quid! Fuck me, that's a lot of dough." She says, "Listen, you see that Mercedes? I bought it by giving blow-jobs."'

Marty pushed his pizza away.

'We should say something,' I said, my voice pathetically low. 'We should say something to these creeps.'

Marty nodded. But he kept staring at his pizza. 'Except there's five of them,' he said. 'Except they might not like it. Except they might have knives.'

'You kidding? These guys haven't got knives. They've got BlackBerrys. What do you think they are going to do? Slash you with their iPhones?'

But for all my big talk, I sat there just like Marty, useless in my disapproval.

There was bedlam at the next table. Red faces. Drunken voices. The joke coming to its punchline. The old ladies were getting up to go. They were telling a confused waitress that they were not so hungry after all.

'And then he goes to the whore and says, "How much for the lot?" And she says, "One thousand quid." And he says, "Fuck my old boots, that's a lot." And she says, "See that big house over there?"'

'She says, "If I had a pussy,"' Marty muttered to himself, '"I bet I could buy that."'

'I feel like saying something,' I said, staring at the suits as I watched the old ladies heading for the door, their big night out already violated.

But I just sat there, and I said nothing.

four

I drove Pat to Soho. He was still not really speaking to me. We were on grunting terms.

I walked him to the door and found the bell with her surname. The name she had before me, the name she had after me. I looked at Pat as I rang it. He was impassive, neutral – the inscrutable offspring of divorced parents.

'Hello?'

It was strange that I had not recognised her face. Because the voice could not belong to anyone else. Pat and I leaned towards the metal grille.

'It's us,' I said.

'It's me,' Pat said.

Gina laughed with delight – a sound that I had not heard in, oh, about a thousand years. 'Great, come up,' she said, and she buzzed the front door open. Pat gave me a blank look and went inside. I stood there for just a moment after the door swung shut.

I don't know what I had been expecting. But I had driven him across town with a mounting sense of dread. And nothing had happened. Had it? I walked back to the car. But I did not get in. I just kept walking. And the reasons that we stay together or come apart just seemed so heartbreakingly random that I could have sat down in Old Compton Street and wept.

Would she take him out to dinner? Or would it be easier for both of them if they stayed home? They would talk, wouldn't they? Or would Gina – would both of them – want to avoid too much talking, and just try to rack up some together time?

It's their thing, I thought. And I was totally lost. I felt flat. And suddenly older.

If I had not slept with someone else, if she had given me another chance, if she had not been so quick to try again with another man . . . not much had to happen to keep us together, I thought.

But I was the child of a nuclear family, and growing up in a family that never comes apart makes you believe in the inevitability of staying together. And I could see that there was a banality about my expectations – like the predictability of the princess stories that my seven-year-old daughter had suddenly grown out of.

Gina came from a family where the father walked out. She did not expect happy endings. She did not expect families to stay together. She expected them to fall apart. I walked out of Soho and into Chinatown, reluctant to start the drive back across town in case it all went wrong, and there were accusations and raised voices and slammed doors and the call to come quick. I kept my phone in my hand in case it suddenly began to vibrate. But I walked all over Chinatown, and it never did.

Five good things about being a single parent.

You are alone now, so you can make all decisions concerning your kid without consultation.

You know, with total certainty, that a child only needs one good parent.

You know that your child is loved, and will always be loved.

There is no need to feel like a freak at the school gates, because the world is overflowing with single parents now.

And your ex is out of your life.

Five bad things about being a single parent.

You are alone now, so you constantly feel like you are the

last line of defence between your kid and the lousy modern world.

You know, with total certainty, that a child is always better off with two good parents.

You know your child is scarred by his parents breaking up, and will carry those scars forever.

You feel like a freak at the school gates, because the world is full of happy, unbroken families.

And our ex can come barging back into your life whenever they feel like it, just by uttering the magic words – 'This is my child too.'

But what did I know about it?

I had not been a single parent for years.

What made me such an expert?

It had been ten years since Pat and I had lived alone – that strange, messy period between my first marriage and my second. A time of raw pain all round, and being unable to wash his hair without both of us having a nervous breakdown, and the slow realisation of how much I had relied on Gina to give shape to my life, and form to our family, and to wash our child's hair and put him to bed while I heard their laughter through the walls.

And what I remembered most of all about that time was the feeling that I had failed. I could still taste it, ten years down the line. The feeling of failure, as undeniable as a broken arm – failed as a father, failed as a husband, failed as a man. Lugging that feeling of failure to the supermarket, to the school gates, to the house of my parents – that's what I remembered most of all. Failed as a son.

But it was all years ago. And although I still noticed the single parents at the school gates – their time much tighter, their love somehow fiercer and more protective and more evident – I could not pretend that I was one of their number.

I had a wife and three children. And they were our children. And if you wanted to be picky, and prissy, and small-hearted, then you could say that the boy was my son and the older

44

girl was her daughter and the seven-year-old was our daughter together.

But we did not think that way.

The whole menagerie had been mixed up for so long – for most of the lives of the elder two, and for all of the life of the youngest – so that we did not think in those terms. Sociologists and commentators and politicians – they think in terms of blended families. In the real world, you just get on with it, and it either works or it doesn't.

It worked for us.

This little post-nuclear family where the females out-numbered the males. It was home. But seeing Gina again had prised open some secret chamber in my heart where I still felt like the father I had been so long ago.

A card-carrying single parent.

Gina made me see that bitter truth.

Once a single parent, always a single parent.

'The whites are worse than the darkies,' Ken Grimwood said, and I did not know where to begin.

He was a time capsule containing everything that was rotten about the country I grew up in. Yet I found myself feeling curiously grateful that he was enlightened enough to see that the morality had little to do with the colour of your skin. But the casual talk of *darkies* – it gave me exactly the feeling of dread that I felt when I saw him producing his tin of tobacco and packet of Rizlas, which he was doing right at this moment. I felt like opening all the windows.

'Please, could you save it until I've got you home?' I said. His home was only in another corner of North London. But it felt like another planet, another century.

'At least the darkies have God and church,' he said, carrying on as if an audience had asked him to elaborate on his feelings about race relations in modern Britain. The roll-ups and the baccy tin sat in his lap, apparently forgotten. 'God and church keep them in line. Nothing wrong with a fear of hell.

Nothing wrong with believing you're going to burn in the eternal fires of hell if you step out of line.'

'I agree,' I said. 'It's very healthy.'

'As long as their God doesn't tell them to stick a rucksack full of Semtex on the Circle Line,' he said.

I looked at him and shook my head. 'How can you talk like that?'

'Like what?'

'All this stuff about darkies,' I said. 'You fought against all of that, didn't you? When the Nazis were building factories to kill people. You were fighting for tolerance. For freedom.'

He smiled. 'I fought for your dad,' he said. 'I fought for my mates. For them. Not for King and country or anything else. We fought for each other.'

I kept my eyes on the road. Where was his son? Where was his daughter? They had never called back. Didn't they love their father? Shouldn't they be doing this chore, instead of Harry's Magic Taxis?

He was looking out the window. The twenty-four-hour shops were lit up like prison camps. And I remembered how my mother and father would look at those same streets, the streets of London where they grew up. The look that said, There must be something out there I still recognise. 'But the whites – what have they got? Cheap booze and talent shows and benefits,' the old man said, looking at me sternly, as if I had just disagreed with him.

'What's the knife for?' I said. 'I can't believe it's just for sticking in your leg.'

'Dogs,' he said. 'The knife is for dogs. Where I live, there's a lot of big dumb animals – and some of them own very large dogs. The kind of dog that gets a kiddy in its cakehole and doesn't let go. You can't pull them off. Do you think you can pull them off? You can't. That's what the knife is for, smart arse. If a dog gets a kiddy.'

'What did you do?' I said. 'What was your job?'

'Print,' he said, cramming sixty years of working life into one syllable. 'That ended.' He laughed. 'The welfare state was

46

built for men like your father,' he said, and then his eyes shone with a sudden flare of anger. 'Gift of a grateful nation. It was meant to be an effing safety net for the needy – not an effing comfy sofa for the effing feckless. Men – like your dad and me.'

Except that my dad would never have said effing three times in the same sentence. That was the big difference between my old man and this old man. I glanced at him and saw him staring out at the city streets, shaking his head.

'Where did England go?' said Ken Grimwood.

'You're looking at it,' I replied.

'This country's finished,' he said. 'Land fit for heroes? They told us we were heroes and then they made us crawl. Told us we were heroes and then they made us crawl! More like a land fit for yobs and scroungers and anyone who just jumped off the banana boat . . .'

'Then why stay?' I said, cheerfully rising to the bait. I had argued like this before. It was like Sunday dinner with Dad.

'I wanted to go,' the old man said, with that same hard, resentful certainty that my father could summon up so easily. 'Fifty year ago. To Australia. That's the place. Got a son out there. Wanted to go myself. We were going to be ten-pound Poms. You went on the boat. Took bloody ages. We had been down to Australia House. Filled in all the forms and everything.'

'What happened?'

'My wife,' he said. 'My Dot.' He smiled, thinking about his dead wife. 'In the end she wouldn't leave her mum.' Then his voice went flat and hard. 'So we stayed.'

'I think they may have one or two immigrants in Australia,' I said. 'In fact, now I come to think of it, the entire country is made up of immigrants.'

'That's just where you're wrong,' he said, and he looked out at the grimy streets of King's Cross but he was seeing Bondi Beach. 'And I fancied seeing the penguins. I always wanted to see that. The penguins on Phillip Island near Melbourne. Thousands and thousands of the little buggers. They come out

47

of the sea when it gets dark. On Summerland Beach. Every night of the year. I always fancied seeing that. What a sight it must be – all the penguins on Summerland Beach.'

'Penguins?' I said. 'In Australia?'

He stared at me thoughtfully.

'Exactly how little do you know?' he said.

The dog was on me as soon as I got out of my car.

A rocket of muscle and teeth and bulging eyes, bounding up on my chest, pushing me back against the car, growling as though it had a human bone lodged somewhere deep in its throat.

Two men were milling around outside the flats. They were not kids with hooded tops that covered their faces and baggy jeans that did not cover their backsides. They were men around my age who had been losing hair and gaining weight for twenty years, so that now they resembled a pair of giant boiled eggs. I could see them tearing up the terraces in their number one crops two decades ago. They were old but they were not exactly adult. They were Old Lads. They looked up at me with their blank white faces. And they smiled.

Ken was ambling across the courtyard, fumbling with his keys. I tried to follow him and the dog shoved me back against the car with an outraged snarl. I looked up at the Old Lads.

'He likes you,' one of them said, and they both had a giggle at that. 'Tyson likes you, mate. If Tyson didn't like you he would have ripped your face off by now. You should be flattered, mate.'

And he did like me. I could tell by the way he suddenly settled down with his hindquarters wrapped around one of my legs. The growling subsided to a romantic moan.

I tore myself away, the vicious creature whimpering with frustration, and ran after Ken. He had paused halfway up the stairs.

'Just taking a breather,' he said, and I remembered how, near the end of his life, every breath my father took had been an effort. I stared down at the courtyard that the low-rise council flats overlooked. The Old Lads were shuffling off, the dog snarling and snorting around their snow-white trainers.

'They should keep that thing on a lead,' I said.

Ken began to get up. I took his arm and helped him the rest of the way.

'They love their dogs round here,' he said. 'Big animal lovers, they are. Those two charmers are in the flat above me. With their old mum. They love their mum and their mutt, but not much else, as far as I can fathom.'

We had reached the first-floor landing. He had his keys in his hand, outside a green door that appeared to be made of cardboard. I could hear what sounded like a hundred television sets. I wasn't used to it. All these people living on top of you.

'Thanks for the lift,' he said. 'Fancy a cup of tea before you shoot off?'

I wanted to get out of here. But I looked down at the courtyard and the Old Lads were still mooching around with their killer dog. They strolled around the double-parked cars as if they owned all they surveyed, their giant bald noggins like twin moons. It looked like a car park in hell.

So I found myself following Ken inside. His flat seemed far too tiny to be the final stop in a lifetime. On the wall was a framed poster of a blonde girl on a white beach. *Australia*, it said. *What are you waiting for?*

There were photos on the mantelpiece. In black and white, a sailor and his bride. Also in black and white, a boxer posing for the camera, trying not to smile. The young Ken Grimwood, fists in a southpaw stance, a glint in his eye, his stomach like a washboard. And in faded colour, three smiling children in the sixties. Two boys and a girl, grinning on the doorstep of a caravan.

'Good to be home,' coughed Ken. 'Take a pew while I put the kettle on.'

I sank into an orange sofa made of some synthetic material that must have seemed modern in the 1950s and now was just a fire hazard. On the coffee table was a copy of the *Racing Post*. The sofa seemed to suck me into its polyester heart.

The telephone rang. Ken was banging around in a kitchen the size of a coffin, busy with our tea. The phone kept ringing. I picked it up.

'Dad?'

A woman's voice. The daughter in Brighton. Tracey.

'I'll get him,' I said, and when she wanted to know who I was, I told her. No apology for not calling me back. No thanks to Harry's Magic Taxis for bringing him home from the hospital.

'Is he all right?' she said.

I looked at the phone. 'He's dying,' I said.

Ken came back into the room with two mugs of tea on a tray. There was the damp squib of a roll-up glowing between his lips.

'I know he's dying,' she snapped, as if I was the idiot home help. 'I mean, apart from that.'

'Apart from the dying? Oh, apart from that, he's great.'

I heard the woman bristling with irritation. 'He's not still smoking, is he?' Then her voice choked and broke. 'Oh, that impossible old man.'

Ken smiled at me and bent to place the tea on the coffee table. When he had straightened up – it took a while – he took the phone from me. I could hear the voice of his daughter. He didn't say much.

'Yes . . . no . . . yes, as it happens . . . no, as it happens.'

He winked at me as he took a long toke on his cigarette and I looked away. I had already decided that I didn't like her very much.

But she was right.

He was an impossible old man.

'She wants a word,' Ken said, handing me back the phone. The daughter's voice was shrill with hysteria in my ear.

'I just can't believe you're letting him smoke,' she said. 'What's wrong with you?'

Then she hung up. Ken was laughing to himself.

'I was married to her mother for near on fifty year,' he said. 'Her and that useless git she married managed about forty-five minutes. And they had a couple of kiddies too. So how come she's the one dishing out advice?'

I sipped my tea. It was scalding hot, but I tried to bolt it down, despite the third-degree burns. I wanted to get out of there.

Ken took off his glasses, picked up the *Racing Post* and squinted at it with his mole-like eyes while patting the pockets of his blazer. He peered blindly around the room and for the first time I thought I saw a touch of fear on Ken Grimwood's face.

'Me reading glasses,' he said. 'Didn't leave them at the hospital, did I?'

He made a move to rise but I held up a hand. Life's too short, I thought, and began searching for his missing reading glasses. The dead air of old smoke stung my eyes and made me want to go home. The doorbell rang and I let him get it. I would find his glasses and then I would leave.

'Try the chest of drawers,' he advised, lumbering to the door.

I opened the drawer and rifled through old bills, a pension book, curling postcards from Down Under.

And a rectangular, claret-coloured box that I recognised from long ago and far away. It was about the size of a palm-held phone. The reading glasses were next to it, on top of a stack of prehistoric betting slips. There were voices at the door.

I looked up and saw Ken letting in another old man. Even smaller than him, and some kind of Asian. His skin was the colour of gold. He was old, maybe only slightly younger than Ken, but his face was curiously unlined by time.

I looked back at the box. I picked it up. As the two old men shuffled into the flat, Ken doing all the muttering, I opened it.

And I looked at Ken Grimwood's Victoria Cross.

51

I felt a stab of – what? Jealousy certainly – my dad's DSM was the second highest award for bravery. The VC trumped that, and the lot. And I felt shock. And shame. It all hit me at once, as real as a kick in the stomach.

I had never seen one before. I had held my father's Distinguished Service Medal a million times, but I had never seen one of these. FOR VALOUR it said on a semi-circular scroll, under the lion and the crown. The medal was suspended by a ring from a suspension bar of laurel leaves. The ribbon was pale pink, but I suppose it could have faded with time. I closed the box and shut the drawer. Then I opened it again and took out the reading glasses.

'This is Paddy Silver's boy,' Ken was saying to the golden old man. Ken was smiling. The other old boy watched me without expression. 'He passed away,' Ken said, and his friend looked at him quickly. Ken smiled and nodded. 'Ten year ago. More. Same as I've got. Cancer of the lung.'

The other old man nodded once, and looked back at me.

'This here's Singe Rana,' Ken said. 'His mob were at Monte Cassino with our mob. Did you know that? Did you know the Gurkhas were with our lot in Italy?'

I shook my head.

'I didn't know that,' I said, and I held out my hand to Singe Rana.

He shook it, a handshake as soft as a child's.

'Nobody knows anything these days,' Ken said. 'Nobody knows bugger all. That's the problem with this country.' He looked at his friend. 'Wanted him to march with us, didn't we? Paddy Silver. March at the Cenotaph.'

Singe Rana confirmed this with a curt nod. If he was upset about my father's death, he gave no sign. But of course it was all a long time ago. All of it.

'But he was never much of a marcher, your old man,' Ken said. 'He was never one for wearing the beret and doing the marching and putting on the medals. But we thought he could come down there. And if he didn't fancy a march, well, then he could just watch.'

He looked at Singe Rana.

The old Gurkha shrugged.

I handed Ken his reading glasses.

'I'll come,' I said. 'I'll come with my son.'

When I was twenty-five years old, and about to become a father for the first time, my mother told me the same thing again and again.

'As soon as you're a parent,' she said, 'your life is not your own.'

What she meant was, Put away those records by The Smiths. What she meant was, Wake up. The careless freedom of your life before there was a pushchair in the hall is about to come to an end.

But I never really felt that way. Yes, of course everything was changed by the birth of our baby boy – but I never felt as though I had surrendered my life. I never felt as though parenthood was holding me hostage. I never felt that my life was not my own.

Not until that night I waited for Pat to come home from Gina's place in Soho. Not until he was absent and I was waiting. Then I really felt it, manifesting itself as a low-level nausea in the pit of my stomach, and nerve ends that jangled at every passing car. Finally, I understood.

My life was not my own.

The sound of Joni came down the child monitor and Cyd tossed aside her *Vogue*. 'I knew it,' she said. '*Dr Who* always gives her nightmares.'

'It's the Weeping Angels,' I said. 'They give me nightmares, those Weeping Angels.'

'I'll lie down with her for a bit,' Cyd said. 'Until she settles.' She stroked the top of my arm. 'I'm sure he's fine,' she said.

It was near midnight when Gina's taxi pulled up outside. She didn't get out but waited until he had opened the front door before driving away. He came into the living room, his face a mask.

'You all right?' I said, keeping it as light as I could.

He nodded. 'Fine.' Not looking at me.

'Everything go okay?'

He was fussing with his school rucksack, checking for something inside.

'I'm going back next week,' he said evenly. 'Gina asked me to go back next week.'

He still wasn't looking at me. 'Well, that's good. That's great.' Then I thought of something else. 'You take your pills?'

He shot me a furious look. 'You don't have to remind me,' he said. 'I'm not a baby.'

He had to take these pills.

A few years ago, just at the start of big school, he had been laid flat by what looked like flu at first and, after he had missed most of the first half-term, began to look horribly like ME. We found out, just after one of the less fun-packed Christmas celebrations, that he had a thyroid condition. So he took these pills and they made him well. But he would have to take them every day for the rest of his life. There are children all over the world who have to deal with a lot worse than that.

But I went to bed knowing that I would be wound too tight to sleep tonight, or at least until it was nearly time to get up.

Because that was another thing that Gina had missed.

five

Tyson saw me as soon as I got out of the car.

At first he just stared — ears back, teeth bared, a long stream of drool coming out of the corner of his vicious maw. As if he couldn't quite believe his luck. The object of his base lust had returned.

Then suddenly he left the side of his Old Lad masters, their huge boiled-egg heads leaning together in hideous fraternity, and bounded across the courtyard, weaving between the brand-new Mercs and rusty jalopies with Polish plates.

Too late.

By then I was halfway up the concrete staircase, already hearing the whine of the dusty wind that whistled down the corridors of Nelson Mansions.

I banged on the old man's door.

It took him an agonisingly long time to open, but I was inside the trapped air of his flat before Tyson arrived. We could hear his meaty paws slapping against the thin door as he howled of his unnatural love.

Singe Rana was sitting on the orange sofa, watching the racing. He glanced over at me, made a small gesture with his impassive face and turned back to the 2.20 at Chepstow.

'I brought you these,' I said, and gave Ken the A4 envelope I was carrying.

He reached inside and took out a handful of black-and-white photographs, pushing his face against them. I found his reading glasses and gave them to him. He took the photographs over to the sofa and I stood behind the two old men as they leafed through them. They picked up the first one.

It could have been a holiday photograph. There were perhaps a dozen young men, tanned and hard, posing in the sunshine on the deck of a ship.

'On the way to North Africa,' Ken said.

'That was lovely trip,' said Singe, and his Nepalese accent had a soft Indian lilt to it. He smiled at the memory. 'There were dolphins swimming and flying fish used to flap about on the deck of our landing craft. We saw a whale and her children.'

And another photograph of men in uniform. Maybe twenty of them. Less smiles here, and less sunshine. But still the shy grins as they stood for the camera recording the moment before they went to war.

Most of the photographs were posed. As formal as a school photograph, and as determined to hold that fleeting moment. Ken muttered the names and nicknames of long ago. Lofty and Albert. Tubby and Fred. Chalky and Sid. And sometimes he would remember where they had died.

Salerno. Dieppe. Elba. Names that I learned in childhood. Anzio. Sicily. Normandy.

Ken tapped the face of a thin boy with slick black hair. He smiled at me.

'Who's that then?' he said.

My old man. Dark-eyed and cocky. A wild boy. The uniform too big, proud of the flash on his shoulder. *R.N. Commando.* Eighteen years old. A boy I never knew. Not much older than my son was now.

'In Italy,' said Singe Rana, 'we passed fields of wheat and many grapes. We drank wine. The women and children stared at us. The men looked away. We did not speak to the girls until they spoke to us.'

I wanted to take them out for lunch. But they said they already had some dinner prepared. Singe Rana collected a plate of potato cakes from the kitchen. I took a bite and stuffed inside the potato I tasted chilli and ginger, turmeric and cayenne pepper. It was like something my wife would have served to a room full of investment bankers.

'Aloo Chop,' Ken told me. 'Spicy potato cakes. Gurkha nosh.'

But both of them ate like my seven-year-old daughter. Taking a bite and making it last forever. I got the impression that eating was something the pair of them had largely given up years ago.

'Keep some of this Aloo Chop for your tea,' Ken told Singe Rana. 'When you're at work.'

I must have looked surprised.

'Got a little job, haven't you?' Ken said to his friend, and Singe Rana confirmed his employment with a curt nod. 'Security job,' Ken elaborated. 'Night watchman. At that firework factory on the City Road.' He turned to me. 'Know it, do you?'

I nodded, vaguely remembering some ugly concrete block surrounded by council flats around Old Street. What I remembered most were the faded images on its windowless walls. Cheery cartoons of rockets, roman candles, sparklers, jumping jacks and bangers, all joyfully exploding, and all so worn away by time that they looked as though they had been painted there by cavemen.

Ken grinned at Singe Rana with boundless amusement. 'Keeps him off the streets,' he cackled. 'Keeps him out of trouble.'

'Gurkha people,' said Singe Rana seriously. 'Always trusted for security position.'

'You don't want to nick a packet of sparklers when he's on guard duty,' Ken chortled. 'He'll slit your throat soon as look at you!' Then he looked at his friend with affection. 'And the money comes in handy. Minimum wage. But it helps when you're having a flutter. And we do like a little flutter, don't we, Singe Rana?'

While we ate the Aloo Chop they consulted the racing pages of their newspapers, and when we had finished they were ready to go to the betting shop.

Ken Grimwood lived at the sharp end of the Angel, where Islington fell away to the borders of King's Cross. We walked slowly past a sad little strip of shops. Everywhere was crowded, everything was worn out. Nail parlours and junk food and mobile phones. Cheap neon on a grey day, some of the lights burned out, as glaring as missing teeth.

Then suddenly the women with pushchairs crowded with children and shopping were jumping out of the way. Something was stampeding towards us – big kids on small bikes, as multi-racial as a Benetton marketing campaign, whooping with joy as the crowd scattered.

I quickly stepped into the gutter, with that easy middle-class cowardice that comes so naturally these days.

But Ken Grimwood dipped his right shoulder, tucked in his chin and stood his ground. They hurtled towards him and it seemed certain they would run him down. He did not budge. And as the lead cyclist reached the old man it was as if he leaned into him, putting the full weight of his short, broad body into the boy on the bike.

It didn't seem like much, but the kid went sprawling.

I stooped to help him up, anxious to avoid an unpleasant scene, and he bared his fangs, backing me off.

His friends had pulled up and they stared at Ken Grimwood in disbelief. We all stared at him. Only Singe Rana looked unimpressed, as though he had seen it all a thousand times before.

'Fool!' shrieked the biggest one. 'Who you think you are, old man?'

And Ken Grimwood just smiled to himself, as though his mind was somewhere far away, with his mob in the sunshine off the coast of Africa, and the flying fish falling into the landing craft.

Gina and I walked out of Soho, turned south down the Charing Cross Road, strolled along the Strand for a bit, and then turned right to the Victoria Embankment and the river.

There was stuff to sort out. In the end, it always comes

down to practicalities with children. Times for pick-ups and drop-offs. Homework assignments and meal requirements. The endless vigilance of the search for nits. That sort of thing.

We were being nice to each other. For the sake of our son. We were trying to be mature grown-ups and keep the party polite.

If you had glanced at us on the street, then you would have taken us for a couple. But it was as if there was somebody walking between us, keeping us almost ludicrously apart, making accidental physical contact impossible.

For we walked the way that old lovers do.

'It's so beautiful, this city,' she said, smiling at the gypsy glamour of the barges and the tugs on the Thames. 'You forget how beautiful. Why is that? Why do we forget? I walked down here with Pat last weekend. And he got it. A lot of boys his age – they wouldn't get it, would they? But he definitely got it.'

I was used to the way she looked now. I had got my head around it. It wasn't complicated. She was a good-looking woman in her forties and everything we had lost was so long ago that it hardly even hurt. It wasn't pain any more. It was more like a memory of pain. I was relieved that we would never have to go through it again.

Besides, when she had suggested meeting, I had been expecting this kind of stuff. The forgotten beauty of our city. The remembered beauty of our son. Philosophical Gina, who had somehow achieved enlightenment while she was working as a translator in Tokyo. That is what I had been expecting. Reflective Gina – sighing at the tugs and the barges and something our son had said.

Maybe even an apology or two. Why not? That would be nice, I thought. For the years wasted on useless men and pointless jobs and faraway places with strange-sounding names. An apology on behalf of her – and all absent parents just like her – for the time when their child wasn't top of the list. It was a good job I wasn't bitter.

But she surprised me. She could do that now, because we

no longer really knew each other. It wasn't like when we were married and you pretty much knew what was coming next.

'I don't like him taking this medication,' she said. 'It's not right. A teenage boy taking pills every day of his life.'

'Thyroxine,' I said. And I actually laughed. 'You make it sound as though he's raiding the medicine cabinet. You make it sound as though the kid lives for chemical kicks.'

She frowned at me. 'No need to get excited,' she said, with a disapproving pout of her lips. Did she used to do that? I didn't remember that move. Someone had taught her that gesture. It was nothing to do with me.

I took a breath. I could do this thing. I could get through this conversation without my head exploding. Probably. We were mature grown-ups. If we were any more mature, we would be fossilised.

'Pat was sick, Gina,' I said quietly. 'As soon as he started big school. He was flattened by – whatever it was. Just exhausted.'

'We spoke, remember?' she said coldly. 'I knew all about it.'

'But you didn't really,' I said. 'Because you weren't here. You were in Tokyo. You were busy with your new job or the new guy in Shibuya.'

'You can't argue, can you?' she said, turning to face me. She had forgotten about the beauty of the eternal river. 'You never learned to argue in a civilised fashion. And it was Shinjuku not Shibuya. And it wasn't some new guy – it was exactly the same useless bastard that I was with in London.'

'My apologies,' I said. And then I was quiet, because I thought about the school year slipping away as Pat stayed in his room, only emerging to haul himself into a cab to see yet another doctor or paediatrician. And I remembered almost sobbing with gratitude when we discovered that he had a thyroid condition that was easily rectified, and that he wasn't going to die. And I understood that there is nothing in this world that has the power to slaughter your heart like having a sick child. Sorry, Gina, but no woman can kill you like that.

'The pills make him well,' I said, very quietly, because I felt so very much like shouting. 'The pills are nothing. I appreciate your concern, Gina. But he needs them.'

She touched my arm. Patted it twice, and then sort of stroked it with the middle joint of her index finger. That was new too. I quite liked it. We smiled at each other, and turned to look at a barge floating by as if on air. She was right. It was beautiful.

'Harry?'

'What?'

'Why are you so angry?' she said.

'Because you didn't put him first,' I said. 'It doesn't matter what else was going on. New man, new job, new life. He should have been top of your list. And he wasn't.'

A kind of laugh. 'Was he top of your list when you were on top of that little slut from work?'

'One night, Gina.'

'One night is plenty.' She shook her head and looked at all the painted barges. 'Don't act as though you were burned at the stake, Harry. You were the one who fucked around.'

Ah yes.

There would always be that.

After the show I was in the studio with Marty talking about airport security. I sat on the desk among the dead microphones, all of them a different primary colour. Like the Teletubbies. Marty swung in his chair, his hands stuffed deep inside his combat trousers.

'When they stop some little old lady who looks like your granny,' I said.

Marty grimaced. 'When they stop some little old lady who looks like your granny but they *don't* stop the guy who looks like Osama bin Laden.'

I laughed bitterly. 'The way they don't let you carry a pair of nail scissors on board in case you burst into the cockpit and give the pilot a quick pedicure.'

Marty laughed at the insanity of the lousy modern world.

61

'The way they don't let you carry a pair of nail scissors on board but they will flog you a bottle of duty-free booze and nobody bats an eyelid.'

'And what would you rather be attacked with?' I asked. 'A dinky pair of nail scissors or a broken bottle of Johnny Walker Blue Label?'

'Let me think about it for a bit,' Marty said. He swung in his chair. 'Shouldn't we be writing some of this down? It's all good stuff.'

'You'll remember it,' I said.

Marty looked over at the gallery. Josh had gone home. The sound engineer had gone home. But through the big glass window we could see some young guy with glasses staring at us. He had a rockabilly haircut and his quiff stood up like a shark's fin.

I didn't recognise him. But that was the BBC for you. There were always new kids fresh from their firsts at Oxford and Cambridge turning up to fetch us a sausage roll.

'Fancy a cup of char?' Marty asked me, and made a 'T' sign with his hands towards the booth. The young guy with glasses and the shark's fin quiff just stared at us. Marty impatiently banged the top part of the 'T' down on the bottom part. The sap on the other side of the glass just smiled weakly, shaking his head. He held up a hand – please wait, o mighty one – and came through to us, his cheeks a rosy glow.

'Come on, you thick bastard,' Marty barked at him, swinging his feet up on the desk. 'You're not taking a punt down the River Cam now. There's no Bollinger on the lawn with the rowdies from the Bullingdon Club.' Marty had dropped out of a comprehensive in Croydon. 'This is the real world. Tea for two and be sharp about it.'

The young man laughed. 'I'm terribly sorry,' he said. They were all posh boys. And even the ones who weren't posh boys had mastered the accent, if nothing else. 'I should have introduced myself but I didn't want to interrupt your editorial meeting.' He glanced at me, as if I might help him out. 'Blunt,' he said. 'Giles Blunt. Controller of Editorial Guidelines.'

I shook his hand. It was soft and wet as the River Cam. Marty was fabulously unmoved.

'And what?' he said, his pale features set in stone. 'Some fancy title makes you too important to get a cup of tea for the talent?'

The silence of the mortuary lab. And then Marty laughed. And Blunt and I smiled, relieved to hear something, anything, to break that awful silence.

'Just pulling your chain,' Marty laughed, standing up to offer his hand. He could ingratiate himself with management when he felt like it.

'We need to talk about the direction of *A Clip Round the Ear*,' said Blunt, regaining his composure, remembering his power. 'If you can find a window for me.'

Marty nodded briskly.

'Let me get my coat and I'll see you in my office,' he said.

The young man looked startled. 'Now?' he said, glancing at the big old-fashioned clock. It was way after midnight. Marty and I smiled at each other.

'Son,' he told Blunt, 'this is not a nine-to-five job.'

The three of us left Broadcasting House and walked down to Mayfair through empty city streets that I had known all my adult life. The streets around here never seemed to change. But I knew that I was changing.

'When you're thirty you want to be free,' I told Marty as we crossed Berkeley Square. 'But when you're forty you want to belong.'

Marty nodded. 'There's a little minx from Vilnius that I've been seeing,' he guffawed. 'I wouldn't mind belonging to her for an hour or two.'

Then he slapped me on the back, and turned to bark at Blunt, who was trailing behind us, worried about what he was getting into.

But I really believed it.

Ten years ago I longed for a life that was limitless and free, even though – or perhaps because – I knew I would never have it. But now, on the edge of forty, I just wanted my family, and roots, and to belong. And I thought that was typical. But Marty was the kind of man who, even at the edge of forty, wanted to belong to a Lithuanian pole dancer.

We came through the door of the Pussy Galore and a young woman in a nightdress took Blunt's arm.

'Want to party?' she said, her accent curiously American, yet ripe with some former Communist hell. 'Where you stay? Want to dance? Want to party?' She leaned in, all close and conspiratorial. 'We party at my place . . .'

Blunt stepped back as if she had a gun.

'Maybe later,' I told her, and put my arm around him, steering him away from the hungry eyes at the bar.

Marty had gone on ahead of us. He had a girl clinging on to each arm and some manager was whisking him off to the VIP area. His office.

'What is this place?' Blunt said, his voice quivering with a heady cocktail of fear and distaste.

'It's not what it was,' I said. 'Nothing like. Come on.'

We hurried downstairs into the blackness of Hades and Marty's office – a cosy VIP cubbyhole behind a red velvet rope. There was a former heavyweight boxer in black tie guarding the rope. He lifted it gently to allow Marty and the girls to enter. We quickly followed him, as if it was the last lifeboat on the *Titanic*.

Marty sat smothered in girls.

A song was playing that sounded like a beautiful heartbeat. It was the one where he says to the girl that he is not loving her the way he wanted to. That one. It's good, I like it.

Blunt and I perched on the end of the curved sofa like maiden aunts at a Roman orgy. Blunt stared at Marty Mann with appalled eyes.

'Ten years ago this place was quite chaste,' I told him, because I felt I should say something. 'Full of local girls who wanted to be models and actresses. Doing a bit of lap dancing so they could pay the rent until they became Dame Judi Dench.'

We turned our heads tracking a burst of hysterical laughter. The two blondes had removed their nightwear and were unfurling themselves all over Marty's grateful face in nothing more than a little strategic dental floss.

'Now it's full of girls who are from out of the neighbourhood,' I said. 'That's one of the things the EU has done for these places. Allowed freedom of movement for prostitutes.'

A waitress in a tutu brought a bottle of Pol Roger in a bucket of ice. She poured five glasses. Blunt shook his head at Marty.

'Relax,' I said. 'Have a drink. The sex is not compulsory. You can still leave these places with your virtue intact.'

'It's exploitative,' he said. 'Degrading. And it treats half the human race as cattle.'

Then he reached for his champagne.

And by the time I left them, Blunt had lipstick all over his gurning face, half of the Baltic hanging on his fragile frame and his BBC credit card in his hand, waving it wildly as he howled for more, more, more.

Outside the Pussy Galore I let the friendly gorilla on the door hail me a cab. And I saw that there was something else that had not changed about these places over the last ten years.

Standing by the taxi drivers waiting for a fare, there were the boyfriends of the dancers. They were as silent and still and alone as they ever were – the fun-loving studs whose dreams had come true, who had landed the girl with the face and the body and the perfect, rock-hard breasts, and it had done nothing but bring them jealousy and despair.

Those men had not changed at all over the last ten years. But now there were more of them.

Pat removed a crushed cider can from the grave of his grandparents.

I looked at the headstone – the name of my father above my mother, four middle names between the pair of them, a relic from the days when the children of the working class

65

were loaded with as many names as a duke or duchess. I looked at their names, and I watched Pat removing the dead flowers, and I felt nothing.

My parents were not here. I didn't know and it did not matter if the divine spark of life that made them who they were had gone to heaven or oblivion. But it had gone, and all that was left were those husks that I kissed, and touched once, and choked over even though I knew they had nothing to do with my mother and father. My mum and dad never looked like that.

I wasn't the grave visitor. Part of me – perhaps a big part of me – wanted to keep the grave clean, but only in theory. The crushed cider can had not been tossed on my parents. I couldn't take it personally. Not the way my son did.

I stared out over the fields beyond. When my parents had been buried – years apart but the same spring month claimed both of them – those fields were bright yellow. Now they were brown and bare.

'But why do we have to go?' Pat said, and I turned to watch him arranging the little bunch of flowers we had bought at a petrol station on the way out of town. 'Why do we have to go to – what's it called?'

'The Cenotaph,' I said. 'It's called the Cenotaph. And we have to go because . . . we owe these old men.'

And because I never talked to my father as much as I should have. And because I never went to the pub with him because I was too busy with work and girls and life. And because I loved him but I didn't really know him at all. I did not even know what had happened on Elba. And then it was too late.

'Pat,' I said, and saying my son's name in this place gave me a good feeling. 'We have to go to the Cenotaph for this one Sunday of the year because this is who we are.'

He straightened up from the grave. I have to admit the kid did a good job of keeping it nice. And although my parents were not here, I was grateful for that.

'But Gina and I were going to go ice skating on Sunday,' he said.

He was about to say more but I did that thing that my father could always do with me.

I silenced him with a look.

six

Joni sat reading the latest copy of *Go Girl* as her mother ran the fine-toothed nit comb through her long brown hair.

'And what do you say if someone says that you have nits?' Cyd asked, not for the first time.

Joni didn't look up from her magazine.

'I say, "Please, miss, but I *don't* have any nits,"' she said. 'I say, "Please, miss, we used the special cream and then the special comb and my mummy checked. She looked all over for the nits, miss, but they had all gone."'

'Very good,' Cyd said.

She began to collect her head-lice equipment – the Nitty Gritty Nit-Free Head Lice comb, the Wild Child hair cream – and stared thoughtfully at Joni's hair. Under the lights of our living room, it looked impossibly glossy, ridiculously clean.

Our little Holloway home wasn't big but we had torn down a separating wall on the ground floor and there was a large open space where we all rattled around – eating, reading, watching TV, hanging out, hunting for head lice.

A small keyboard was shoved up against a wall, and Peggy sat playing. You would think a piano would get in the way, but somehow it seemed natural to us. Pat and I were reading at opposite ends of the sofa – *Broadcast* for me, Edward de Bono's *Lateral Thinking* for him – as Peggy carefully picked out the same snatch of melody.

'Joni?' Peggy said, not lifting her eyes from the keys.

Joni put down *Go Girl*. 'What, Peg?'

'Have you got nits?' Peggy asked.

Cyd shook her head at the general laughter. 'Don't make fun of her,' she said, kissing Joni on the back of her bug-free head. But our youngest was proudly flashing her vampire smile.

'I have no nits,' she said. 'I am a nit-free girl. There are no nits on me.'

She jumped down from the table and got herself a banana. Pat and I went back to our reading. Peggy carried on producing the same little ribbon of notes.

'Oh, that's nice, Peg,' Pat said. 'Mariah Carey?'

Peggy snorted. 'Mariah Carey? This is Mendelssohn, sunshine.' She delicately picked out the same few haunting notes. '*Lieder ohne Worte.* "Songs Without Words" to you.'

'Sounds like Mariah Carey,' Pat said good-naturedly, grinning at me.

'What do they teach you at Ramsay Mac?' Peggy said.

'Not much,' he said, returning to his *Lateral Thinking*.

Joni appeared before me with a banana in her hand. She bared her fangs at me. 'Don't forget,' she told me, 'the Tooth Fairy still hasn't been yet.'

Pat and Peggy were watching me, poker-faced and unsmiling.

I nodded. 'I'm on it,' I said. Joni went off to sit next to her sister on the piano stool.

'Give me your hands,' Peggy said. 'I'll show you how to do it.'

'Joni,' Cyd said, 'don't play the piano when you're eating a banana.'

I followed my wife to the kitchen. She was experimenting with some dips. All these different little pots of something between red and orange. It looked like Thai sweet chilli sauce to me.

'This Tooth Fairy stuff,' I said.

Cyd's eyes widened. 'You didn't lose her teeth, did you?'

I held up my hands. 'Got them in a matchbox up in my

room,' I said. 'But I remember how scathing she was about Father Christmas in Selfridge's. I thought she was going to tear down Santa's Grotto. And that was – what? Nine months ago.'

'Ah,' Cyd said. 'But that's because it wasn't the *real* Father Christmas. Don't you get it? She believes but she doesn't believe,' my wife said. 'Don't you ever feel that way?'

Marty had sunk three Red Bulls and he was ready to take on the most powerful nation on the planet.

'Obama removing Churchill's bust from the Oval Office,' he said, shaking his script at the mic. 'What's all that about?' He crumpled an empty Red Bull can in his fist. 'You heard about this?' he said. 'Bronze bust of Winston Churchill by Sir Jacob Epstein – worth hundreds of thousands of pounds, as it happens – loaned to the Americans after 9/11 – and this guy Obama decides he doesn't want it in the White House . . .'

He looked up at me through the glass. He was waiting for calls from outraged listeners eager to give the American President a clip round the ear. I shook my head. The subject wasn't making the lights come on. Marty continued with his riff.

'Who does Obama think is out there dodging the roadside bombs in Afghanistan? The French? The Germans? The Belgians? No – it's our boys. Standing side by side with Uncle Sam, just as we always do, in good wars and in bad. And then Obama has the brass neck to leave a bust of Churchill out for the bin men.'

This wasn't strictly true. Obama had given the bust back to the British Ambassador and replaced it with one of Lincoln. But Marty was so steeped in American culture that he could not fail to be hurt. He felt rejected. He took the return of the Churchill bust as a snub, and that was good – good for the show. What was bad was that his listeners apparently did not care what the American President had sitting on his mantelpiece. When he went to Mariah's 'I Stay In Love', I hit the button.

'They're not going for it,' I said. 'We've got a guy on line one who wants to talk about inconsiderate parking. Sid from Surbiton.'

Marty cursed. 'Our nation is publicly humiliated by the American President and this guy wants to talk about Mr Jones from next door parking his Vauxhall Fiasco over his drive?'

'Yeah,' I said. 'Line one, after Mariah Carey. Coming back in ninety seconds.'

Marty tore the final can from his Red Bull four-pack, popped it and took a swig. Then he meticulously tore the cardboard packing to little pieces as Sid from Surbiton told us about his next-door neighbour parking across his drive.

'I'll tell you what we should do with someone like that, Sid,' Marty broke in. 'He should be shot.'

Then he reached for the switch to cut off Surbiton Sid, but somehow backhanded the last can of Red Bull. It clunked against the live mic and toppled over, its contents spreading over the script before him.

Like blood sitting on a pavement, I thought.

I reached for my wife and she did not even turn away. She did not have to. It was as if I had not touched her, and so I retreated to my side of the bed. I was just sliding into sleep when she started talking.

'How did stepmothers get such a rotten reputation?' Cyd said in the darkness. 'How did that happen? For years and years you cook fish fingers and do the laundry and sew the name-tags on for someone else's kid and it's never enough. And it's never appreciated. And you do it all for a child who is not your own, and even after you learn to love them, you can never be number one. You can never be good enough. You wipe their nose and treat their nits – their nits, Harry, remember the nit comb, when it was Pat and Peggy who were giving a home to the nits? – and yet you still get treated as if you just dumped Hansel and Gretel in the forest.'

I turned on the light.

'You're right, baby.'

'Don't "baby" me, Harry. And turn that light off, will you?'

I turned the light off and lay on my side, one hand stroking her arm, but ready to withdraw at the first sign of hostility.

'You think you've got it hard, Harry? Try being a step-mother for ten years. Try being the wicked witch whose only crime is not being the mother of the kid she's trying to raise.'

Cyd was great with Pat. She had never forced it. They had been friends and, over the years, it had become more than that. The only thing missing was the blood. If you ask me, the blood is overrated. It's the fish fingers and the name-tags and the nit comb that count.

'You think it's easy for me, having Gina come back and start playing happy families? And seeing Pat torn between his mother and his father? And me as the meaningless bit player in the family drama. You think I like it?'

'We appreciate it,' I said. 'All of it. Everything you've done. Just being here.'

It was true. We appreciated it. But we also took it for granted. Especially now that Gina was back. The fish fingers and the name-tags and the nits were being consigned to history. 'I'm sorry,' I said.

'You don't have to be sorry. Just a little less self-absorbed would be good. Would be nice. Would be appreciated. And have a word with Pat. He's started bringing his phone to the dinner table just in case she calls or texts or deigns to get in touch. He never did that before. You think you're the only one. And it's hard for all of us.' Her pillow rustled as she shook it. 'Gina,' she said. 'That bloody . . .'

But she couldn't find the words. There were no words. And then she let me take her in my arms and I loved my wife. And that was the way I always thought of her – my wife. I never thought of Cyd as my second wife, because that made her sound like some kind of consolation prize, or runner-up, or second best, and she was never that. Cyd was not my second wife. She was my wife. Although where exactly that left my son, I never really knew.

But wherever it was, I could see that it wasn't a great place to be.

'You can't smoke in pubs?' Ken Grimwood said, the glowing roll-up halfway to his incredulous mouth. 'Since when can't you smoke in pubs?'

'It's been a while,' I said, and I looked up at the barmaid as if she might make an exception for someone who had lost a leg freeing the world from tyranny.

But she just stood there staring blankly at the offending fag until the old man holding it had stubbed it out. Then she turned away.

And I realised that Ken Grimwood was having me on. He knew very well that there was no smoking in pubs.

The old men in their green berets all chuckled. On their chests their medals glinted in the twilight of the little brown pub. There were six of them plus Singe Rana. They all wore shirt, tie and blazer, making me feel ludicrously underdressed in my leather jacket and black jeans. They all wore the green beret of the Royal Naval Commandos, apart from the old Gurkha who wore a bush hat with a cotton hatband, the rim pinned up on one side. It had a square patch of green felt with a silver badge – two crossed kukri knives under a crown.

'Careful, Ken,' one of them said in a Glasgow accent, 'you'll have the Health and Safety inspector down on us.'

They were having a good time. They had not seen each other for a while.

A few years before smoking had been banned in public houses, and everywhere else, the Royal Naval Commando Association had been disbanded, due to the toll of the years. There were not many of them left. The youngest of them – the ones who were teenagers in the war – had to be in their eighties now. They sipped their half-pints of mild and bitter and laughed together in the Trafalgar Square tourist pub.

I looked at Pat sipping his lemonade. He was smiling.

'Singe Rana,' Ken said. 'Tell us the one about the three Germans at Monte Cassino.'

The old Gurkha frowned at his orange juice. He was the only one of them who wasn't drinking beer for breakfast. I had tried to buy some food but they had little interest in eating. I had tempted a couple of them with a bag of cheese-and-onion crisps, and I had a feeling they would call it a meal.

'That story is worn out from the telling,' Singe Rana said in his quiet sing-song, and the other old men protested in their voices from the Clyde and the Taff and the Tyne, and the Trent and the Mersey and the Thames. Tourists at the bar turned to look at the noisy band, and then looked away. They were just a bunch of old men in their Sunday best. If the tourists saw the green berets and the medals, they gave no sign.

'Go on, Singe, one more time, for your old mates,' Ken said, getting out his tin of Old Holborn. Had he forgotten that there was no nicotine in here? No, I think it was simply that he did not care. The pathetic, semi-skimmed little rule-makers of the lousy modern world – he genuinely did not give a toss about them. He made a small gesture at Pat and me. 'And for some new mates, too. They haven't heard it.'

Singe Rana held his glass of orange juice and looked at it as he began talking. The old soldiers smiled and nudged each other with delight. But they let him tell his story without interruption.

'We were on night patrol at Monte Cassino,' he said. 'Our colonel liked to use us for night patrol. He knew the Gurkhas were good mountain troops and that the night held no fear for us.' He peered with interest at his orange juice. I looked at Pat. He was holding his lemonade and staring at the old man with a fixed smile. Ken Grimwood was chuckling to himself as he made himself a roll-up.

'On our first night patrol at Cassino we found three Germans asleep in a slit trench,' Singe said. 'We took the two men on the outside and cut off their heads.' His voice was very quiet. 'The one in the middle we let sleep on. So that when he awoke,

74

he would find his friends sitting with him.' Singe allowed himself a small smile at this point. 'And tell the others.'

The Gurkha sipped his orange juice as the old Commandos fell about laughing. I saw Pat still wearing his frozen grin, uncertain how to react, a little white around the gills. As if he thought he was missing something, as if the old men might be having him on. He looked at me for guidance then quickly stared down at his drink, suddenly knowing that every word of Singe Rana's story was true.

We stood among the silent crowds on Whitehall and squinted against the bright November sunshine as the soldiers came marching past.

THE GLORIOUS DEAD, it said on the Cenotaph, and the poppies and the flags were bright splashes of colour against the pale Portland stone, and the three words burned my eyes.

I looked at my son's face and I wanted to believe that he felt it too. All of it. The sacrifice, the courage. How ridiculously easy it would have been for my father to have died at Anzio or Elba or Monte Cassino, shot in a ditch or bleeding out in a landing craft or drowning in a dock choked with smashed men and machinery, how easy it would have been for my dad to die aged eighteen, and for neither of us to ever be born.

Pat felt it too, I thought, despite not growing up with it the way I did, despite not being taught about it at school. He got it. The heroism, the wild reckless courage. The armies of boys who never came home, or who came home with their bodies in shreds. And all that we would forever owe to these old men.

He leaned towards me. 'It feels a bit like being in church,' he whispered, with a little half-smile, and I felt a flash of irritation. But then I nodded and touched his shoulder. Because he was right.

Despite the light breeze on our faces, and the dazzling winter sunlight in our eyes, it was exactly like being in church. The quiet awe, the reverence of the crowd. The sense of being in the presence of something monumental, the way that being in this sacred place did something to your breathing, and to your heart. My father felt very close.

The soldiers were old now – more than old. And surprisingly small. Almost like a different species of man. They reminded me of school field-trips and dinky suits of medieval armour gawped at inside glass cases. A race of pint-sized warriors.

They were stiff-limbed, self-conscious. It was more than old age. It was more than the memory of military bearing; it was as if they were self-conscious at being watched. Not by us, not by the crowds on Whitehall. But by the others. The ghosts of that Sunday morning. All of their fallen brothers.

I looked at Pat's face. He had loved his grandfather more than he loved anyone in the world, but he had lost him when he was too young to understand. And I wanted him to understand. Because I could see that it was fading among his generation. All that priceless knowledge. The memory of what they did, and the awareness of our debt. Did he remember the way his grandfather looked when he took off his shirt in his back garden? Did Pat remember that terrible starburst of scar tissue that almost covered my father's upper body?

'Here they come,' he said, and I turned back to the serried ranks of soldiers, scanning the row upon row upon row for the green berets.

I could see them too, and I felt my heart beat faster at the sight of what my dad called 'my mob'. The Royal Naval Commandos. The bravest of the brave. *In primo exulto.* Rejoice in being first.

They were almost level with us when Pat's phone began to ring.

Playing more than ringing.

It was that song again.

The song that sounds like a heartbeat. 'Love Lockdown' by Kanye West. *Dun-dun-dun*, it went, and the heads of the crowds turned towards us. *Dun-dun-dun.* Just like a piercing electronic heartbeat. And as Pat fumbled in his pocket, the people around us shook their heads and went *tch-tch-tch* and snorted with disgust. And someone behind us commented, 'Oh, for God's *sake!*' as if we knew nothing, my son and I.

He had the phone out of his pocket, so it was suddenly louder, but in his rush to turn it off it squirted out of his fingers and fell to the pavement. You would think that might shut up old Kanye West, but it didn't. The phone went on as if it was what in the old days we used to call the twelve-inch disco mix. *Dun-dun-dun*, it went, as Pat fell to his knees – not easy in those packed crowds at the Cenotaph. *Dun-dun-dun*. Pat's face burning like my blood.

I looked back at the old soldiers just in time to see Ken Grimwood and the others from the pub marching past. Pat picked up his phone and squirmed through the crowds, getting away. I called his name but he did not stop. I looked back at the Commandos, hoping that their hearing might have faded to the point where they could not hear Kanye West's 'Love Lockdown' at the Cenotaph. But their hearing was not that bad.

And I could read their faces, the faces of the old men, those beloved, unforgiving old soldiers, just as I could read my father's face when I broke a window, or dropped out of school, or got divorced.

For this?
For this?
We did it all for this?

Somewhere beyond the Remembrance Day crowds, and where the idling tourists began, I caught up with my son.

'Give me that thing,' I said. He did not move. I turned up the volume. 'Just give it to me,' I demanded, my voice way too loud, and tourists gawped as if we were a Covent Garden mime act.

The tears welling up, Pat gave me his phone.

I looked at it.

ONE MISSED CALL FROM GINA, it said.

My fist tightened on the bloody thing as if to crush it,

and I held my hand above my head, truly meaning to bring it down on the pigeon-flecked pavement and smash the phone beyond all repair.

Then I looked at my son and he looked at me.

I watched him wipe his nose on the back of his sleeve and choke down the tears. I looked at the poppy sticking awkwardly out of the buttonhole of his school blazer. I sighed and shook my head.

Still white with fury, I slowly lowered my hand and gave him back his phone.

'Come on, kiddo,' I said, putting my arm around his shoulders, not wanting him to start crying, and suddenly, desperately, wanting to be away from this place. 'Let's go home.'

But as we walked in silence to the tube station, I could feel it between us.

It did not really matter that I had given him his phone back.

Something had been broken.

seven

I sat in the kitchen hunched over the glow of the laptop's screen as my wife moved through the house locking up, checking windows and turning off the lights. She hovered in the doorway, tomorrow's school satchel in her hands.

'You coming up then?' Cyd said.

'I'll be right up,' I smiled, and she nodded and moved away. Then I could hear her out the back, the recycled bottles clinking like wind chimes. She came back inside, and I heard the key in the lock.

I typed 'Commando' into the search engine and waited.

And then I sighed.

Type 'Commando' into a search engine and what you get is old Arnold Schwarzenegger product, violent video games and cheerleaders with no pants.

Going Commando once meant risking your life to save the free world. Now it means dispensing with your underwear.

Cyd came back and stared at me. I pressed quit and the cheerleaders were instantly gone. My wife folded her arms and leaned against the doorjamb.

'Interesting?' she said.

'Not really,' I said. Then we both looked at the child monitor as Joni began to call out in her sleep.

'I'll get her,' my wife said. 'Don't worry, Harry. You just carry on with what you're doing.'

When she was gone I typed 'Beach Parties' into the

search engine. I was offered just over 30,000 sites featuring people with no pants.

And soon I could hear the sound of my wife soothing our daughter on the child monitor, the little green lights rising and falling with the sound of their voices.

But long after their voices had faded to silence, and the house was still, I sat in the kitchen, looking for the ghost of my father.

'We love edgy,' Blunt said, speaking for the station, for the corporation, for the entire BBC. He gave Marty a professional smile. 'We love controversial. We love danger. We love all those things.' Another smile that glittered with frosty familiarity. Then he looked down with some distaste at the newspapers spread across his desk. 'But we don't like trouble. We don't like anti-BBC leaders in national newspapers. We don't like the media ripping out our liver and feeding it to the dogs.'

Sid from Surbiton had taken Marty's advice. He had attempted to solve the parking dispute with his neighbour by shooting him in the face with a starting pistol.

Sid blamed Marty. SHOOT THY NEIGHBOUR, SHOCK JOCK TOLD ME, a tabloid screamed. The papers blamed Marty. The broadsheets had debates about the licence fee being used to promote gun crime. The tabloids just went bananas, absolutely ape-shit with righteous rage, choosing us as this week's telling vignette from badly mangled Britain.

Pictures of Sid being hauled off to the cells shared front pages with Marty photos from the archives. He picked up a copy of the *Daily Mirror* that had a picture of him arriving at some forgotten premiere. He shook his head and looked at me with desperation in his eyes.

'Am I losing my hair?' he asked. 'Have I put on a few pounds?'

I ignored him.

'How bad is it?' I said to Blunt.

'The neighbour has a damaged retina,' Blunt said. 'It gets

80

worse if he loses the eye. If he keeps the eye – that would be helpful. So we want him to keep the eye.'

I placed my hands on the pile of papers, fighting the rising tide of panic. The car was still parked across Sid's driveway. So a fat lot of good shooting his neighbour had done.

'Some of these reporters talked to other residents,' I said. 'Nobody liked this guy. The guy that got shot. They call him a neighbour from hell.' There was a photograph of a front yard with a refrigerator dumped on a shabby lawn, and a pack of unwashed, unsupervised, sugar-crazed children clambering all over it. 'Inconsiderate parking was just the start. He has kids running wild. One of those amusing signs saying, *Beware of the Children*, which is never funny if you actually live next door to the little bastards. Music turned up to eleven. A dog that had apparently been trained to pee through your letterbox.'

'The usual,' Marty said, making no attempt to stifle a yawn. 'Chav scum.'

'Popular opinion is definitely with Sid from Surbiton,' Blunt conceded. 'But I am not sure the response was commensurate with the crime. After all, the show is called *A Clip Round the Ear*. Not *A Gun Blast to the Face*.'

'It's a – what do you call it?' Marty said. 'An aphorism. A maxim. If you want to start getting all literal-minded then we could call it *Hanging's too Good for the Chav Scum*.'

We both ignored him.

'So it doesn't help us,' I said to Blunt. 'It doesn't help us that everyone hated this guy.'

'It doesn't help you,' he corrected.

And we stared at each other across a BBC desk covered with the morning papers, and we understood each other perfectly.

I stood in the newsagent's looking up at the shelves of tobacco. SMOKING KILLS, it said under a leering skull. SMOKING HARMS YOURSELF AND OTHERS. YOU ARE GOING

TO DIE NOW. DEATH. DEATH. CERTAIN DEATH.
PUFF, PUFF – YOU'RE DEAD.

'Is it for yourself?' said the boy behind the counter.

'No, it's a gift,' I said.

I thought that I would buy Ken a tin of Old Holborn. The kind of tin that he carried, and that I could clearly remember my father having – yellow and white, with a drawing of a Ye Olde Georgian street on the front, and 'Old Holborn Blended Virginia' written in that fake fountain-pen font, as if nothing in this universe was more tasteful and sophisticated and classy than rolling your own soggy little man-made snout.

I thought that I might be purchasing the last loose tobacco in captivity. But the newsagent's was full of the stuff. Just not in tins.

'You could try eBay,' the kid behind the counter told me. 'They sell them on eBay. But we got these.'

The kid made a gracious gesture with his hand, like a proud sommelier presenting me with his extensive wine list. Amber Leaf. Golden Virginia. Van Nelle. Samson. Domingo. Drum. And Old Holborn itself – still going strong but in small packs rather than big tins now, and given new brave new world colours of orange, black and blue, kin to a lovely pack of Jaffa cakes.

'You want some skins with that?' said the kid behind the counter.

I stared at him, struck dumb by the fact that the baton dropped by my father's generation had been picked up by what my dad would have called the pot heads – the kind of people he despised above all others. Apart from men who wore dresses. And Germans.

I got a 500-gram pack containing ten convenient grow-your-own-tumour sachets. It wouldn't make up for Pat's phone going off at the Cenotaph. It would not make up for smashing the silence with 'Love Lockdown' by Kanye West.

But I didn't know how else to say I was sorry.

* * *

82

At Nelson Mansions, Tyson dozed at the foot of the concrete staircase, his enormous front paws clamped possessively on some hideously chewed object, possibly a human bone.

I stepped over him and skipped up the stairs, passing a couple of children huddled in their elf-like hoods, like some Tolkien nightmare. It felt much colder than November, but that might have been just the ceaseless wind that always whipped through Nelson Mansions, whatever the weather.

I rang the doorbell and a man in his early fifties answered. He looked soft and rich, like a banker enjoying his day off in lime-green Lacoste, a man whose life had treated him well. His thin lips and little eyes made three slits of his face, and he could be nobody else's son. I held out my hand and introduced myself.

'Ian Grimwood,' he said, and his accent was different to his father's – a classless modern drawl. 'Thank you for – you know. Everything.'

I saw him looking at the Old Holborn in my hands. 'No problem,' I said.

Singe Rana was just leaving. He turned his soft golden face towards me. 'I'll come back when it's over,' he said.

'I wanted to say I was sorry,' I told him. 'My son's phone – it rang as you were marching. And – I felt bad. I felt terrible. About all the old soldiers.'

Singe Rana smiled gently. 'Don't be so fretful,' he said. 'Half of them are so deaf they couldn't hear a bomb go off. And the other half don't care.' He tapped my arm fondly with his rolled-up copy of the *Racing Post*. 'They have seen worse things.'

Then he slipped away.

Voices were being raised in the kitchen. Ken's unmoving, old man quaver and, much louder, the voice of a woman. She had the same accent as her brother. One of those accents that sound as though you come from nowhere.

'I don't know how you can even think such things,' she said, coming out of the kitchen. She was a bit younger and in much better shape than the man. A good-looking fifty-year-old

83

woman. But she had the same small slash of a mouth, and the same slightly squinty eyes as her brother, and her father, who followed her out of the kitchen with a bread knife in his hand.

'Go on,' Ken invited her. 'Stick it in me. Right there, girl.' He gestured at the crest on his blazer pocket. 'Then you'll all be happy.'

The son held up his hands. 'Come on now, let's all calm down,' he said, and I could see that it was the daughter who shared her father's temper.

Ken leaned against the television set for a breather. The woman was looking at me.

'Tracey,' her brother said, 'this is Mr Silver, who brought Dad back from the hospital.'

She was shaking her head. 'Please don't tell me this is for him,' she said, snatching the 500-gram pack from my hand. 'Don't tell me that.'

I felt a flare of resentment. 'Well,' I began.

'He's got cancer,' she said, very slowly, as if English was not my first language. 'Lung cancer. Caused by this stuff.' She threw the pack back at me. It hit me on the chest but I caught it.

'I know,' I said.

'What's going on in there?' Tracey Grimwood said. She tapped her temple with an impatient index finger. 'Are you as stupid as he is? You give Old bloody Holborn to a man who is dying of lung cancer? What are you thinking?'

I took a breath.

'I was thinking that it wouldn't make much difference,' I said, more calmly than I felt. I remembered my own parents giving up their Bogart-and-Bacall smoking fantasy before they died. And a lot of good it did them.

She threw up her hands and went into the kitchen, where I could see her putting the kettle on. Ken took the tobacco from me and winked.

'Just go easy with it, Dad,' Ian said, gazing anxiously at the kitchen.

'A little of what you fancy does you good,' Ken said, settling

84

himself on the sofa. He expertly cracked open the 500-gram pack and began emptying the sachets into his battered tin, the kind you can only find on eBay. He turned towards the kitchen. 'I deserve a few small pleasures.'

Tracey's head appeared from the kitchen.

'If you wanted pleasure, then you could have been a real grandfather to your grandchildren,' she said. Then she looked at me. 'Do you see any photos of my kids? Or Ian's children?'

I looked up at the mantelpiece. There was the young boxer. And the three children in the faded colours of the sixties. And in the middle, the one of Ken Grimwood's wedding day. I looked at it now. He wore his naval uniform and stood proudly in his bandy-legged gait, his shy bride almost covered by the waves of her white wedding dress.

Tracey came into the living room. 'Beautiful grandchildren, he has,' she said. 'Beautiful, they are. Or were – they're grown-ups themselves now. But did he ever take them to the park or read them a story? Did he ever do all the normal granddad things? No, he was too wrapped up in himself. Horses. And greyhounds. And gambling.'

Ken was frowning at his tobacco. 'Punk rockers, they were,' he said. 'Punk rockers and skinheads.'

Tracey exploded. 'That was years ago!'

'I'll make the tea,' Ian said, scuttling off to the kitchen.

'And Suzy was a Goth, not a punk rocker,' Tracey said. 'Now she's married with a kid of her own. And does he show a blind bit of interest?' She watched him unloading the sachets into his tin and sighed – a lifetime of frustration in one long breath. 'And why are you here, Mr Silver? Apart from encouraging this silly old goat to smoke himself to death.'

I thought about it.

I didn't know how to explain it.

'He – Ken – was with my father,' I said, and he didn't look at me but I thought he was listening. 'In the war, I mean. They fought together.' I looked at her. 'My dad was a Royal Naval Commando too,' I said.

She nodded, calmer than I had seen her. She picked up the bread knife from where it was sitting on top of the TV.

'And your father passed away, I presume?'

I was watching that knife.

'Ten years ago,' I said. 'From lung cancer, as it happens. And he had stopped smoking in the final years. Not that it did him any good.'

'Paddy Silver,' Ken chuckled. 'Hard as teak, that boy. A very good boy, old Paddy.'

'Then you are one of those,' Tracey said, tapping the bread knife in her palm. 'I've seen a few of your type over the years.'

'And what's my type?' I asked. I didn't want to argue with her. But I felt I was going to.

She looked at her father.

'Men who think the old medal he's got stuck at the back of some drawer holds the meaning of the universe.' She smiled with vicious amusement. 'Well, thanks for stopping by, Mr Silver, and thank you for your inappropriate gift, which I am sure is given with the best intentions. But let me tell you something about my dad, so that you do not leave here under any illusions.'

'Ian!' Ken barked. 'That bleeding tea ready yet?'

A plaintive voice from the kitchen. 'Coming, Dad,' the son said.

Tracey took a step closer to me, the bread knife hanging by her side. I wanted to step back but I stood my ground.

'He's not a hero,' said the old man's daughter. 'And he's not your father. So if you are here looking for a hero, or you're here looking for your father, then you have come to the wrong place. He's just a stupid, selfish old man who is waiting for death.' She pointed at me with the bread knife. 'And you can have him.'

I stood in the doorway of my son's bedroom and I didn't turn on the light. Everything was *Star Wars*. Everything was still *Star Wars*. Shouldn't it be something else by now?

But grey plastic X-wing fighters and a big *Millennium*

Falcon hung from the ceiling. The classic poster was above his single bed. Luke aiming his gun at the camera, flanked by Han Solo wielding a pink-beamed light sabre – when did Han Solo ever use a light sabre? I didn't remember that – and Princess Leia blasting away. And the glorious bit players – Obi-Wan Kenobi, and the two droids, and Chewbacca. And looming above them all, the patron saint of lousy fathers – Darth Vader, gazing blankly at the Death Star.

Something had been arrested in this room. A clock had stopped. It was as if time had stood still at the point in my son's childhood when things had still been uncomplicated.

He had started sleeping over at Gina's. On a school night, it was just about do-able, the run from Soho to Islington. If he skipped breakfast, or stuffed down an almond croissant on the tube, then he could make it to school on time. There were no lifts to school from his mother. Gina did not own a car. As far as I could tell, there were multiple reasons for the lack of a car – because you could walk most places if you lived in Soho, because she had a bit of a phobia about driving, and an even bigger phobia about parking. And so I kept my mouth shut. And he started to make himself at home at Gina's place.

Cyd appeared at my side and put her arm around me. A moment later, Joni squirmed between us, wearing her pyjamas and brushing her teeth.

'You should do that in the bathroom,' Cyd said.

Joni looked at her brother's *Star Wars* bedroom, still brushing her teeth. Then she lifted her face. There was toothpaste all around her mouth. It looked like ice cream.

'But why can't Pat's mummy come and see him here?' she said. And we didn't have an answer. Joni wandered back to the bathroom. Soon we could hear her elaborately spitting into the sink as she rinsed out her mouth.

'He's fine,' Cyd told me. 'You know he's fine, you good man. And you are a good man. And you are a loving father. And that beautiful boy will be all right. And it's good that he knows his mother, Harry. And it is very necessary.'

I swallowed.

I should have done something, I know. Or said something. Showed her that I was happy and grateful she was on my side. But I just kept staring at Luke Skywalker pointing his gun at me. I could feel my wife's patience being tested.

'Is it going to be like this every time he sees her?' Cyd said. 'Don't you *want* her to know him? She didn't leave him, you know.' I knew what was coming next. 'She left you.'

That was true.

But there were times when it felt like she had left both of us.

And sometimes they lasted for years.

eight

We were at a Lee Marvin double bill at the NFT when he told me.

The Dirty Dozen and *Hell in the Pacific*. Lee Marvin in Nazi-occupied France on a suicide mission with a bunch of doomed misfits and psychopaths. And then, after a twenty-minute break, Lee Marvin stranded on a desert island with a fanatical Japanese soldier. A perfect Saturday afternoon for a father and son. We could spend hours together without hardly ever being required to actually talk.

'*We got enough here to blow up the whole world!*' I quoted as we came out of *The Dirty Dozen*, and Pat smiled shyly.

The booksellers were packing up their stalls. It was getting dark early now and the lights were coming on all along the Thames. The dome of St Paul's shone dully in the last light of the day. Ancient brown barges drifted down the river. I bought hot chocolate for Pat and a tea for me. The giddiness from the film started to wear off. We looked at the river rolling towards the night.

Pat sipped his drink and stared back at the cinema, a white moustache of cream on his upper lip.

'We've got a break before *Hell in the Pacific*,' I said, and he nodded. There were a few blond hairs on the side of his face, like the fuzzy fluff you get on a new tennis ball. He would have to start shaving one day. Give it a year, I thought. He wiped the foam from his lip and looked at me.

I saw him draw a breath.

'I've been thinking,' he said.

'You've been thinking?' I said, all startled.

Pat nodded. 'I might move in with Gina for a while,' he said, giving a little nod as if the idea had just occurred to him. 'See how that goes.'

I stared at him for a bit and then I looked away. 'What about school?' I said. 'You going to make that journey every day?'

'I've done it already,' he said quickly. He had thought this out, anticipated my questions.

'But not every day of the week,' I said, aware that I was somehow getting this all wrong. My son, who would clearly carry the weight of his parents' divorce to his dying day, was telling me that he wanted to live with his mother.

And I was talking about bus timetables.

'The thing is,' he said, 'I want to know her, properly know her. Not just the bits and pieces of her that I've had over the years. But properly know her. Like normal people.'

'If it makes you happy,' I said, and all those wasted years made my heart feel like lead. I never felt more like holding him. But I didn't touch him. 'Of course you should know each other. And she loves you. Of course she does. I just worry, that's all.'

His face furrowed in a sort of babyish scowl. 'What do you worry about?'

I shook my head. 'Exams,' I said, feebly. 'School. Just – all the disruption, Pat.'

'I don't want disruption,' he said. 'I want the opposite of disruption. Whatever the opposite of disruption is, that's what I want.'

The opposite of disruption, I thought. Stability? Normality? Happiness? A quiet life.

'When's all this going to happen?' I said.

He looked hopeful. 'Next weekend?' he suggested.

Then I exploded. 'But that's our weekend for the Clint Eastwood double bill! *Where Eagles Dare* and *Kelly's Heroes*!'

'To be honest,' he said, 'I'm not really that crazy about war films.'

90

I was dumbfounded. 'You don't like war films?'

'Not really. I mean, they're okay. *From Here to Eternity* was all right.'

'All right? All right? *From Here to Eternity* was all right?'

He shrugged. He drained his hot chocolate. 'Pretty good, then. The bits with Frank Sinatra in his Hawaiian shirt. And the bits with James Dean when he refuses to join the boxing team.'

'That's not James Dean,' I shuddered. 'That's Montgomery Clift. Then what are we doing here, if you don't like war films?'

'We go because *you* like them,' he said. 'And because it's a way for us to – you know – do stuff. We can't just kick a ball around forever, can we?'

We stared at the river in silence.

Pat cleared his throat. 'Lee Marvin starts in a bit,' he said.

'Bugger Lee Marvin,' I said. But he was right. Faces that I recognised from the audience of *The Dirty Dozen* were necking their skinny lattes and going back inside. But still I watched the river flow.

'I'm sorry it wasn't more settled,' I said, and I meant it, and I could feel it sticking at the back of my throat. 'I wish – I don't know. I wish it had all been more settled for you when you were growing up.' I felt a quick sting in the eyes and then it was gone. So I looked at him. 'I'm sorry, Pat. I really am.'

He laughed. 'That's okay,' he said. 'I'm fine. It's just . . . I don't remember that much. Of me and Gina, I mean. I think a lot of what I remember is just photographs I've seen. Sitting on a horse when I was four. Climbing over the back of a brown sofa with a light sabre. On a trampoline in the back garden. But I don't think I really remember that stuff. I've just seen the photographs.' Then he touched my arm lightly. 'Come on,' he said, his ludicrously blue eyes under his dirty blond fringe, his slow, all-knowing smile creeping across his face. 'Let's go and see Lee Marvin. You know you want to.'

'What about Elizabeth Montgomery?' I said, playing my

trump card. 'You'll be living further away from Elizabeth Montgomery. I mean, I know you'll still see her at school, but you'll be living in different parts of town.'

I didn't want him to get hurt. It was just that, wasn't it? That's what I was worried about.

But now he really laughed.

'Elizabeth Montgomery?' he said. 'She's not interested in me, Dad.'

Sid's neighbour did not lose his eye and we did not lose our jobs.

Marty and I sat across from Blunt, but the tension was gone. There were papers on the desk but they contained think pieces and leaders hailing Sid from Surbiton as a defender of decency, an honest man pushed too far by the feckless, a lonely dissident voice armed with nothing but a starting pistol, standing against the yob values of mangled Britain.

'We could get Sid into the studio,' Marty said. 'He's a have-a-go hero. Let him choose his top ten tracks from the eighties and talk about what's wrong with the lousy modern world.'

Blunt laughed. 'Let's not push our luck,' he said, and he smiled at us. It looked like a real smile. 'I wanted to invite the pair of you to the conference in Glasgow this weekend,' he said. 'It's the largest digital media industry event in the country.' We looked blank. 'I'll be making a speech about the next generation of video and audio content across multiple platforms,' Blunt said.

But still we looked blank.

Then Marty leaned forward, straining to decipher what Blunt was saying. Was it something to do with telly? And I thought of my son's bedroom. Would he take everything – just clean it out? Would he want me to help him move? Why hadn't he told me that he didn't like war films?

My phone began to vibrate and I looked at it. UNKNOWN NUMBER, it said, and I rose from my chair.

'I have to take this,' I said.

'This is Singe Rana,' he said, and it took me a long moment to connect the old Gurkha with the voice on the phone. 'You have to come. I can't talk to him today. You have to come. They have taken everything.'

When I hung up, Blunt was looking at me.

'This weekend?' he said, waiting.

'What about it?' I said. This weekend was when it all happened. This weekend was when my son moved from my life to his mother's life.

'Will you come?' Blunt said, testier now. 'It's the world's largest digital media industry event, attended by leading media, entertainment and communications professionals.' He visibly preened. 'I'm giving the keynote speech.'

'This weekend?' I said, shaking my head. 'Can't make it. Sorry.'

The BBC man looked at Marty. He shrugged and laughed. 'I can't make it either,' he said. 'I don't know why. But I'll think of something.'

When we were out of his office, Marty took my arm and snarled. 'They want you to open up a vein these days,' he said. 'They want to own your life. We do the show and then we go home. That's enough, isn't it?'

The phone in my pocket began to vibrate again.

'That's more than enough,' I said.

I called his daughter on the way over.

'What does he expect?' she said. The phone was removed from her mouth and I could hear her encouraging a grandchild to take just one more bite. Then she came back. 'He should have moved out of that dump and into a home years ago.'

The door was open when I arrived.

Not so much open as shattered.

Hanging off its hinges at a sick angle, the smashed wood below the frosted glass bearing the imprint of a large trainer. US size 12. It looked like a pitifully inadequate door to keep out the wicked world. I could see figures moving about inside.

Singe Rana. A young policewoman with a notepad. I rang the doorbell. Nobody responded so I went inside.

They had made a mess of the place.

Everything was spilling out of itself. The guts of the slashed sofa where Ken was slumped, small and unmoving, staring off into nothing. The contents of the drawers, their ancient gas and electricity bills and postcards from Australia covering the carpet like propaganda leaflets. And the life that had been lived here. That felt as though it had been dragged out into some harsher light, and smashed to pieces.

Singe Rana acknowledged me with a nod of his head.

There was a rolled-up *Racing Post* in his hand, and he held it like a sword. The policewoman carried on taking her notes. I picked up the photo of his wedding day, the glass a broken spider's web, and as I replaced it on the mantelpiece I saw the TV set.

It was one of those old-fashioned televisions that I had not seen in years – as deep as it was wide. They had not bothered to steal it, just rammed a pink figurine of a ballet dancer through the screen. She lay surrounded by shards of broken glass, one of her thin legs snapped off below the knee.

I sat down next to Ken. His breathing was more laboured than I had seen it. For the first time he looked like what he was – an old man with a tumour that was killing him. He looked beat.

'It's not as though there's even anything worth nicking,' he said. His fingers toyed with the tobacco tin on his lap but he made no attempt to roll a cigarette.

And my stomach fell away. Because I remembered that there was something worth stealing.

I quickly crossed the room to where the little chest of drawers had been ravaged. The remains of old age were still there. His reading glasses. More utility bills, preserved for posterity. Curled postcards, fading photographs of grand-children who were grown up now. It was all there.

But the medal was gone.

* * *

94

In the end it wasn't much. Pat just went.

I brought down two suitcases from the attic and he stuffed them and his school rucksack with all the clothes and books they could carry. He was leaving behind more than he was taking. I stood in the doorway of his bedroom and watched him hefting the bags. On the wall, Luke Skywalker and Han Solo and Darth Vader looked down, as forgotten as the toys of childhood.

A taxi pulled up outside and sat there with its engine idling, ready for a quick getaway. I went to the window and Gina was in the back of a black cab, dressed for the gym and frowning as she tapped out a text message. Waiting. Our front door opened and Cyd appeared, coming down the path to the waiting cab. I heard the voices of the two women, but not their words.

'I guess that's it then,' I said, a breezy note in my borrowed voice. 'Ready?'

He nodded, all business, and I took one of the suitcases and followed him out of the room, the eyes of the Jedi Knights upon us.

His sisters were waiting at the foot of the stairs. The big one and the little one. Peggy and Joni were both crying, and I felt my heart slide, wanting it to be over. Peggy threw her arms around his neck and Joni wrapped her arms around his thighs.

Pat smiled, dry-eyed but touched.

'I'm just down the road,' he said.

Then Cyd was there, standing in front of him and doing the things that it would never cross my mind to do. Pushing the hair off his face, untwisting the strap on his rucksack. Why couldn't I do that stuff?

'You take care, Pat,' she said, and she kissed his face, and she gave him a squeeze. And I knew her well enough to know that she wasn't thinking of the things she shouted at me about, she wasn't thinking about nits and fish fingers and dirty laundry. She was just thinking what a lovely kid he was and how we were all going to miss him.

95

He turned to look at me. I smiled and nodded encouragement, and for want of anything else to do, I held out my right hand. He gave it a soft little shake and then we let go of each other. We had never shaken hands before.

The front door was open. His mother was waiting. His sisters wiped their eyes, and said his name, and Joni was suddenly babbling something about Christmas, and we all had to reassure her that nothing had changed. Even though everything had changed.

'Okay,' I said, and we carried his bags out to the waiting car. And my son left home, and I watched him go, my throat all choked up because I had absolutely nothing to say.

I went into Joni's room and found her sitting up in bed waiting for me, hugging her knees, glowing from her bath, all smiley and smelling brand new. I sat on the edge of her bed and she snuggled down as I opened the book in my hands.

'Are you sitting comfortably?'

'Not really,' she said. That vampire smile. 'Just kidding.'

I laughed for the first time that day. And we began where we had left off.

'Fancy the happiness of Pinocchio on finding himself free,' I read. 'Without saying yes or no, he fled from the city and set out on the road that was to take him back to the house of the lovely Fairy.'

This is what we had settled for, in the time between princesses and hot vampire boys. This is the way we chose to go – back to the good stuff, the ones that had lasted. The princesses – and the mice in tutus, and the crocodiles on tractors, and all the animals who had the power of speech – were over, and there would be time enough later for the hot undead boys.

For now we would stick with books that we thought we knew because we had seen the Walt Disney movie, but that we didn't really know at all.

'Pinocchio, spurred on by the hope of finding his father and of being in time to save him, swam all night long.'

This was better than all those princesses and their chisel-jawed princes with a private income. This was the real thing.

Wanting to be a real boy. Wanting to be like all the other real boys. Carlo Collodi made that simple wish feel like an impossible dream.

And my daughter stared up at me, her eyes shining, as our heads struggled with the knowledge that not all stories have the same happy ending.

nine

My father's medal sat at the back of my desk.

I could not remember the last time I had looked inside the claret-coloured box. Long enough ago for me to forget that there were also three rings in there. My mother's engagement ring, her wedding ring and her eternity ring. They were very small, like trinkets for a child's hand. They were all made of low-grade wartime gold, hardly metal at all, and the cheapness of them made something stick in the back of my throat, and block my chest, and burn my eyes.

Yet my mum and dad were together from school to the grave. So who was I to put a value on those rings?

I took out the rings and stored them carefully in the back of the desk. Then I looked at the medal.

There was a blue ribbon with two parallel white stripes that had been darkened by the sixty years that had passed since it was pinned on my father's chest by the King. The worn silver had the face of the king on one side and on the back there was a crown, and laurel leaves around the tiny words FOR DISTINGUISHED SERVICE.

I closed the box and slipped it into the pocket of my jeans.

I wanted to give it to Ken Grimwood. It felt like the least I could do.

Downstairs, Joni was hunched over the coffee table, pens scattered all around. She was in her school uniform, ready to go, but busy working on a card that said – *It's your birthday! – Don't be sad! – Eat cake!* On the front of the card was a cartoon cake and a sad-looking little cartoon man. She was adding dozens of multi-coloured candles to the cake, making it look like a fire hazard, and she was making the sad little cartoon man smile by turning his mouth around. She saw me coming and hurriedly threw an arm around the card.

'Nothing, nothing, nothing,' she said breezily, as her mother called her name.

And I thought – Oh, yeah. Now I remember.

Tomorrow is my birthday.

The thing about turning forty is that you are looking your life right in the eye. You are still young, but you are too old to kid yourself. It is when you know what you have made of your life.

It didn't bother me. There were things I would have liked more of, and things I would have liked less of. More money. Less weight. More hair. Less work. But I didn't believe in the mid-life crisis. I thought it was a myth. When I was barely thirty, my life fell apart around me. What could be more of a crisis than that?

'Daddy, you didn't look, did you?' said my daughter.

I smiled and shook my head. 'Didn't see a thing, angel.'

'Good.'

I went to work.

'You know we love you,' Blunt said, his soft mouth twisting in a grotesque parody of affection. I could not imagine him loving anyone.

'I think I might have the shark and pumpkin ravioli,' Marty said, looking around for the waiter. Totally oblivious. But I knew. At the BBC they never tell you they love you until the day that you are dumped.

I love you. So now you must die.

And I suddenly took in the venue – a wood-panelled Italian fish restaurant in Mayfair that was inexplicably popular with the movers and shakers of our business – and realised that making any kind of scene would be self-defeating. We would look like sore losers. And nobody is going to give a gig to sore losers.

There was bread on the table. It was not sliced. It was torn by hand, and meant to represent the way the Italian peasants would eat their bread.

'Could we get this bread torn a little smaller?' Marty asked a passing waitress, and she took it back to the kitchen.

'The post-watershed demographic is changing,' Blunt was saying. '*A Clip Round the Ear* does what it says on the tin – but should we really be pandering to baby boomers who want to kill someone they see using a mobile behind the wheel of a car?'

'Definitely,' I said, even though in my bones I suspected it was too late.

'Are you going to have a starter?' Marty said. He patted the growing equator of his trouser line. 'I might skip the starter.'

'Marty,' I said, looking at Blunt. 'Marty – we're being sacked.'

It was a loud restaurant. The places we went to were all like that. It was as though nobody was actually using their mouth for anything but talk. But Marty continued to wave his menu at harassed young East Europeans in white aprons. I stared at Blunt.

'Because we didn't come to your crummy speech?' I said. 'Your big-swinging-media-dick speech? Because we weren't available around the clock? Because we have lives? Because we have families?'

Blunt flushed. 'Oh, that's not it.'

'But it didn't help, right?'

'We just want to make a few changes.'

'Why is it when people say that, the changes are never to your advantage?' I said. 'Why do changes always make life worse? Why can't things ever just stay the same?'

It would have been a good item on our show. Our audience would have loved that.

* * *

100

At Pussy Galore there was a problem with Marty's card.

A waitress in a tutu brought it back with an embarrassed smile and a bouncer. He hovered behind her, waiting to see which way this thing was going to go.

'Do you know who I am?' Marty said, staring down at the card on the silver tray, and the brute lifted his enormous head, as if sniffing prey. Then I was by Marty's side, laying a soothing hand on his arm and reaching for my wallet. We had only had one bottle. I would pay cash.

'Come quick,' called the bouncer to a brace of his Neanderthal mates. 'There's a man here who doesn't know who he is . . .'

'How much is it?' I said, and the waitress in the tutu helpfully shone her torch on the bill. Marty and I stared at it blindly. The truth was we both needed reading glasses in the Pussy Galore but we did not want to admit it. The Pussy Galore would be the last place we would wear any reading glasses.

But I didn't have enough cash. Nowhere near it. A bottle of fizz at Pussy Galore was surprisingly steep. So I pulled out my own card, already with a sinking feeling, and laid it next to Marty's.

The waitress went away. She returned with both our cards cut in two.

'Company cards,' I said to Marty, as the bouncer reached out with huge meaty hands and seized our collars. 'They stop those pretty quick.'

He dragged us through the crowds of almost naked girls asking men in suits if they wanted to party. He did it alone. That was humiliating. I think it would have been much better if we had had a bouncer each. And it would have been better still if Marty hadn't picked up that ice bucket and swung it in his face.

They all came running.

And then they took us out the back way. It was dark, but only just. We could hear the traffic going mental in the surrounding streets as the rush hour kicked off.

A chef from the restaurant next door was smoking a

quiet spliff in the alley. He took one look at us and scarpered. I watched the bouncer who had been hit in the ear with the ice bucket knee Marty between the legs. He went down hard.

Another bouncer appeared in the doorway carrying two brown boxes. The contents of our desks. We had left them in the club. That was thoughtful, I thought, bringing those for us. Then I watched the bouncer empty the boxes into the rubbish-strewn alley. That wasn't very nice. Then someone hit me once in the ribs and I never knew it was possible to feel such pain.

'Not in the head,' somebody said. 'Kick them anywhere but the head.'

I stood outside Ken's front door, trying to stop myself from being sick.

The day had somehow slipped away. How long had we been in Pussy Galore? And how many hours had we waited to be patched up in Accident and Emergency? The day had dwindled down to next to nothing. There was hardly any day left.

And I felt the same way. I was worn out, weak from drink and the beating. My nose, my throat – full of gunk. One side of my rib cage felt like it was on fire. I wiped a patch of something wet from my chin and gingerly touched my front teeth with the tip of my tongue, feeling all sorts of strange new peaks and valleys.

But I still had the medal. Somehow I still carried my father's medal. Everything had been lost – my job, my dignity, my tooth – but the medal remained. And I believed that some good could yet come out of this rotten day if I could only give my dad's DSM to his old friend.

And so I rang the doorbell. Then I rang it again. And only then did I notice that the flat was in darkness. It looked abandoned, because the council had taken away the smashed door and put up a thick slab of wood enmeshed in a metal grille. The place looked like a derelict prison. I turned away, the eternal wind of those flats bringing tears to my eyes, and I wondered if I would ever see Ken Grimwood again.

For once the concrete stairs were empty of all life forms. I increased my pace, hearing distant cries and laughter. The flats were sometimes empty but never silent. Then I saw him at the bottom of the steps, flat on his belly, chewing on a dead tennis ball.

Tyson.

'Good dog,' I said, stepping over him and simultaneously pressing my car key. The car beeped and the orange lights flashed twice. Oh, let's get out of here right now, they seemed to say.

But Tyson growled from the back of his throat, leapt up and wrapped his mighty front legs around my thigh. His hind legs began pumping furiously. I looked down at his blank features, the tongue lolling hideously from his wet mouth, the dull gleam of lust in his eyes.

'Bad dog,' I told him and I kept walking.

Tyson held on to my leg as if he would never allow us to be parted.

I came home as a distant church bell began to measure midnight.

I stood there for a moment with the key in the lock, controlling my breathing, feeling my forties begin.

My head spun with questions. Did I have more years behind me than in front of me? Would I ever get another job? And what was I going to say to my wife? And my dry cleaner?

The house was black. Not the forsaken, vacant blackness of Ken's home. The blackness of sleep, and rest, and peace, and children tucked up for the night. I was glad and grateful, and I let myself inside as quietly as I could.

I caught a glimpse of myself in the mirror in the hall. Even with all the lights off, I could make out the scuffed, misshapen look of my face, as though I had been shaving with a bread knife. One eye was closing. There was blood on the front of my shirt. There was a love token from Tyson staining the leg of my jeans. I shook my leg, grimacing with disgust. My cardboard box was falling to bits. I stared at it with numb disbelief. I could not understand why I had not thrown it away.

I listened to the sleeping house, hearing the rasping sound of my breath, and I felt like a creature of the night.

Then I went into the living room and turned on the light.

And there they all were, waiting for me with champagne and big smiles and presents. Waiting for me to come home from work. Waiting to celebrate the day I was born.

My wife. My beautiful wife. My big daughter, looking like a young woman. My little daughter, struggling to stay awake so far past her bedtime. Ken Grimwood, in his striped tie and blazer. Singe Rana. And even Gina, with a smile that I remembered, a smile that I knew, as though our marriage had been an honourable defeat, and no worse than that. And my son, by his mother's side, instinctively tipping his head forward so that his flaxen fringe would shield his eyes.

But they were all smiling. I watched their smiles freeze at the terrible sight of me.

And Cyd advanced with the cake in her hands, the candles flickering as if they might expire at any moment, as the church bell in the distance tolled one last time.

I am forty years old, I thought to myself. How did that happen?

'Surprise,' said my wife.

part two: *spring term —*
if i were a boy

ten

They stared straight through me. That was fine by me. I did not want them to look at me. I wanted to be invisible. I preferred it that way.

The party was on the thirtieth floor of some shining glass tower high above the river. These were the last of the fat years, before the area would be decimated by the money meltdown. Before too long many of these men – and they were mostly men – would be carrying their belongings out of this building in an old champagne box from Berry Brothers. But that was all in the unimaginable future. Tonight they were celebrating their bonuses. And my wife was doing the catering.

Cyd appeared at my side, smiling as she gave my arm a squeeze.

'Do you want me to get some more vegetable samosas out here?' I said.

She patted my bum. 'First clear up the empties,' she said.

They were used to being served, these people, and they did not even notice me as I moved among them, collecting the plates scattered with the picked-clean sticks of yakitori and the rice crumbs of sushi. Some guy in an apron. Nothing special. Not like them.

I piled up the dirty plates and headed for the kitchen. You would not think that there was a kitchen on the thirtieth floor of one of Babylon's shining towers. But apparently they had lunches and dinners in the boardrooms up here. Sometimes these big shots just couldn't be bothered to make it down to a restaurant. It was another world.

I shouldered my way through the door and then I just stood there, the plates still in my arms, because I had caught my reflection in the window. It was an incredible view of London from up there, one of those views to make you believe that there is nothing more beautiful and romantic in this world than a big city at night. London shone like God's own jewel box.

But I did not see any of it. Not now. All I saw was myself.

And I got that feeling – the feeling you get when you look down at the city, and it seems to be calling you, and providing all the answers as it tells you to step out the window and just do it, just fall through the air, just jump. That feeling we all get when we look down at the pavement from a great height.

Or is that just me?

I felt the air leaving me. All of it, all at once. Like a man drowning in his own life. Oh bugger, I thought. Just what I need. A panic attack.

Cyd came into the kitchen and stared at me as she picked up a tray of samosas.

'Harry,' she said. 'Are you all right?'

But I didn't reply.

I just stood there, the dishes in my arms, looking at the man in the glass, and trying to get my breath under control, and wondering if I was going to have a heart attack. She left, looking concerned. But, slick with sweat and breathless, I did not move.

The man in the glass looked back at me, like a shadow of my former self.

Because of the boy I was a better man, I thought. Because of the boy I was more patient, and less selfish, and a kinder human being. Because of the boy I had grown up. Because of the boy I had learned how to put someone above myself. Because of the boy I had learned how to love.

And then the boy was taken away from me. It had been

two months since he had moved in with Gina. Almost two weeks since I had last seen him – his Christmas Day with us, and then back to Gina on Boxing Day.

It was a different life now, and a different way of being a father and a son. It is not the things you do with them that count – the Lee Marvin double bills, the trips to football and the theme parks, all the fun family outings that are so much fun that you never have to actually talk to each other – it is the day-to-day confluence of everyday life that matters, the unadorned fact of living together, that is what makes your souls stick to each other.

And now all that was gone and I wondered where did that leave me? What did that make me? What was the good of me? What was I for? Losing my job hadn't helped fight this feeling of being lost. But it was not the work thing. I could always find another job. But the boy was irreplaceable. My sense of myself was wrapped up in the boy. My measure of my worth. And with the boy not around, what was I worth? What was the point of me?

I stared at my mirror image for a moment longer and then I felt the stack of dirty dishes slipping from my fingers. No paper plates in here, so the noise was shattering, followed by appalled silence. A ripple of nervous laughter, and then the rest of the hired hands went back to work. It was just a waiter having a nervous breakdown.

I slumped over the sink and after an unknowable stretch of time I felt my wife at my side.

'That's one way of doing it,' Cyd said. 'Or you could just put them in the dishwasher. That works, too. Come on, let's get you outside.'

And the bankers or brokers or whatever they were stared at us and moved aside as we walked through them to the lift. Cyd took my hand and smiled as we went down to the ground level, and she kept telling me that it was okay, it was all okay. I wasn't so sure. There was nowhere really to sit when we reached the lobby so we went outside and stood looking out at the river as we had long ago, as we had on our very first date, when we were just starting out. The river made me feel better. The river and the way she would not let go of my hand.

'Pat will be all right,' she said.

'I know,' I said, very quickly, almost before it was out of her mouth.

'It's just hard,' she said. She smiled, shrugged. Trying to explain. 'All of it, I mean. Always. The way we build our lives. Work. Home. Having a career. Raising kids. Doing the lot. Like the song says – caught between the longing for love and the struggle for the legal tender.'

'I know that song,' I said. 'That's a good song.'

'I mean, our parents and grandparents had it hard, but it was a different kind of hard.'

'You mean the possibility of nuclear holocaust? The Great Depression? Hitler and Stalin? All that twentieth-century stuff?'

'All that twentieth-century stuff,' she said. 'War. The Bomb. Buddy, can you spare a dime? I am not minimising it. But things were simple. For men and women. Nobody thought they had to do it all.' She put her arm around me, and it was as if there was nobody left in the city but us. 'It's hard,' my wife said. 'It's just hard, having it all.'

And I thought – *having it all?*

I wouldn't mind having just a bit of it.

Marty held up his hands, anxious to share his vision with the commissioning editor.

'*Whose Tattoo Are You?*' Marty said excitedly. 'Panel game. I chair two teams of comedians. You know the sort. Smug, edgy comedians who dance on the borderline of good taste. But who desperately need the work.'

The commissioning editor frowned, not really getting it. 'And they . . . get tattooed?'

Marty laughed like a maniac. 'No, no, no,' he said. 'They have to *identify the owner of a tattoo.*'

I cleared my throat. 'So you would see a close-up shot of

110

a bar code on somebody's neck,' I said. 'Or a butterfly. Or one of those, you know, Chinese symbols.'

'It could be live!' Marty said. 'Doesn't need to be a photograph! Could be a live feed from the green room!'

'Put people in masks,' I suggested.

'Masks are good!' Marty said. 'Those sort of Venetian masks – you know what I mean? The masks they wear in Venice. At the festival. Spooky, sexy masks. Then after some witty exchanges from the two panels we pull back the curtain to reveal . . . *David Beckham. Or Amy Winehouse. Or Cheryl Cole. Or Samantha Cameron.* The great thing is – everyone has a tattoo these days.'

The commissioning editor looked doubtful. 'I don't,' he said. 'And do you really think you can get Beckham?'

'Well, Beckham might be a booking too far,' I said. 'But all these Premiership footballers have got bar codes and barbed wire and Chinese dragons tattooed somewhere. So if we can't get Becks, we can at least get someone who wants to be him.'

Marty smiled at me. 'It's a gap in the game-show market,' he said. 'A yawning chasm.'

The commissioning editor touched his watch. 'Or perhaps a bottomless abyss,' he muttered.

'*My So-Called Teeth*,' Marty suggested. 'I go undercover to investigate why the British have the worst teeth in the world. Posing as a dental hygienist, I infiltrate –'

'Don't like it,' the man from the BBC said.

I sipped my tea. It had gone cold.

'Or, or, or – *Marty Mann's Binge Britain*,' Marty said. 'I go undercover to expose Binge Britain – but I do it while drunk . . . absolutely rat-faced . . . while binged out of my brilliant mind . . .'

The commissioning editor looked as if he was in pain.

'Or animals,' Marty said, his voice rising high with panic. '*How Clean is Your Hamster Cage? Britain's Most Embarrassing Animals . . .*'

The commissioning editor frowned. 'What – you mean a

dachshund called Darcy who has developed a taste for his own excrement? And an oversexed corgi called Colin?'

'Exactly!'

'We did that already,' said the man from the BBC. 'And we did *Help Me, Anthea, I'm Infested* and we did *Dog Borstal* and we did *My Life as a Pig*, where celebrities that only their mothers have ever heard of sleep among pigs, eat like pigs and even learn to converse like pigs.'

'I remember that show,' I said. 'It was pretty good.'

'So the animal thing,' said the man from the BBC, 'has been pretty well covered.'

'Then – let's take it to the next level,' said Marty. 'The new generation. A talent show – but for dogs. We are talking post-Simon Cowell – broadcasting that has assimilated the lessons the Einstein of light entertainment has taught us. Dogs! Skilful dogs! And rubbish dogs that – you know. We can laugh at it. They can pee on me! I don't mind! Really! The audience will love it!' Marty shot a sideways look at me with the eyes of a seal that is cowering under a baseball bat. 'Monkeys?'

I felt like hugging him. Instead I smiled and nodded. 'Monkeys,' I said with slightly more enthusiasm than I felt. 'Monkeys are good. Monkeys are classic.'

'*Britain's Monkeys Got Talent*,' Marty said, and the idea immediately evaporated in the thin air of the commissioning editor's office.

'Or something else,' I suggested.

'We were programme makers,' Marty said. 'Mad Mann Productions.' There was defiance in his eyes now. 'Ever heard of *Six Pissed Students in a Flat*?' He tapped his chest. 'We invented that format. We sold that format all over the world. *Six Pissed Norwegian Students in a Flat. Six Pissed Australian Students in a Flat. Six Pissed Poles* . . . That show went around the world!'

'Reality TV,' said the man with the power to change our lives, parroting this week's party line, 'has peaked.'

'Ah,' I said, 'there will always be a place on the schedules

112

for cheap programming full of people who are willing to make complete idiots of themselves.'

'We did one of the first CCTV shows,' Marty said.

I nodded. *'You've Been Robbed!'*

Marty got misty-eyed at the memory. 'Just edited high-lights of crime caught on camera,' he said. 'But it was – you know – a savage indictment of our, er, violent society.'

'But you're talking about twentieth-century television,' said the man. 'You're talking about ancient history.'

'No, I'm trying to show you how broad our range is,' Marty said. 'You can't have all your eggs in one chicken, right? We did the irreverent late-night arts show, *Art? My Arse!* The quiz show, *Sorry, I'm a Complete Git.* We did *Wicked World.'*

The man looked interested. 'Was that the one with Terry Christian and Dani Behr?'

'You're thinking of *The Word,*' I said. 'Our one had Eamon Fish and Hermione Gates and Wee Willie Hiscock, the love-able Geordie cook.'

Wee Willie Hiscock clearly did not ring any bells.

'Don't you remember us?' Marty said, begging now, all defiance gone. 'We won BAFTAs. Back in the day.'

The commissioning editor stood up, and I realised that it was a new day. I stood up too. The meeting was over. Marty remained in his seat.

'Just give us a job,' he pleaded. 'We're dying here.'

And that was the problem.

They only wanted you when you did not need them.

We came up the steps and when we got to the top the greyhound stadium was spread out before us.

I remembered Thursday nights as a kid, at the dog track out at Southend, collecting armfuls of losing tickets with my cousins while my dad and my uncles studied form, and my mum and my aunts bet on their lucky numbers. Did we really do that on a school night? We must have done. A lot of it was shockingly unchanged. The smells of tobacco and perfume and beer, the accents and the laughter. Hard men in their day-off clothes and pretty women done up to the nines. After-shave and dog shit. The working class at play.

'I thought this world was gone,' I laughed. 'I thought it went years ago.'

'No, this world is still here,' Ken said sharply. 'It's you that buggered off, sunshine.'

What was different was that we were here in daylight hours. They called it a BAGS meeting – Bookmakers Afternoon Greyhound Service – and entrance was free, designed to entice the real hard core.

We picked up Singe Rana after his shift as a security guard at the firework factory on the City Road, and I took them to the Badham Cross dog track. There wasn't a lot else I could do with them.

They did not like restaurants because they did not really eat – even when they had personally selected some greasy café in their own neighbourhood, they only picked at their food like fussy toddlers. They preferred staying in Ken's flat and grazing on Aloo Chop potato cakes, or Nepalese curries called Mitho Chat and Aloo Dum.

Gurkha food. Lots of potatoes. And spices.

They did not like pubs because Singe Rana did not drink alcohol and Ken could not smoke. They did not like walking. They had no interest in movies. It was all rubbish after *Casablanca*, according to Ken. Television bored them, apart from the horses on Channel 4.

But they liked gambling.

So I took them to this dog track out on the borders of the East End and Essex that I remembered from my childhood. I thought it might have disappeared around the same time as the New Romantics, but when I Googled Badham Cross Greyhound Stadium it was still there.

In a bar that smelled of fish and chips, Ken removed one of those tiny biros that builders use from behind his ear. He licked the tip of it and bent over his racecard. As always, he was immaculate in his blazer, shirt and tie. I believe he may have slept like that. Singe Rana stared out at the track, and

114

then up at the sky. His bets were placed on form, weather conditions and a meticulously calculated weighing of risk and reward. Ken was more superstitious. He chose his runners on the basis of names, portents, hidden omens. Ken rarely won and Singe Rana won all the time. But the amounts they gambled were so tiny that it did not make much difference.

'Lonesome Traveller,' Ken said, watching the dogs as they were paraded past. 'Number five. Look at him.'

Number five was sniffing the air, but apart from that he looked exactly like the other greyhounds. They were built more like missiles than dogs.

Singe Rana shook his head. 'The going is too soft for Lonesome Traveller,' he said. 'He likes the ground to be hard. But there was morning rain.'

'He smells the blood,' Ken insisted. He turned to me. 'Some of them train with real rabbits, see. Makes them run a lot faster, because a real rabbit tastes a bit better than a metal rabbit. When they've trained with real rabbits, we say they can smell the blood.'

Again Singe Rana shook his head. 'Not that one,' he said. 'Not after the morning rain.'

'I came here with your dad once,' Ken told me. 'Before you were born. We bumped into Alf Ramsay. Before he was Sir Alf Ramsay. You heard of him, have you?'

I was slightly offended. 'Manager of the England team that won the World Cup in 1966,' I said. 'I know my dad was at school with him.'

Ken nodded. 'Alf had started to change his accent. What do you call it? Evolution lessons. He was very keen on his evolution lessons, old Alf. So he could natter like the toffs.' Ken chuckled at the memory. 'Your dad thought that was priceless.'

I thought of my father in this place. How old would he have been? Younger than I was now. A metallic parody of a rabbit rattled past. A cry went up as the dogs burst from their traps.

'I never told him I loved him,' I said.

Ken looked askance. 'Alf Ramsay?'

'My dad,' I said. 'Apart from the once. At the end. In the hospital. When I knew he was dying. I told him then. But I only ever told him the once. And I regret that.'

Ken Grimwood grimaced, straightening up inside his blazer. He looked a little nauseous.

'I wouldn't worry about it,' he said. 'Your father wasn't the kind that needed a hug. He wouldn't have thanked you for slobbering all over him every second of the day.'

Voices were raised. The metallic rabbit came rattling past, followed by the soft thunder of the greyhounds after it. Number five, Lonesome Traveller, was nowhere to be seen. Ken began ripping his betting slip into tiny shreds. Singe Rana laughed. The dog at the front of the pack wore black and white stripes with a red number six.

'Six!' cried Singe Rana, bouncing up and down. 'Come on, you number six!'

Ken Grimwood sniffed, not looking at me.

'You told him you loved him once,' he said, his builder's biro flitting across his betting slip, ready for the next race. 'And for a man like your dad, believe me – once is plenty.'

There was a pack of them, methodically destroying the bus stop.

Hooded and beanie-capped in deference to the CCTV cameras on every corner, but beyond that quite brazen as they skimmed lumps of concrete through the panes of glass. It smashed like an explosion of diamonds under the yellow streetlights, and they whooped with pure joy.

I had dropped Ken and Singe Rana off at Nelson Mansions, and I was glad they were not with me. That was one good thing. They would have done something stupid. Like trying to stop them.

They seemed to be multiplying before my eyes. They were spilling out into the road, ducking and shrieking with delight as the glass sprayed around them. I put my foot on the brake, and I could feel my breathing. I wanted to turn around and

116

find another way. But it was too late. My headlights caught them, trapped them in the accusing glare. And, as if they had one mind among them, they turned to look at me. And then I saw him.

In the middle of the pack.

A thick wedge of blond hair sticking out from his beanie cap.

A lump of concrete the size of a pizza in his hands.

He bit his bottom lip as he tossed the concrete through the last of the glass. Then they were gone. Back into the warren of flats. And I sat there with a million diamonds in my headlights, thinking, It was a boy who looked just like him. That's all. A white kid in his mid-teens with long fair hair and a face that was young for his age.

There must be a million kids who look like that.

eleven

There was the full-throated rumble of a Harley-Davidson outside our house, and then the immediate sound of footsteps on the stairs. Peggy gave me a quick hug and the motorbike helmet she was carrying pressed against my ribs.

'He's here,' she said, giving me a peck on the cheek, and a smile that looked as though it was trying to hold itself back. 'My dad's here.'

'Have a good time,' I said, but what I thought was, You can't compete with blood. Well, you can compete, but you will always lose. Straight sets. TKO. Ten–nil. Take on blood and you do not even make it to a penalty shoot-out.

I went to the window and gazed down at Jim's face, so familiar from his leading role on the hit TV show, *PC Filth: An Unfair Cop.* Jim Mason, heroically beautiful in black Belstaff leather from tousled hair to the adorably scuffed toes of his biker boots, sat astride his mighty steed, leathery legs spread wide, smiling at his daughter. And her mother. He had removed his helmet and his face was red and sweaty but still dead gorgeous.

And more than that – instantly recognisable. I mean, I am not one of the millions who tune in to watch his clichéd cop show (alcoholism – check, divorced – check, dead partner – check, long-running feud with a genius serial killer – check) but even I knew every contour of his high-cheekboned face.

And as the three of them stood there – Jim and Peggy in

their leathers, Cyd with her arms folded across her chest – I felt a hard lump form in my throat. They looked like a real family.

Cyd and Jim had had a traditional divorce – casual infidelity (his), bitter recriminations (hers) and a growing sense of bafflement (his and hers) that they had ever managed to be in the same room together, let alone have a crack at the marriage game.

And they had fought for their love. They had met in her hometown of Houston, Texas, where Jim was working as a despatch rider and seemed to young, impressionable Cyd as if he was an incredibly glamorous postman.

They married, but when he failed to make the kind of impact on America that he made on the tall, leggy brunette he danced with at the Yucatan Liquor Store, Jim came home to England with his leather tail between his legs and she came with him, facing poverty, rain and the ritual humiliation of immigration officers who refused to believe they were really in love.

But it was the real thing. Until Jim, after an unhappy spell delivering takeaways for the Double Fortune restaurant on the Holloway Road, began having a thing with the manageress, a nubile Kowloon lass. And then one of the waitresses, a native of Kuala Lumpur. And then her younger sister.

'He's into the bamboo,' Cyd told me when explaining why her marriage had broken up.

But now I watched Cyd with Jim and there was clearly a restored affection between them. It was as though they were engaged in a second courtship – the relationship that is formed after you go your separate ways. He was grinning at her, wiping sweat from his forehead in a gesture that was almost shy. She reached out and rubbed his arm. Softly, twice. Blink and you would have missed it. The gesture was so shocking that I almost looked away. But I couldn't.

Because I could see what was happening.

There was a secret chamber in my wife's heart that longed for her old life. When she was with the only man that she had ever married. When they had a baby girl that shared their blood. When there was nobody else around – refugees from broken homes, wounded stragglers from the divorce courts dragging their confused, wounded children behind.

I watched them down in the street and I knew.

Cyd – or at least a part of her – wanted a family without any sharp, jagged edges. It did not seem like much to ask for.

And between you and me, I could see the appeal.

There was a rustle by my side and suddenly Joni was there, clambering up on the sofa to look out the window. She took my hand.

'Looks dangerous,' Joni said thoughtfully. 'This motorbike lark.'

We watched Jim and Peggy ride away. Cyd stood in the street until they were out of sight, and when she turned back to the house Joni slammed the palms of her hands against the window.

But Cyd didn't look up.

'It was easy in your day,' I told the old men, not looking them in the eye, but studying the form for the afternoon's racing at Goodwood. 'The men and women thing. The parents and children thing. It was all so much easier.'

Singe Rana stared at me with those kind, soulful eyes that revealed absolutely nothing. Ken gave no indication that he had even heard.

'What do you fancy for the three thirty, me old china?' he said, narrowing his eyes at his *Racing Post*. 'Only Boy?'

Singe Rana turned his face towards the open door of the bookmakers. A grey drizzle was falling on Essex Road.

'Yes,' he said. 'Because Only Boy likes the going soft.'

Ken nodded thoughtfully at this sage advice. He tapped the little pen he was holding against the rim of his glasses. I had always thought of those small, child-sized biros as builder's pens. But I saw now that they were bookmaker's pens. The builders just nicked them from the bookies.

'Easier?' Ken reflected, smiling at his *Racing Post*. 'Don't know about easier. Simpler? I would give you simpler. I would grant you that. All those women stuck in marriages where they were knocked about from their wedding night to their dying day. We didn't have domestic abuse. We had the wife getting knocked about because the old man was back from the boozer, or there had been a bad day at the races, or the boss had treated him like dirt. Or just because he felt like it. Just because he wanted to remind her of her place – under his boot heel. And all those men – the ones who got married to someone they knocked up at seventeen and still didn't know fifty years later. The ones who made a bad choice and lived with it because they didn't know what else to do.'

He looked at me and then up at the TV suspended high above our heads. Horses were being led to the starting line, or whatever they called it. This was all still quite new to me.

'I can see why you're sorry you missed it,' Ken said. 'Marriages that were a life sentence. Marriages that were like prisons. Children who got knocked about or worse.'

'But the children,' I insisted, 'the children were better off. Even if the adults were trapped and miserable. The kids were the great benefactors of those old families.'

'Sometimes,' Ken said. 'In the good homes. Not in the bad ones. We didn't have sexual abuse in our day. We had fiddling about. Brothers. Uncles. Dads. Fiddling about, some of them. And nowhere to run. Nowhere to go. No way out until they carted you off in a wooden box.' He jabbed his baby biro in my face, momentarily lost for words, and I wondered if it had happened to him. His childhood was beyond my imagination. Then suddenly he grinned at me, his false teeth as white as bone.

'Oh yeah, I remember,' said Ken Grimwood, nudging Singe Rana as Long Shot appeared on screen, a faint mist rising from his sleek, chestnut-coloured shanks. Ken began to laugh, and the laughter became a cough, and I could hear the fluid clogging his lungs.

'The good old days,' he said.

*　　*　　*

121

In the film we had somehow found ourselves watching, the seas rose and the cities fell. In a peculiarly photogenic manner.

The dome of the White House was carried off like a ping-pong ball. The Eiffel Tower collapsing like a reed breaking in a stream. The Taj Mahal, Big Ben, the Sydney Opera House – all washed away like flecks of dandruff.

And the fires came, burning like the ovens of hell. And the smoke billowed through the canyons of skyscrapers like clouds at the end of the world. And the earth cracked. And the human race perished in their millions. And the rains lashed the ravished earth.

'They've been unlucky with the weather,' I whispered in the darkness, but Pat did not laugh.

I could feel him stir in the seat beside me, half-heartedly rifling his mega-bucket of sweet popcorn. After a while the glow of his mobile phone appeared in his palm.

'Why don't you watch the bloody film?' I snapped, still keeping my voice down, although it seemed a spectacularly old-fashioned convention, like giving up your seat on public transport, or opening the door for a woman. All around the cinema there were phones glowing in the dark, and people enjoying their main meal of the day, and engaging in animated conversation. Not even the end of life on Earth could distract them.

'You know why?' Pat said, and he glanced at me. 'Because it's just – I don't know – 9/11 porn or something. All these images – people jumping from buildings, the buildings collapsing, clouds of smoke coming down the street – it's all lifted from the news, innit?'

'Don't say *innit*,' I said.

'To give some moron his kicks,' he continued. 'To give some popcorn-chomping thicko his cheap thrills. Know what I mean? It makes me sick to my stomach, if you want to know the truth.'

'But apart from that,' I said. 'Do you think it's quite good?'

'An instant classic,' he said with contempt.

I got up and started working my way down the aisle. There was a time when this would have caused mild outrage among my fellow cinemagoers. Like talking too loud in a library. This shower did not even lower their kebabs.

I stood outside, looking out at Leicester Square, waiting to see if Pat would join me. We had never walked out of a picture before.

And we had always had the movies. When Gina left, back when Pat was four, his *Star Wars* obsession turned into something else. Something more. Another world he could retreat into when the real one was too much. There were the toys – eight-inch Han Solos and Luke Skywalkers and Darth Vaders, battle-grey models of the *Millennium Falcon* and X-wing fighters, and plastic light sabres that were dented forever if you stood on them.

But above all there were the films, which he would watch on video until he was dragged away, and which we went to see in double and even triple bills. Once a year you could catch the entire trilogy in some mad corner of the West End. *Star Wars. The Empire Strikes Back. Return of the Jedi.* And at an age when other fathers were taking their sons to the football or fishing – other pastimes where there is not much call for conversation – Pat was building up an enormous capacity to spend hours sitting in the darkness, sustained by Fanta and milk-chocolate-coated raisins and some $100-million fantasy. The cinema had been our thing. And now, it felt like it was all coming to an end.

Then he was there by my side, both of us embarrassed, anxious to avoid a fight. Because what exactly would we be fighting about? A distant voice told me that we should be laughing about this end-of-days, Book of Revelations rubbish. But neither of us was smiling.

'Chinatown?' I said.

He grimaced. 'Not really hungry,' he said, his hair over his eyes. He looked at his wrist. He was not wearing a watch. 'School night. Getting late.'

I nodded, as if all things were settled.

'Then home,' I said, and the word tasted toxic in my mouth.

Gina opened the door.

She smiled and hugged him and kissed him even as he was brushing past her. He did not say goodbye. She transferred her smile to me as she half-closed the front door, obscuring my view.

'What's wrong with him?' I said.

The smile faded. I could hear him banging about in the kitchen. It sounded like he was getting something to eat. So the not-really-hungry thing was a big fat fib for a start. He just did not want to go to Chinatown. He did not want to be with me.

'There's nothing wrong with him,' she said, and there was sudden frost in her voice. Oh I remember you, I thought. 'Pat's fine,' she said. 'He's settled in very well. He's become great friends with Peter.'

'Peter? Peter? Who the fucking fuck is Peter?'

'Can you watch your language? Peter is my boyfriend.'

I sighed. 'Funny, isn't it? Someone in their forties having a boyfriend. And are you and Peter dating? Or are you just going steady? Do you neck – or do you just make out? How's the heavy petting going? Jesus Christ, Gina – come up with some new terms. You're not a teenager.'

She erupted. 'Even now!' she said. 'It never ends with you, does it?'

'It ends, it ends,' I said, suddenly afraid the door would slam in my face before I had the chance to tell her what I had realised in the sad, silent walk back to Soho. But she had something to tell me first.

'Do you know what your trouble is, Harry?'

'Enlighten me.'

She stepped outside the door, not wanting Pat to hear. I gave her credit for that. It would probably not have occurred to me.

'It's straightforward when there's just one parent,' she said, lowering her voice but spitting out every word. 'For all your

124

Olympic-standard hand-wringing.' She did an imitation of my voice that sounded nothing like me. '*Oh, poor little me. Oh, poor little Pat.*'

'Olympic-standard hand-wringing,' I said. 'I like that, Gina. That's good. I'm going to write that down.'

'So glad you approve, Harry. I live to make you happy.' She took a half-step beyond her door. 'But for all the self-pity, Harry, you actually loved it when it was just you. It's simpler when there's just one parent. You can play the Great Dictator. What you say goes. The single parent is God.'

'Yeah, single parents,' I said. 'What a bunch of selfish bastards.'

'Goodnight, Harry.'

She stepped back inside and began to close the door. I stuck my foot in it, like some psycho door-to-door salesman. Gina looked at it and laughed with disbelief.

'I don't want to fight, Gina,' I said, and I searched for the words. I knew how I felt but I had trouble turning it into words. That seemed to happen all the time these days. 'I just – I don't want his life to be about us.'

She waited. I took my foot away. It actually hurt quite a bit.

'I want Pat to have his own life,' I said. 'I don't want his life to be about his mother or his father or what happened between them. Our divorce. All the rest of that mess. We have to let him have his own life, Gina. We owe him that much.'

She smiled and drew back and then I was staring at the closed door. I could hear her double-locking it, and then her footsteps as she went inside. And she didn't get it. Or perhaps the thought was too unbearable to contemplate.

That Pat's life would be forever shaped by our failure, stamped on his heart for the rest of his life, as indelible as a teardrop tattoo.

twelve

I began to fear the postman's step.

It turned my guts to clay. That heavy-footed shuffle down our garden path, the metallic clack of the letterbox, and then there they were, my problem now, the red bills in brown envelopes, sitting among the restaurant menus and junk mail, as conspicuous as a rash. Symptoms of a sudden outbreak of poverty.

But worst of all was the white envelope containing a letter from the mortgage company. And the language – so stilted, so tired, the mechanical response of a database that had seen losers like me many times before.

If you are encountering difficulties in paying your mortgage . . .

Cyd came down the stairs, watching me, and I quickly folded the letter.

'Harry,' she said. 'We need to talk about money.'

I laughed and took her in my arms. 'No, we don't,' I said. 'Because something will turn up. Something always turns up.'

She slipped her arms around my waist. She laid her head on my shoulder. But she wasn't smiling.

'It's not the way it was before,' she said. 'I can feel it in the City. Something is coming. You can't just walk into a job. A man your age . . .'

Oh, that was low. I let her go. Now neither of us was smiling.

The phone in my pocket began to vibrate and I took it out. Usually any call on my mobile caused a frisson of irritation – good item for *A Clip Round the Ear*, I thought, momentarily forgetting that our little show was history – but now I flipped it open with gratitude, because it meant I did not have to think about money.

UNKNOWN CALLER, my phone told me, and it wasn't kidding.

'You don't know me,' said a cool, middle-class male voice. 'But my name is Peter Groves. I am the, uh, boyfriend of Gina.'

Cyd was watching me. I headed down the hall.

'Hello?' I said.

It creeped me out. All of it. The fact that this guy could just pick up the phone and call me in my home. The fact that he could refer to himself as Gina's boyfriend without any apparent shame or embarrassment. The fact that he must have met my son by now. The boyfriend had probably spent the night with the girlfriend – with the son asleep in the room next door. What did the boyfriend and the girlfriend call that? A sleepover? A playdate?

'My name –'

'Yeah, I got that bit,' I said, heading out to the garden. I dipped my head under the eaves of the Wendy House. I wanted to keep this conversation out of my home. 'What do you want?' I said.

'What do I want?' He seemed taken aback. 'Well, if it is possible, I would like to meet you. To talk. To discuss where we are and how we may resolve any issues.'

This was another language to me. One I didn't speak. I felt the blood rising. My mouth was dry. I realised that this calm, reasonable man filled me with a murderous rage.

'I don't want to meet,' I said, and it came out a bit more sulky than I would have liked. Cyd was at the kitchen door, watching me with concern. Her arms were folded across her chest. That gesture always tugged at my heart a bit, to tell you the truth. It was as if she was trying to protect herself.

I could hear him sighing. I loved that. The sound of him sighing in my earhole.

'I think it would be beneficial for Gina,' he said – the voice of reason. 'And for her son, too.'

Her son. Not Pat. Not your son. Everything this guy said annoyed the hell out of me. But I knew that I would meet him. I knew I had to.

'Okay,' I said, and I thought of a dozen cafés that I knew around my old place of work. Just north of Oxford Street, the great civilised sweep of Marylebone from Portland Place to Baker Street. The area was full of them, and I suddenly missed being in gainful employment more than ever. I named a café on Marylebone High Street and a day and a time.

'It's all fine apart from the time,' he said. 'Could we make –?'

'No, we couldn't,' I said. I looked at Joni's Wendy House. The door had swung open in the night and some dead leaves had blown inside. I began kicking them out. 'You called me, remember?' I told the guy, the Peter guy. 'Can you do it or not?'

A beat of silence.

'Very well,' he said. 'I will see you there.'

'And come unarmed and alone,' I said. 'Or your girlfriend will never see you again.' More silence. 'Just kidding,' I said, and I hung up on the creep.

Then I went back inside the house, where my wife was waiting for me with the mail.

Pat was standing at the bus stop on the Tottenham Court Road.

There were other kids there, but none of them were wearing the uniform of Ramsay Mac. It was quite a hike he had to do every morning.

'Hey,' I said, reaching across to open the passenger door. He slid inside, the rucksack between his long, coltish legs. He got those from his mother. He half-smiled and dipped his head. I stuck the car in gear and laughed.

'I was just passing,' I said.

'Just passing?' he said. He looked as though he hadn't

combed his hair. I felt like hugging him, but instead I just pointed the car north and turned on the radio.

'Yeah, I had a breakfast meeting. It went very well. Marty and I have a lot of projects we're excited about. These people – the people we saw for breakfast – they seemed pretty interested.'

He touched the wrist where a watch should have gone.

'It must have been a very early breakfast,' he said, seeing right through me.

I glanced at him. 'What's this?' I said. 'The Lateral Thinking Club in action? It was coffee more than breakfast, smart arse. Aren't you happy to have your old dad drive you to school?'

'Sure,' he said, and he smiled, leaning back with a sigh. It was a drag catching that bus every day. He was way outside the catchment area.

The traffic was very light. I was driving against the big commute to the city. And still early. We passed the Abbey Road Studio in St John's Wood and there were no tourists walking across the zebra crossing, pretending to be John, Paul, George and Ringo. That's how early it was.

'So how's it going?' I said, one of those meaningless parental questions that usually provoke a non-committal grunt. But Pat's slow, shy smile began spreading across his beautiful face. And he was still beautiful. Even now, with a lone spot on his forehead and a few white whiskers on his upper lip. He was still my beautiful boy.

'I made the team,' he said. 'The Ramsay Mac football team.'

I began pounding my steering wheel with joy. I whooped. I slapped his thigh. He shouted out in protest, but he was laughing too.

'I knew you would,' I said. 'I knew you could.'

And then he was off – telling me how the usual first team goalkeeper tore a cruciate ligament on a skiing trip, and that had given Pat the chance that he had been waiting for. And I nodded enthusiastically, asking him the odd question – the date of the next fixture, if he was all right for boots and gloves, all that stuff – but mostly just letting him talk. And that lasted all the way to the gates of Ramsay Mac.

'Thanks for the ride,' he said, and I got out of the car with him. We stood facing each other and the blue blazers swirled around us. I knew I was not allowed to embrace him. I wasn't that stupid. But I loved him so much.

'I'm proud of you, kiddo,' I said. 'You made it in the end.'

He shrugged, the hair tumbling over his eyes. But he pushed it back with a grin. 'Just one game,' he said. 'There's someone else the coach is looking at.'

A couple of big lads brushed by. One of them caught Pat with his shoulder and knocked him sideways. My boy was tall but a strong wind could blow him away.

'Hey,' said the big lad, and I saw it was William Fly. He had a six o'clock shadow at eight thirty in the morning. 'Watch where you're going, Sick Note,' he said.

Sick Note? Is that what they called him? Because he had been sick? They gave him that name? I stared at William Fly, but I knew I was not allowed to say anything. The other lad – it was Spud Face – was chuckling away as though Fly was a comic genius. And I saw now that they were not both big lads. Only William Fly. Spud Face was the kind of little weasel who becomes big by association.

And I sized up this William Fly. Despite his freakish bulk, and the bluebeard stain on his chops, he was nothing special. There was one just like him in every school in the country. And hanging around every strip of shops, and in every playground, and in every park. They all had their William Fly.

We watched them go. Maybe ten seconds had passed. But it felt like the world had changed. Pat brushed at his blazer and did not look at me. And my rage knew no bounds. I was even angry with him.

'Stand up for yourself,' I said. 'Can't you do that?'

He shook his head. 'Stand up for myself?' he said, and he laughed, but the sound of the laughter was different now.

'Yes,' I said. 'When they call you names. When they bang into you. Just stand up to them.'

Pat picked up his rucksack and swung it on his back. 'What do you expect me to do?' he said. 'Beat them up?'

I took a step closer to him. I didn't want to make a scene. Kids were looking at us. But this mattered to me. I found that this mattered to me more than anything.

'Just stand up for yourself,' I said.

'But I'm not a tough guy,' my son said, and the bell began to ring. 'That's Granddad. That's Clint Eastwood. It might even be you. But it's not me, and it never will be.'

He walked away. I watched him go. I was still standing there when I saw the tears come and the boy making every effort to fight them back. Angry with me and angry with the wicked world. But angry with the tears most of all.

'And I don't need a lift in the morning,' he said. 'I can get the bus, thank you very much.'

Thank you very much.

It was the thank-you-very-much that killed me.

I spotted him as soon as he came through the door.

He was tall, and looked like he worked out, but the glasses softened the effect. He was dressed for the office, suited and booted under a winter coat, but not wearing a tie. He looked like he probably had one in his pocket.

Peter.

For a few seconds I did nothing, just watched him, tempted to leave without talking to him. But then he was looking at me, sitting by myself at a table in the back, and raising his paper in acknowledgement. He came across and I stood up as we shook hands.

'Thanks for coming,' he said, but then we had to pause as a waitress appeared. He ordered his complicated coffee and then held his hand out to me, as if he was an attentive host. I shook my head and sipped my tea. The waitress went away and Peter laid the palms of his hands on the table. He was ready to call the meeting to order. I grinned stupidly at him, wondering what would happen if I flung my English Breakfast Tea in his face.

'It has not been easy for Gina,' he said. 'Having her son – having Pat – move in. Attempting to establish a relationship.' He looked at me meaningfully. 'Not easy.'

I laughed. 'Gina's not my problem,' I said. 'Not any more. I just care about my boy.'

Peter looked as though he was seeing me for the first time. 'But you care about Gina? Presumably. You want her to be happy . . .'

I thought about it. Do we want our old loves to be happy? Do we really?

'I guess so,' I said, and then I smiled. 'But not too happy, of course.'

He wasn't smiling. This wasn't going how he had planned. 'She told me about you,' he said.

I nodded. 'I bet she did.'

'She struggled for years to find happiness after your marriage broke up,' he said. 'Obviously I only hear her side of events. But as I understand it, you were the one who was unfaithful in that relationship. She was never anything less than a loyal, loving wife.'

He had wiped the smile off my face. Good for you, I thought, and then came the first flash of real anger. Who was this guy anyway?

'I don't want to be rude,' I said.

'Really?' he said.

'But what do you want?' I said.

'Just to talk,' he said, holding up his hands. 'Just to have a quick word, mate.'

I laughed at that. 'I'm not your mate.'

He shook his head. 'Why are you so hostile to me? Because I have a relationship with your ex-wife? Because she has introduced me to your son?'

I had an image of him strolling around the kitchen in the morning, all bleary-eyed from Gina's bed, and my son packing his rucksack for school.

'I think you're a prince,' I said. 'A fucking prince, all right?'

He leaned forward. I sipped my tea. It was tepid now. I drank it anyway. But I preferred it when it was so hot that it scalded my throat.

'I just want you to please try to be a little more understanding,' he said. 'Gina has so many issues she is working through.'

'Issues? What are you? Her shrink?'

'Do you have something against therapy?' he snapped. 'Because I think it would be a very good idea for Gina.' The waitress brought his complicated coffee. He did not say thank you. He did not even look at her. I hate it when people treat waitresses like that. 'And Pat, too,' he added.

'There's nothing wrong with my son,' I said, and he chuckled, and I felt like breaking his neck.

'Both Gina and Pat have serious abandonment issues,' he said.

'Then she shouldn't have abandoned him, should she? She shouldn't have wasted so many years trying to find fulfilment – or whatever the crap expression is this week.' He waited. I went on. A bit more slow and measured now. Harry Silver – the voice of reason. 'After the marriage came apart – and, yes, I carry the can for that – there was always something more important than our little boy. Japan. Career. The latest guy. Some guy who looked a lot like you.'

I must have raised my voice towards the end there, because people were starting to stare at us.

'Can we be polite?' Peter asked.

'I don't know,' I said. 'Can we? You call me at home and ask me to meet you, and then you sit there talking in your soft, reasonable voice about Gina and Pat as if you know them better than I ever will. Can we be polite, Peter? I don't think so.'

'I just want you to understand what Gina is going through,' he said. 'I would appreciate it if you could be a bit more understanding. I know how much it upsets her when you argue.'

'Poor thing.'

'Yes,' he hissed, and I saw that I had got to him. Somewhere deep inside – beyond the sensitive specs and the business suit – there was a temper wanting to get out. 'You're right. Poor thing. Abandoned by her father when she was a little girl. And then her husband cheats on her because he is having some pathetic, premature mid-life crisis.'

I grinned at him. 'Keep going. You're doing good.'

He pushed his coffee cup aside. 'Look, I don't actually care about you. Or your son.'

I nodded. I put down my teacup. 'Okay,' I said.

'But I love Gina and I want her to be happy. Your son is clearly a very troubled boy –'

That's when I reached across the table and grabbed him by the collar of his open-necked shirt. A tie would have made it easier. But I got a good fistful of blue-and-white striped cotton from Paul Smith. There was a crash as something hit the floor. A milk jug. We were both on our feet, our chairs scraping back and everybody staring now. I didn't let go.

'All right,' he said. 'All right now.'

I could feel my anger for him closing my throat. The feeling was a black, bitter chunk that made speech impossible. I wanted to tell him so much but I couldn't get the words out. So I let him go. Then I picked up the sugar bowl and hurled it as hard as I could at the wall behind his head. It exploded and he cowered beneath the shrapnel of sugar lumps.

'Watch your mouth,' I said, and I did not recognise my voice. I pulled some notes out of my pocket and threw them on the table. 'Say what you like about my ex-wife. And say what you like about me. But when you talk about my son, you just watch your fucking mouth.'

When I got home the street where I lived looked strange to me. The years spent toiling at the coal face of TV and radio meant that I was used to seeing it at all hours of the day and night. But I was accustomed to seeing it from the perspective of someone in work. The street in the middle of a mid-week morning, with no work that day, or the next day – it was like another planet.

Or perhaps that was just because Jim Mason was parked outside our house. Sitting astride his bike, the engine throbbing between his legs. Did he ever get off that thing?

He was part-man, part-Harley.

Cyd was with him. Her arms folded across her chest. Long-limbed and coatless, the laces of her trainers undone. I loved the dimensions of her. Just the way she was – the heavenly engineering of her body. It knocked me out. Still.

They did not see me. Jim's bike was pointing in the opposite direction and they both had their backs to me. And so I stopped, conscious that I was interrupting something. This is the way to do it, I thought. When love has flown but you have a child together, this is how you do it. Not like me and Gina, who had happily danced across the thin cliché separating love from hate. You do it like this, I thought, and then I may have gasped as Cyd reached out and touched his face.

He did nothing, just let her hand stray across his lovable stubble for a few moments before it withdrew. And then he kicked his bike into roaring life and was gone, and she watched him for a moment and went back inside the house.

When I came through the door seven minutes later she was reading the newspaper. She looked up at me and smiled.

'What's happening?' I said.

She shook her head. 'Nothing.'

I nodded and looked away.

You touched his face, I thought.

Pat came round for dinner.

We were celebrating his birthday late. We had missed it because Gina had suddenly whisked him off to some ski resort in the dying days of the Christmas break.

I did not want it to be a major production. I mean, I wanted us all to give the kid a great birthday dinner, but I didn't want anyone holding their breath and afraid to speak. The best thing would have been if Pat could have just come round for dinner and everything be normal. I really missed normal. Pat having dinner with us – it should not have been a big deal. But it was a big deal.

His sisters were waiting for him in the hall with their presents when the mini-cab dropped him off.

'Pat!' cried Joni.

'Hello, gorgeous,' said Peggy.

'Hello, ugly,' said Pat, and then he picked up Joni and kissed her on the cheek. 'Hello, you.'

She squirmed from his arms, averting her face, kissing still being gross.

Cyd came out of the kitchen and the three of them held him. Joni hugging him around the thighs. Peggy with her arms wrapped around his neck, and crying a bit. And Cyd laughing with her arms thrown around the whole scrum.

I hung back, feeling wound up and weird.

My son was coming round for dinner.

That's all.

He unwrapped his presents as we all slowly trailed into the living room, Joni holding on to his leg and Peggy with one hand resting lightly on his shoulder, Cyd and I bringing up the rear. She slipped her arm in mine and smiled at me.

'What have we got here?' Pat said, opening up Joni's tatty, falling-to-bits, self-wrapped package. His eyes widened at the sight of a Pussycat Dolls CD. 'Wow, *Doll Domination*,' he read, impressed.

'I know you maybe don't like the Pussycat Dolls, but they're really great,' Joni said quickly. She pointed at a girl on the cover. 'I like that one. She's very pretty.'

'I might keep it here,' Pat said. He looked down at his sister. 'Will you look after it for me?'

She snatched the Pussycat Dolls from his hand and ran off.

'I'll keep it in my room,' she shouted. 'You can listen to it whenever you want.'

Pat began to unwrap Peggy's immaculately wrapped present. It even had a ribbon and a bow.

'I didn't know you could ski,' she said.

'I can't,' he laughed, not looking at her. But then he smiled as he unwrapped a DVD of the first *Star Wars* film.

Peggy looked embarrassed.

'It's the enhanced version of *A New Hope*,' she said, looking sideways at it. 'And it's got, er, the theatrical version on there too – but you've probably got it already.'

'No, I haven't got it,' he said, studying the cover like a wine expert sniffing a rare Margaux. Then he looked her in the eye. 'It's great, Peg,' he said quietly. 'Thank you.'

He was a very gracious kid. He made a polite fuss of all our presents. Cyd and I gave him a watch – one of those watches that look like they will tell you the time at the bottom of the ocean, and he put it on and admired it, even though I knew he had never worn a watch in his life, and might not start now.

Cyd slapped the pair of us on the back.

'Eat,' she commanded.

Cyd was cooking chicken curry – Pat's favourite, and I felt a real stab of gratitude as the smells filled the house. Turmeric and peppers and ginger and garlic and onions and coriander. It would have been no different if he was our own child. She could not have loved him more.

Dinner was fine. Dinner was good. Cyd made a killer curry and Pat ate like a horse. We all laughed about his appetite, the way we always used to.

And he was lovely. Appreciative of the food, keen to help – he had always been quick to clear up the table and cart the empties to the kitchen. In the past it had sometimes made me uncomfortable – if Cyd had been his real mother, would he have always been on such perfect behaviour? But tonight I was grateful for my boy's good manners.

Peggy turned off the lights and in the darkness Cyd brought out a chocolate cake with fifteen candles. We all sang, 'Happy Birthday, dear Pat,' and after he had blown out the candles – in one go, to wild applause – we all had a slice.

After dinner Peggy slipped off to do her homework and Pat sat on the floor with Joni. She was showing him some dog game on her Nintendo DS, and every now and again the game gave a very authentic yelp.

'So you've got two homes now,' Joni said, not looking up from her dog game.

Pat laughed. 'I've got no homes now,' he said, and smiled when Joni lifted her serious, seven-year-old face to him. 'Show me how you take Bouncy for a walk,' he said.

But it was a school night and after a while Cyd called to Joni to go and brush her teeth.

'Can I stay up late?' she said, her vampire mouth pleading. 'As Pat's here? As it was his birthday some time ago?'

'You are staying up late,' Cyd said. 'Clean those teeth and get your pyjamas on.'

The evening was winding down. Joni reluctantly went off to the bathroom. I went to help Cyd in the kitchen and Pat wandered out to the garden.

Through the kitchen window I saw the security light come on and illuminate him, all slouching limbs and uncombed hair, looking up at the house as if he was remembering something. Then the light went off and all you could see was his silhouette, lit by moonlight and the orange glow that always hangs over the city.

I felt almost relaxed. He could come round and eat dinner with us and it was as if nothing had changed. I could hear Peggy's music filtering down from upstairs. The sound of Joni spitting in the downstairs bathroom. I watched Cyd rinse a pot and when she had finished I took her wet hand and held it against my face.

'Thank you,' I said.

'Don't be silly,' she smiled. 'I love seeing him.'

Then her smile faded. She squinted at the garden. And I saw it too. The faint red glow in Pat's mouth.

As if the silhouette in the garden knew that it was being watched, it quickly slipped into the Wendy House. But even inside the little wooden playhouse, you could see the red glow in the darkness as it rose and fell from my son's lips.

'Does he smoke now?' Cyd said.

I shook my head. 'Not that I know of,' I said, and I made a move to the garden and then felt her stop me.

'Let me talk to him,' she said. 'It will be better coming from me.'

So I watched her go.

And I watched her long-limbed shadow cross the garden and enter the Wendy House. And after not very long at all she came back, holding something that emitted a faint red glow in the darkness. She burst through the door and I don't think I had ever seen her so angry. I recognised that sickly sweet smell immediately. She held up a soggy hand-rolled cigarette, her eyes blazing.

'Mexican weed in the Wendy House!' she said. 'Very nice! Smoking Mexican weed in the Wendy House!'

Then Pat burst into the house, tears streaming down his face and chin trembling. Hardly what you would expect from a hardened user who had turned his sister's Wendy House into a drug den.

I said his name but he kept heading for the front door. I went after him. Joni appeared in the door of the bathroom, an electric toothbrush vibrating in her hand. Peggy was on the stairs. I looked back at Cyd. She shook her head, the joint extinguished but still in her hand.

The front door opened and closed with a bang.

I called his name again. And then I went after him. I chased him down the street and I could see him ahead of me for a while but then we got to the Holloway Road and I lost him. He must have jumped on a bus or in a cab. I walked the streets until I knew that he was gone, calling his phone again and again even though it always went straight to the answer machine. And then I went back to the house.

It had been a while. Joni had been packed off to bed. The music had stopped in Peggy's room. And the only sounds I could hear were the dishwasher and the muted, troubled voice of my wife on the phone. She hung up when she saw me.

'Wrong number,' she said.

Liar.

thirteen

Even the parents looked different.

We all shivered on the same muddy touchline, the February wind whipping through our winter coats, stamping our feet against the cold as we waited for the teams to appear. But there was no mistaking the parents of the three-grand-a-term UTI kids from the mums and dads of Ramsay Mac. They looked as though it wasn't just a different education they were buying, but a different life.

We looked poorer. We looked fatter. We looked pastier – even though we were a far more multi-racial bunch. Our hair was thinner, gone or bleached to the point of wispy no return. Their hair was long and lustrous, falling in magnificent curls and ringlets – especially the dads. We looked not quite mature – there were lurid tattoos, and replica football shirts – especially among the mothers. And there were more of them – the UTI families bred like pampered rabbits, and younger brothers and sisters frolicked at the feet of their affluent parents, a few of them holding babes in arms. You think that we would have that over them – that at least the Ramsay Mac parents would be able to knock out more kids than they could. You would think that at least we could procreate better than them. But, you see, the UTI parents stayed together. And at Ramsay Mac, we came apart. I inhaled deeply, smelling their swimming pool, and I felt the sharp pang of chlorine and envy.

Their playing fields went on forever, and the cries and

shouts of other matches drifted across as the teams made their way to the pitch. UTI in their red-and-black stripes, and Ramsay Mac in all white. Apart from Pat, who sloped round-shouldered near the back of his teammates as if wishing that his limbs were all slightly shorter. He was wearing a bright orange top, black shorts and socks. Plus his Predator boots, newly cleaned. He looked great. I laughed and applauded wildly. Kill these rich spoilt bastards, I thought, sportingly.

UTI sprinted on to the pitch. They began knocking a few balls about and doing some elaborate stretching. Ramsay Mac were slower, more sullen, trying to act as if this was all slightly beneath them. I recognised a few of them. William Fly was the big striker up front. Spud Face hovered by his side, doing some surprisingly impressive keepy-uppy, his pock-marked face frowning with concentration. As Pat dumped his towel in the back of the goal and tried on his gloves, a small, dark-skinned youth held back, dragging deeply on a Marlboro Light. The referee, a huge red-bearded man all in black, turned on him, eyes blazing.

'Put that fag out, Patel!' he bawled. It was the legendary Ramsay Mac sports teacher. Jones the Psycho, in the flesh.

The boy ground the cigarette out under the heel of his boot, grinning with embarrassment. The sports teacher glared at him as he joined his teammates. And then I saw her.

Elizabeth Montgomery and an older UTI lad, maybe as old as eighteen, his arm draped casually around her shoulder, her hand slipped inside his red-and-black blazer.

'Come on, UTI!' he shouted, but Elizabeth Montgomery turned her back on the field and snuggled up inside his blazer.

Patel, still coughing a bit from his cigarette, shirt cuffs pulled over his hands to keep warm, peppered shots at Pat's goal. My boy tipped them over the bar, pushed them round the post, caught them good and solid, wrapping his body around the ball. He was soon covered in mud, sweating hard, his breath making mist in the cold.

Then it was time to kick off.

Pat wiped the damp from his brow and crouched low,

watching carefully as UTI surged forward. Jones the Psycho's face was scarlet, keeping up with the action. Elizabeth Montgomery languished inside the red-and-black blazer of her mannish boyfriend. Pat had not noticed her.

UTI's number nine was the problem – a hefty blond lad with not much skill but plenty of heart. He shrugged off a couple of tackles, heading straight down the middle, until Ramsay Mac's own number nine – William Fly – brought him down with a sliding tackle from behind. The referee's whistle peeped in protest. Both of the number nines writhed in agony. When they got up, Jones the Psycho showed Fly a yellow card.

'What, sir?' Fly said, spreading his hands with outraged innocence. 'What? What? What?'

Patel and Spud Face made for a surprisingly nippy pair of wingbacks, sprinting down their respective touchlines and tormenting the UTI defence with crosses that swung teasingly away from the goalkeeper. But William Fly was slow and lumbering, better at sticking his elbow in someone's face than getting on the end of a cross, and if it wasn't dropped on his head or his right boot then he floundered and fell, rising to scream abuse at Patel and Spud Face, and beseeching Jones the Psycho for justice.

Now the UTI number nine had the ball again and was ploughing through the middle of the Ramsay Mac defence. Past one defender, and then another, with William Fly chasing back and then giving up in the centre circle, puffing and cursing.

I looked at Pat and he was crouched like a cat, ready to pounce. Patel and Spud Face were clinging to the men they were marking on the wing, looking at each other, waiting for the other one to do something. Then it was too late. UTI's number nine was through on an open goal, his right foot swinging at the ball, his mouth grimacing, the braces on his teeth gleaming in the pale winter sunlight.

He shot.

The ball arced slowly through the air towards the goal.

Pat was up on his toes, ready for it, glancing side to side to make sure there was nobody coming in to challenge him.

Then he saw her.

His true love inside the blazer of another.

Her skirt hiked up to new heights.

Her high heels sinking into the mud of UTI's impressive playing fields.

It was just a moment.

But it was quite long enough for him to take his eyes off the ball and let them settle on the girl. When he looked back the shot was on him, and directly above him and he closed his eyes against the sun, his hands flapping wildly for the ball even as it bounced off the back of his head and dribbled into the goal.

Pandemonium.

The parents going mental. UTI jumping on top of their number nine as Patel threw himself to the ground, his fists pounding against the mud. Spud Face ran towards Pat, screaming abuse.

Pat fumbled among the netting, retrieving the ball. When he fished it out, William Fly was standing in front of him.

'Sick Note,' he said, as I read his lips. 'You really are Sick Note, ain't you, Silver?'

Pat threw the ball in his face.

It hit Fly flush on the nose and the blood was already starting to flow as the bigger lad shoved his goalkeeper back into the goal and began to pummel him with fists and boots. Pat cringed under the assault, retreating into the back of his goal and squirming in the netting, like something that had been caught.

I was on the pitch and running towards the goal. But Jones the Psycho was already there, between them, pushing them apart.

Then he took out his red card and showed it to both of them. William Fly turned away in disgust, ripping off his white Ramsay Mac shirt and throwing it to the ground, to a chorus of boos. But Pat was tangled up in the netting, trying not to cry as he attempted to free himself. Jones the Psycho seized him by the scruff of his orange jersey and hauled him into the six-yard box.

'Off you go,' he said. 'Early bath, Sick Note.'

And that is when Pat hit him.

A wild, swinging punch that Jones the Psycho could have easily avoided if he had been looking. But he did not give my son that much credit. So Pat's tearful haymaker caught Jones the Psycho on the point of the chin just as he was turning away. And he dropped to the ground like a sack of very red potatoes.

Pat did not cry. I was happy about that. White with shock, he was way beyond crying. He collected his belongings from the back of the net – his Predator water bottle, his Predator beach towel, his spare pair of Predator gloves – and stepped over the prostrate figure of Jones the Psycho.

He did not look at me as he passed.

He did not look at anyone.

But as he brushed past Elizabeth Montgomery and her three-grand-a-term boyfriend, I could have sworn I saw her swoon.

fourteen

I followed my wife.

It was actually quite difficult. In the films they make it look easy. You just have to be ready to duck inside a doorway or bury your head in a newspaper when your prey turns around, their suspicions momentarily aroused.

But it wasn't like that at all.

Cyd had taken her Food Glorious Food van. I followed in my car, pulling one of Pat's old beanie hats over my head for a cunning disguise and giving her a five-minute start.

I thought I would struggle to keep up with her. But that wasn't the problem. As soon as we hit the Holloway Road, she ground to a halt in the mid-morning traffic jam, while I hovered dangerously close behind. I had to pause at a green light, provoking the wrath of my fellow motorists, to avoid catching up with her.

She was seeing 'a friend', she'd said, a wonderfully vague appointment. Perhaps she did not want to lie to my face. Perhaps that is what they all say.

I was hanging back, beanie hat pulled down, watching the back of her car, and watching the back of her head too – her hair worn up, her neck showing – and I marvelled at that curiously upright gait she had, and I felt this numb ache inside me just looking at her, and ducked my head every time she glanced in the rear-view mirror.

And I did not want it to be true.

Oh, Cyd, I thought, I love you so much, but then I had

145

to pay attention when I was nearly sideswiped by a bendy bus turning off for Kentish Town.

Then I lost her.

At the great screaming hub of Archway, she put her foot down on a yellow light – that naughty girl – and I had to pull up, although a flock of cyclists blithely kept going, shaking their fists and screaming their murderous curses at motorists with the right of way.

The traffic was clearer beyond the junction, and the road rose with Cyd as she climbed the hill towards London's leafy highlands.

And then she was gone.

But it did not matter, because here was one more thing that was different from the films.

I knew exactly where she was going.

It was one of those big white houses in Belsize Park. Nice neighbourhood. Nice architecture. Nice life.

The street was quiet and calm and rich. Far too affluent to tolerate a man in a black beanie hat lurking in the shadows of its sturdy trees. So I took to driving around the block. Even that was risky – a young dog-walker with half a dozen pampered mutts on a lead paused to watch me going round in circles for the third time. But when I went round again the dog-walker was gone, and there was just me and the house where Jim Mason lived, and the terrible knowledge that Cyd was in there with him. I parked in a residents-only bay down the street. And after an hour, the front door opened.

I was stretching my legs under one of those old trees and I watched them come out. Cyd first, her arms folded across her chest in that way she had when the world needed to be kept at bay. And then him, then Jim, his handsome head down, all serious. No sign of Liberty, his nurse from Manila.

So no surprise there then.

And so the world turns.

On the top step Cyd turned to look at him. I held my

breath, waiting for them to kiss, but instead they embraced – or rather, they held on to each other, as if each was preventing the other one from falling. Somehow that was worse.

I don't know what happened after that because I didn't stick around to find out. I got in the car, did a three-point turn and went back the way I had come, heading downhill to London's lowlands, the great black hole of betrayal in my chest, sticking two fingers up at all the crazed cyclists, and my eyes half-blinded by the tears.

The three of us sat outside the headmaster's office, a family once again.

Gina and Pat and I – when was the last time we had sat together like this? It was beyond memory, it was another lifetime. Some family dinner, before the fall? But no – because those three people no longer existed. The young husband and father. His tall, radiant wife. Proud parents of their mop-topped little *Star Wars*-barmy boy. Where were they today? They were not outside the head's office.

School sounds, school smells. Laughter and threats. Food and chlorine. Pat slumped low and unmoving in his chair, as if trying to disappear, as if he was a boy in a coma, the only sign of life the occasional flickering of his gaze as some giant child ambled by – the boys mean and hard-looking, quick to take offence, the girls with their skirts hiked up, wearing their sexual power like a prefect's badge. And they looked at the boy humiliated by sitting with dear old mum and dad, but I could not tell if their gaze meant everything, or nothing.

Gina was impassive, strangely calm considering the circumstances. All charm with the head's secretary when we were told that we had to wait, Mr Whitehead was running late, Gina all smiley understanding, not remotely defensive or surly, every inch the good parent.

And as we bided our time, waiting to be summoned into the head's office, I felt strangely elated – this wild, mad joy welling up inside me.

I thought it was because Pat was fighting back. But perhaps

147

it was something else. Perhaps it was just sitting there with my son and his mother, and a glimpse at the old comforting symmetry of our long-lost family, like a dead loved one met again in a dream.

'Mr Whitehead will see you now,' we were told, the old secretary's rheumy eyes staring at us over the top of her reading glasses, seeing right through us, but Gina was all smiles and thanks, gently indicating that Pat should snap out of his coma, and that I should get to my feet, and that we should both follow her into the headmaster's office.

He was charming. I mean, we were not offered tea and crumpets, but he was friendly enough in a stern, Victorian dad sort of way, and he did not treat us like the scum of the earth because my son had flattened a sports teacher. I suppose he saw a lot worse than that every day.

'We take any form of violence against a member of staff very seriously,' he said, his gaze moving from concerned parents to troubled child. Pat stared beyond his shoulder and out of the window, taking great interest in the totally empty playground and the playing fields beyond, as if this had nothing much to do with him.

'It was an accident,' I blurted, and Gina's head snapped in my direction. 'But it was,' I said feebly. 'He didn't mean it.' I looked at my son. 'Did you?'

Pat shrugged. 'It doesn't matter,' he said. 'They all hate me anyway.'

'How are you, Patrick?' Mr Whitehead said, and I realised with a shock that he actually seemed to like our son.

Pat nodded, still intent on the empty playground. 'I'm all right, sir.'

'You were doing so well,' the head said. 'Japanese – that was your subject, wasn't it?'

'Sir,' Pat affirmed, still not looking at him. And I could see that the boy was prepared to endure everything today, apart from a little kindness.

The headmaster even smiled. 'And as I recall, you were a leading light in . . . the Theatre Club?'

148

Pat finally looked at him. 'The Lateral Thinking Club, sir.'

Mr Whitehead nodded. Then he looked at Gina and I and his smile grew wider. 'I'm not even sure I know quite what they do in the Lateral Thinking Club,' he confessed.

Nervous laughter all round.

'Me neither!' I offered, a note of total hysteria in my voice.

'There have been bullying issues,' Gina said, and she looked at Pat and for a second I thought she was going to tell him to sit up straight. 'Issues of bullying that have been going on for quite a while.'

'He has to learn to stand up for himself,' I said, and she was on me.

'You think that's the answer to everything,' she said, biting my head off. 'But what if someone can't stand up to the bullying, Harry? What if they are too gentle or too timid or too alone? What happens then?'

'I don't know,' I said. 'I suppose then you get your head pushed down a toilet.'

Mr Whitehead raised his hands, like a marriage counsellor calling time out.

'We do not tolerate a culture of bullying at Ramsay Mac,' he said. Pat snorted with bitter laughter, and for the first time the headmaster looked as though he was ready to kill someone. 'You are suspended for one week, young man,' he said, jabbing an angry Parker Pen at my son. 'And I am taking into account that you did not intentionally strike Mr Jones and that for the last four years you have been a good, hard-working student.' He shook his head. 'I don't know what's happened to you this year, Patrick. But if your behaviour doesn't improve then you will give the school no option but permanent exclusion.'

Pat got a secret little smile on his face. He looked up at his mother.

'We have been thinking about changing schools,' Gina told the headmaster. 'My husband and I are no longer together.'

The headmaster nodded. 'I gathered that.'

Was it so obvious? I couldn't believe that it was only the

couples that broke up that got on each other's nerves. I thought that everyone did it.

Mr Whitehead shook his head. 'But this is a big year for Patrick,' he said. 'An exam year.'

'Well, then it would happen on the other side of exams,' Gina said. 'Probably.'

'I can tell you've really thought this through,' I said, looking from my ex-wife to my son. 'When did we start thinking about changing schools?' Neither of them would look me in the eye. 'Because I don't remember that conversation.'

'The travelling has become difficult for my son,' Gina said, ignoring me. 'There are these bullying issues. And now this suspension.' She cast down her eyes, and then shyly looked up at the headmaster. Ah, Gina. She still had that old magic. The headmaster put down his Parker Pen. 'I do appreciate your understanding,' she said quietly.

'Well,' Mr Whitehead said, 'you must let me know what you decide. But I strongly recommend sticking with us until the end of the academic year.'

'Thank you,' Gina said sweetly, as if she had just been told, Go ahead, love, do what you like.

But my blood was up. A new school? Who mentioned anything about a new school?

'There are bullies in every playground,' I said, immune to the power of Gina's eyelashes. 'In every playground in every school in the country. There will always be someone.' I shook my head. 'He can't just run away. It doesn't work like that.'

'Do you want him to go around punching everyone?' she said, as if I was some kind of psychopath. 'He's not like your father, Harry. And you know what?' The trouble with old partners is that they know what will hurt you the most. 'Neither are you,' she said.

Then Pat and the headmaster looked away, the pair of them embarrassed to be in the same room as us.

We lingered at the school gates, car keys in our hands, reluctant to go our separate ways with so many angry words still unsaid. I shuddered with the cold. Winter felt as though it was never going to end. I looked at Gina.

'Have they got any good schools in Soho?' I said.

She looked at me sharply. 'Have they got any round here?'

'Ramsay Mac is not so bad,' I said. 'You should see their A-Level results for Crack Dealing and Knife Fighting.'

Her mouth hardened. 'You think this is funny?'

I took a breath. Should I suggest coffee? A pint and a game of arrows? We seemed beyond all of that. But I didn't want to fight with Gina any more. I had a wife. I could be at home fighting with her. What was I doing expending all my energy on this stranger? But of course I knew the answer to that. It was because of the boy. Without our son Gina and I would be happily living on different planets.

'We're in this together,' I said, and I almost reached out to touch her arm. Luckily I managed to restrain myself.

'In it together,' she said, all numb. 'Yeah – like two ferrets in a sack.'

I stared back at the school where my son had returned to his unknowable day. Double maths and a ducking in the toilet? Abusive text messages and a kicking by the bike sheds? Collecting his rucksack and starting his suspension? I looked away, ashamed of myself, wondering when I had lost the power to protect him.

'I should have mentioned the change of schools,' Gina said, thawing a bit. 'I'm sorry, Harry, I really am. But this is not working.'

Everything was working fine until you decided to make a guest appearance in our lives, I thought. But I said nothing, and felt suddenly empty. The one thing left of our love was our ability to argue about anything.

'Do you ever wonder,' Gina said, 'what life would have been like if we had stayed together?' She half-smiled, and I had no idea what was in that smile. 'Do you wonder what would have happened, Harry, if you hadn't fucked around and I hadn't fucked off?'

'That's beautifully put,' I muttered, and I let a long breath ease out, and another long breath ease in, as I remembered the uncomplicated past, the unbroken and enduring past, with the little blond boy and the knock-out young mother, and the proud, capable father who loved them both, and never thought they would slip away when he wasn't looking.

I saw all of that letting one breath out, and one breath in, but it was always sliding away from me, like trying to remember the kind of dream that fades upon waking. I did not love this woman before me. I loved Cyd. I loved my wife.

I looked Gina in her blue eyes. They did nothing for me now.

'No,' I said.

I had forgotten about hospitals. The waiting around. The endless bad tea. The mind-numbing bureaucracy of terminal illness. How bored you could get in death's waiting room. Ken and I sat outside his doctor's office. He studied his *Racing Post* while I read my copy of Matthew Parker's *Monte Cassino*.

Only the bloodbaths of Verdun and Passchendaele, or the very worst of the Second World War fighting on the Eastern Front, can compare to Monte Cassino. The largest land battle in Europe, Cassino was the bitterest and bloodiest of the Western Allies' struggles with the German Wehrmacht on any front of the Second World War. On the German side, many compared it unfavourably with Stalingrad.

'I quite fancy Lucky Sue in the two thirty at Haydock Park,' Ken said, more to himself than me.

'Dad,' a woman's voice said, and we looked up to see Tracey and Ian bustling down the corridor. Then they had to press against the wall to let a man with a trolley-load of blood samples pass by, his little bottles rattling away, but they never stopped smiling at their father.

'Sorry we're late,' Tracey said. 'The traffic.'

'Hanger Lane was a nightmare,' Ian said. 'Chock-a-block, it is.'

152

Ken grunted, and turned back to the *Racing Post*.

'You haven't missed much,' he said.

I went to get tea for the four of us. When I came back, they were still waiting to see the doctor. Tracey was banging on about some homeopathic quackery she had just read about, while Ken rolled his eyes and stared at a point somewhere over her shoulder. Ian smiled nervously, trying to soothe the troubled waters that raged between them.

'It's really hot,' I said, passing the white plastic cups around. 'Give it five minutes.'

But Tracey was still talking about this miracle cure for cancer. She took a big gulp of molten tea and then jumped up as if she was choking.

'Told you to wait a minute,' I said.

She turned on me. 'And – sorry – remind me,' she said, 'why exactly are you here?'

'Tracey,' said her brother, not the first time, I'll warrant.

I cradled my boiling hot cup. 'I drove your dad here,' I said quietly.

'That's not it,' Ken said with a chuckle. He folded his *Racing Post* and looked at me. 'He's looking for his dad. Aren't you?'

I said nothing. I held my book and my tea. It was still too hot to drink. But I brought it to my lips anyway, just for something to do.

'He's looking for his dad but he's not going to find him here,' Ken said. An emphatic little gesture with his head. 'He's gone, your dad,' he told me. 'There's just me and my tumour.' He looked pleasantly surprised. 'Here – sounds like a song.' He began to sing, to the tune of 'Me and My Shadow'. *'Me . . . and my tumour . . . strolling down the avenue.'*

Tracey covered her face. 'Dad,' she said. 'Please. Don't.'

Ken smiled. 'You can say what you like when they're digging your grave.' He raised his hands in exasperation. 'Oh, here we go,' he said. 'Here come the waterworks. Here comes Niagara Falls.'

Ian had begun to cry. More of a weeping and a wailing.

Great wet tears coursing down his big round face. I swallowed hard. I looked away. But then I had to look at Ken.

'Your dad's gone,' he told me. 'Get it?'

'Got it,' I managed, and I necked my tea in one go as the nurse stuck her head around the door and said, 'Mr Grimwood?'

He stood up, straightened his tie and tugged at the hem of his blazer. 'Here, miss,' he said. I watched the Grimwoods troop off to the doctor's office. Ken turned and beckoned me to join them.

'But what does he need to come in for?' Tracey demanded. 'He's not family.'

'Oh, come on,' Ken chuckled. 'Let him have a bit of fun.'

Tracey shook her head, and bit her lip. Her brother patted her arm and we all went in where the doctor showed us X-rays of the old man's lungs, black with primary tumours and foggy with the fluids that clogged his chest.

The doctor was very nice. He pushed a box of Kleenex across his empty table for Tracey and Ian when they really started to sob. And he told us that only twenty per cent of lung cancer cases are ever suitable for surgery, and explained very patiently why chemotherapy and radiotherapy were inappropriate for an elderly man at this late stage of the disease. So he told us that there was hope. But not today, and not in this room, and not for this old man.

'You have perhaps nine months,' the doctor said, and Ian and Tracey were leaning out of their chairs, hugging each other.

I gripped my book with both hands.

But Ken Grimwood sat there dry-eyed.

'Thank you, Doctor,' he said. 'Can I go home now?'

That was the day that I really saw the hardness in him. Not the hardness that I had always admired – the hardness that gave him and all the men like him the courage to stand up to poverty and war and cancer and death – but the other hardness, the kind that kept his children at a distance, and his wife a little in fear, no matter how much she was in love.

As though something inside him was forever frozen, and

154

could never melt, and could never be reached. Perhaps they were the same thing, the good hardness and the other kind, and perhaps they had always been the same thing.

And he might have felt that my father was not there, but I could sense my old man muttering in the wings. I could almost smell the Old Spice and Old Holborn and the brown ale on his breath. And I could see him – I could see ten thousand nights of him eating his dinner on his lap in front of the TV, and I could remember the one special night when he was stone-faced with fury as I told him that my marriage had died, and then near the end, I remembered the nights when he was pumped full of morphine in a hospital ward, and still fearless, still hard as teak, and still totally incapable of tears, or of ever being touched.

So the old man was wrong.

My father was there all right.

fifteen

Cyd and I were home alone.

It was one of those rare moments of peace that descend on any busy household. When you suddenly find time on your hands, and stillness in the house, and the children all elsewhere.

A Saturday morning, and suddenly I had nothing to do today. In a terse text message, Pat had cancelled our trip to the NFT for the director's cut of *A Bridge Too Far*. Peggy was at her salsa class. And Joni had not yet returned from a sleepover at a friend's house.

I placed two cups of coffee on the little table in our living room. There was a catalogue on the table for serious kitchen appliances – fridges that can hold enough canapés to feed a thousand, that kind of thing.

I settled myself on the sofa with my copy of the *Racing Post*.

I felt good. I felt calm. I noted that Marley's Ghost had been found wanting in its last three starts but had now dropped some weight and was expected to get involved in the 1235 at Limerick.

Interesting, I thought. Very interesting.

Cyd walked into the room towelling her hair. It was still wet from the shower. She was barefoot, half-dressed, her limbs long and coltish in white shorts and black vest. She knelt on the floor in front of the big wall mirror, lifting her bottom in my general direction as she plugged in the hairdryer.

It was a bit like one of those mirrors you see in dance studios. A mirror that dominates a wall, and lets you see everything. And I saw how my wife's body had changed over the years. She was rounder now, made of more curves. Time did that. A baby did that.

I liked the way she was before and I liked the way she was now. If anything, I liked her more now. Cyd was always lovely, but she was one of those women who grow into their beauty. And she looked great in her white shorts and black vest, her hair all wet and mussed up. I had quite forgotten about Marley's Ghost getting involved at Limerick.

She caught me watching her and smiled at me in the mirror.

'What?' she laughed.

As if she couldn't tell.

I crossed the room to her, the *Racing Post* still in my hand. She shook her head and turned on the hairdryer. I knelt by her side, feeling a blast of hot air on my face. Her black hair was flying, all wet and glossy. I threw aside my paper and touched her hair with the tips of my fingers.

'Want me to do that for you?' I offered, looking at her bare legs. There was a long muscle on the top of her thighs and it really stood out when she knelt down like that.

'You want to blow-dry my hair?' she said. 'Thanks, but I think I'm starting to get the hang of it.'

I nuzzled the side of her face, her hair damp against my nose and mouth.

Then I slipped into my Barry White voice.

'You know, baby, no matter how many times I've blow-dried your hair, it just never seems like it's enough . . .' I shook my head like the great man. 'It's just not enough, baby.'

Cyd turned off her hairdryer.

'What do you really want?' she said, and she tilted her head as I kissed her mouth. A perfect fit, as always and forever. She stroked my arms as we knelt side by side, our foreheads touching, looking at each other in the mirror.

'Saturday morning?' she said. 'Come on.'

157

'Why not?' I said. 'Nobody around. We're an old married couple. We have to take our pleasures where we can.'

Her eyes got that sleepy, knowing look that I loved.

'You don't need any of those little blue pills yet, do you?' she said.

That kind of lavish sexual praise always gets me going.

'Not if you catch me before noon,' I said.

She laughed. 'Then we've got sixty minutes.'

I slipped back into Barry White.

'That's good, baby, because you know I'm a sixty-minute man.'

'Promises, promises,' she said, and laid her hairdryer to one side and put her arms around my neck.

Then we were rolling around on the floor, and every now and again I would stop kissing her to look at us in the mirror. And Cyd would look too. And what we saw in the mirror would make us want to kiss some more.

We were just about to get down to the serious stuff when Cyd said, 'Ouch.'

Something was sticking in her back.

She rolled on her side and pulled my scrunched-up *Racing Post* from beneath her.

She frowned. Then grinned.

'The *Racing Post?*' she said, with genuine marital amusement. She held it between her thumb and index finger, as if about to conduct a forensic examination.

'Since when did you start reading the *Racing Post?*'

I had actually been reading it for quite a while. She just hadn't noticed.

'Oh,' I said. 'Every now and then.'

I kissed her neck, her forehead, her ear.

But she was laughing quite hard by now. It's difficult to stay completely in the mood when someone's having a good old laugh.

'Hilarious,' she said.

Have you noticed that when anyone says, 'Hilarious,' it is never, ever even remotely funny? Saying *hilarious* is the kiss of death to humour. And everything else. I rolled on to my back. Cyd crossed her legs and actually began flicking through the *Racing Post.*

After a while I realised she was looking at me.

'What are you doing?' she said. She wasn't smiling now. It wasn't hilarious now. None of it. 'You're not . . .? I don't believe it, Harry. You're not actually . . . *gambling*, are you?'

I sat up. 'I never actually thought of it as gambling,' I said. 'It's just – you know. Having a flutter. A bit of a laugh.'

She stood up, smoothing her white shorts. She flopped down on the sofa. She took a sip of coffee, still examining the *Racing Post* as if it revealed some dark secrets about my soul. Then she put down her coffee, too hard. Some of it splashed over the little table. 'A bit of a laugh?' she said. And then the same again, but with the volume turned way up. '*A bit of a laugh?*'

I got up off the floor and lifted my coffee just as she chucked her kitchen appliance catalogue at me. It only brushed my arm but it was like being hit by a telephone directory, or a very large brick. I cursed, and cursed again, most of my coffee sloshing down the front of my jeans and shirt.

'Jesus Christ, Cyd,' I said and put down the cup, and went off to clean up. She came after me.

'Have you seen all the bills in the top drawer?' she said. 'All those red-coloured bills, Harry? Those bills from gas, electricity and every other bastard we owe money to?'

I was at the sink tearing off kitchen towel. It was no good. I was going to have to change, shower, start again. 'I'm going to get a job,' I said. 'And until I do, I'm going to get a loan. From the bank. I keep telling you.'

I turned to go but she barred my path. 'Yes, you keep telling me,' she said. 'That's all you ever do – tell me. Tell me how everything's under control and everything's going to be good tomorrow. What is it you bloody English say? Jello tomorrow. That's what my life with you is like, Harry. It's all bloody jello tomorrow.'

I pushed past her, glad our kids were not here for this. 'Jam tomorrow,' I said. 'The expression is jam tomorrow.'

'You're the expert.'

I went to the bathroom and began taking off my clothes. I thought she had left me alone but after a while she appeared in the doorway, a sheath of papers in her hand. She began throwing them at me one by one.

'British Gas,' she said, and for just a second I remembered how much I loved her crazy accent. The way she said 'British'. It made something inside me ache. But then the moment was gone, gone the moment she threw the bill at me. It fluttered between us. 'Eastern Electricity . . . Virgin Media . . . Vodafone for Joni . . .'

I stood there in my pants, my hands held up in bewilderment. 'Vodafone for Joni? Why is a seven-year-old girl receiving a bill from Vodafone?'

'For her *cell*, stupid,' Cyd said. And then, switching to a grotesque parody of a London accent, like Dick Van Dyke in *Mary Poppins*: 'For her *moh-bile fone, mayte, innit?*'

She kept reading the names of the bills and throwing them at me. When she began reading out a letter from the Cheltenham and Gloucester about our mortgage, I decided I had had enough. I started putting my coffee-soaked clothes back on.

'All on me, Harry,' she said. She was calmer now, but that was somehow worse. 'This house needs two incomes. This house needs both of us contributing. But it's all on me. We're lucky I'm busy right now. We're lucky Food Glorious Food has more work than it can handle. Otherwise – I don't know.'

'I'm sorry,' I said. And I truly was sorry. 'I know it's hard.' I zipped up my jeans, adjusted my penis. 'I'm doing my best.'

'Then don't gamble, Harry,' she said, pleading now. 'It's insane, baby! Can't you see that? We have no money – we are right at the limit – and you are starring in a remake of *Casino Royale*.'

'It's not like that,' I said. 'It's just a few quid, now and then.' I left the bathroom and walked, just wanting to get some distance between us. 'It's a bit of fun. Some light relief.' She was right behind me, following me. I turned to look at her. 'God knows I deserve some.'

She nodded, as if she understood everything. 'Living with me, you mean?'

'I didn't say that, did I?'

'I do my bit for this family – and plenty more,' she said. 'Don't you ever forget it, mister.'

We were on the stairs. Going nowhere. I turned to look at her. We were right by the alcove that contained all my prizes. My BAFTA from the long lost era of *The Marty Mann Show*. My glass earhole from quite recently. A glass pigeon from somewhere that I couldn't quite recall.

'And what about me?' I said. 'I've worked like a dog for years.'

'What kind of dog would that be, Harry? A Chihuahua? A little Shih Tzu?'

I gestured at my illustrious prizes. 'They don't give these away for serving chicken satay,' I said, because I knew it would hurt her. But I could not stop myself. We had got to that point where we could not stop ourselves from hurting each other. It was all we wanted now.

Cyd looked at my prizes, less than impressed.

'It's a glass earhole, Harry,' she said. 'It's just a glass earhole.' She saw my face turning red. She saw the little vein in my right temple start to throb. And she laughed. She knew she had scored a bull's-eye. 'What shall we do, Harry? Shall we try to pay our mortgage with your glass earhole?'

My voice was very quiet. 'If you don't like it,' I said, 'then why don't you go back to fucking Jim?' We stared at each other. 'Your ex-husband. If you've had enough of me, then why don't you drag the carcass of that marriage around the block one more time?'

'What?' she said.

I pushed past her. Going back down the stairs now. Over my shoulder. 'You heard,' I said.

She sat on the stairs. I went to the kitchen and ripped off

a rubbish sack. Then I went back to the alcove that displayed my prizes. Cyd was still sitting on the stairs, her face in her hands. I began tossing my prizes into the rubbish sack. The glass earhole went first. Cyd looked up with wet eyes as we heard it explode.

'What are we doing to each other, Harry?' she said, and her lovely face was all twisted with what we had become. 'Oh, please don't throw away your pigeon.'

'Too late,' I said, and the pigeon went in, followed by my BAFTA from the days when we thought that TV would always love us – my beautiful BAFTA! – and it smashed the pigeon and the earhole a bit more. I hung my head and I covered my face too.

Then the doorbell rang.

Cyd and I looked at each other and then slowly descended the stairs. The doorbell was still ringing. I was still holding the rubbish sack, and the broken glass tinkled like jewels. The sound of the shattered prizes made Cyd cry a bit harder. There was a sob the size of a ten-year-old marriage in my throat.

I opened the front door.

There was a smiling Japanese woman holding a newborn baby, and a shy-looking Japanese man behind her, dressed for the golf course. I couldn't work out what was happening. Then Joni and her friend Asuka jumped out whooping from either side of the door, surprising me, and then standing there jumping up and down and hugging each other and chanting this mantra.

'Best friend,' the two girls sang. 'Best friend, best friend.'

'Very good playdate,' said the smiling Japanese lady, and the tiny mop-haired baby in her arms began to mew. Her husband nodded shyly in agreement. Joni brushed past me.

'Can Asuka have a sleepover with me next weekend?' she said.

'Very good girl,' said the kind, sweet Japanese lady, and her decent, golf-playing husband nodded again.

Then the shy, smiling, decent Japanese family looked at

my wife and me, really looked at us for the first time, and their smiles faded.

They saw it all. The coffee on my unbuttoned shirt. The grief on our faces. The red bills that were scattered across the hall like the betting slips of lost races. And in the rubbish bag I held, they heard all the glittering prizes, reduced to jingling-jangling pieces of trash.

They gathered up their children.

They nodded a polite goodbye, as if we were normal people too.

And then they got out of there.

sixteen

I sat up in my office, watching DVDs of *PC Filth: An Unfair Cop*. It was a depressing business. But I was going to an interview for a production job on the show and they always expected you to know the thing inside out.

I knew exactly what some sniffy little twelve-year-old executive producer would ask me. How did you feel when PC Dibbs got shot at the end of the fourth series? How about the sub-plot of the cross-dressing copper? Should DCI Rooney still be struggling with his booze problem in series five? How about reconciliation with his estranged wife? Is the police dog a distraction from the action, or does it rope in the animal lovers? Should we hang a hoodie in the cells? Or just beat the crap out of him in the police canteen? They wanted you to share your ideas. They were very big on sharing.

And they got massively offended if you weren't totally up to speed with their little show. If they knew that I would cross the road to avoid watching it, I would have never got through the door. So I bought the boxed set online – *PC Filth: An Unfair Cop*, series 1 to 5 – 'Well Worth Getting Nicked For!' – and I studied it, and I made notes, and I knew that in the end they would still give the production job to someone else.

I pressed pause when I heard the delivery van, feeling as if I was coming up for air. I went to the window and down on the street four men were easing a giant box off the back of their lorry. I went downstairs, eager to help, and even more eager to escape *PC Filth: An Unfair Cop.*

Because I wanted to be good. I wanted to provide and protect. I wanted to try to be the man that my father was without trying. I wanted to watch over my family like a statue of a Golden Retriever.

I could hear Polish voices in the hallway. The box was on its side and being eased through the front door. It seemed to be stuck. Cyd stood watching with her arms folded across her chest. She did not look at me as I came down the stairs.

They got the box through the door and stood it up. It was ten feet tall, almost touching the ceiling. Joni came downstairs and we all stood watching as they got the box on to a trolley and wheeled it into the kitchen, giving a light bulb a whack on the way.

Joni danced after her mother and the men and the box as I steadied the light. I followed them into the kitchen. One of them began disconnecting the old fridge while the rest of them cracked open the box. It was a new refrigerator. The King Kong of fridges. A double-doored American monster in stainless steel.

Joni crawled into the box and looked out.

'Like a Wendy House for indoors,' she said. 'Can we keep it? Can we keep the box? Can we?'

'No,' said Cyd, and she took a step closer to peer at the magnificent fridge with her wide-set brown eyes. I had once lost myself in those eyes. It seemed like a long time ago.

'Beautiful,' I said, above the babble of Polish and Joni pleading to keep the box forever. 'But can we afford it?'

Cyd glanced at me with those far-apart eyes and then she looked away.

'Let me worry about that,' she said.

And suddenly the room was so quiet that you could have heard my penis dropping off.

I waited for Peggy outside the club.

I stayed in the car, the engine running, and the only time

I took my eyes off the door was to quickly glance at my watch.

Ten to midnight. She was meant to come out at twelve. There was a big man on the door, a giant skinhead in a black Crombie, and he lifted and lowered a red velvet rope with surprising delicacy. He stared impassively at the kids in the queue, letting them advance when the mood took him, a Pied Piper with a history of steroid abuse, and I willed the minutes away.

Then I saw Peggy and her friend. Skirts too short and heels too high. But laughing, happy, which was good. And with a group of boys, which was bad. One of the boys was doing all the talking, trying to sell them something. A ride, a party, the notion that the night was still young.

I recognised him.

The bulk of his body – big for his age – and stubble like a black cloud on his face. William Fly did the talking, while Spud Face and the others held back, fixed grins on their ugly mugs, content to let the big man do the talking. And he did. Peggy turned to look at him, throwing back her head with a laugh.

She was a good, sensible girl. And there were boys around every day at her school. But not that kind of boy. She shook her head, her smile fading, and turned away.

William Fly reached out and held her wrist.

And I was out of the car, calling her name. I stepped forward and nearly went under the front wheels of a lorry. The driver leaned on his horn, and by the time it had passed Peggy and her friend were crossing the road towards me.

The pack of boys were watching them go, grinning and sharing their witless observations.

'Thanks for coming, Harry,' Peggy said, and then looked at her watch. 'We're not late, are we?'

I got them in the car and hit the button for central locking. Two children dressed like women. My daughter watched my face in the rear-view mirror.

'What's wrong?' she said.

'Nothing,' I said. 'Put your seat belts on.'

* * *

166

'Look at my house, Daddy,' Joni said.

I got down on my hands and knees and peered into the giant cardboard box that had held the refrigerator. Joni had lined the walls with stuffed animals and assorted dolls. At seven, she was getting a bit old for this stuff, and she could feel it. The pressure to grow up was all around, and it made her nostalgic for earlier times. She missed being a little girl. She was nostalgic for the simple pleasures of Ken and Barbie.

'You can come and visit, if you want,' she said, rearranging a couple of Bratz and a monkey from London Zoo.

I crawled into the box, and Joni had to shuffle to one side as I turned around. It was the size of a telephone box. We peered out, both of us laughing. Cyd walked into the room and stared at us.

'Hard at it?' she said to me. She had her coat on. She was going out. It was the first I knew about it.

'I was just making a cup of coffee,' I said. 'Then I was going back to work.'

I crawled out of the box. The new refrigerator hummed self-importantly. Cyd opened the door and took out a bottle of water. 'Watching old episodes of *The Bill* all day long?' she said. 'Nice work, if you can get it.'

'It's not *The Bill*,' I said. 'It's *PC Filth: An Unfair Cop*. You know that one. I thought you were a fan. And I'm only –'

'Yeah,' she said, cutting me off. 'I know.' The fridge bathed her in a golden light. She closed the door and the light was gone. 'Peggy's got her eye on Joni, so don't let her stop you.'

'Daddy was just visiting,' Joni said.

Cyd bent down to kiss the top of her head. 'We're not keeping this old box in the house forever,' she said, and stood up as Peggy drifted into the room.

Peggy did this sort of spin, like a lazy ballet move, and crouched down in front of the box.

'Would you like to visit?' Joni said.

'Love to, darling,' Peggy laughed, and she crawled into the box.

The front door closed quietly behind Cyd and I stared at

it for a while. I went into the kitchen and put the kettle on, not really hearing the sound of my daughters playing or the unbroken hum of the fridge. My mind was elsewhere, to tell you the truth, up in the leafy highlands of North London. I walked back down the hallway and stared at the door.

I felt for her. I really did. This was not easy for her. This was not something that she could do lightly.

And I could hardly blame her. Truly.

Overlooking the fact that she was ripping out my heart, and tearing it into a billion tiny pieces, I could even understand it.

Because how can it be infidelity when you have had enough of someone?

I stood across the street from the house in Belsize Park.

I didn't care if the neighbours looked at me as if I was a master burglar casing the joint. And I didn't care if they saw me from his flat. I was beyond caring about all that stuff. I wanted it all out in the light, no matter how ugly it looked. I was sick to my stomach with all the things that were being left unsaid, unseen, unknown.

It began to rain, and still I stood there. Then it got dark, and still I stood there. In the end, after a lifetime or so, the door opened. And this time there were three of them. Cyd and Jim and a woman that I did not recognise at first. But then the last time I saw her was many years ago, sitting on the back of a motorbike on her wedding day.

Liberty, still in her nurse's uniform.

You can buy that kit on the Internet, I reflected. A nurse's uniform – that's sex wear for some sickos. How do we know she's a real nurse? We just have her word for it.

They were locked in a group embrace. Heads down, hugging.

The three of them?

What kind of evil was abroad in Belsize Park?

I stepped forward, realising that I was soaked to the bone. They all looked at me as I crossed the road. Then I realised that Jim was crying. And Liberty. Only my wife was dry-eyed, and she looked at me with an expression that I could not read.

In a dream I drifted up those few steps to the front door, and Jim put an arm around me, drawing me into their group embrace.

'Harry,' he said, all choked. 'Cyd's been so great. Ever since we found out. She's been there for me. We're working out how to tell Peggy. She doesn't know a thing. She's going to be . . .'

He shook his head, gulping it down, overwhelmed.

'She'll deal with it,' Cyd said. 'Peggy's strong and smart.' I could see her making the physical effort to keep the tears at bay. 'I'll tell her. It will be okay. Everything will be okay.'

Then I took half a step back, and it sort of broke up the group hug. The three of them kept their arms around each other, but I was out of it.

I looked at Liberty, not understanding anything. How she became this nice middle-aged lady, how they could look at me with total innocence, how the time can slip away when we are not even looking.

'Jim's got Parkinson's,' Cyd said flatly. 'Diagnosed –' She looked at her ex-husband for confirmation. 'A month back?' Then she looked at me.

'Parkinson's disease,' I said, pointlessly, taking another half a step back and almost falling backwards down the steps. Which was not what the moment needed. Cyd took my arm, preventing me from falling. 'I don't really know . . .' I began.

Jim was staring at his hands. 'It's the nervous system,' he said. 'Affects the brain and the spinal cord. Nobody knows how it will progress. Your mobility, your speech . . .'

Liberty hung her head.

Cyd took a fistful of his shirt and shook it. 'That's right – nobody knows how it's going to progress,' she said. 'Not even the doctors. So stop imagining the worst, okay?'

Jim looked at me. 'It's the work, Harry – you understand? The idea that it could stop me working.' His voice choked, broke. 'You know?'

I knew.

And when Cyd and I walked away, I put my arm around her and she neither pushed me away nor encouraged me to carry on holding her. She just kept walking. My arm fell away. It seemed only natural, that falling away.

'Poor Jim,' I said. 'I thought . . .'

She shook her head. 'I know exactly what you thought,' she said evenly. 'You thought I was coming here to have sex with him.'

'No,' I said. 'No, no, no.'

'Oh, yes, yes, yes,' she said. 'My ex-husband! I don't even know how a mind can think such a thing. Or how you can think such a thing of me. And what about Liberty? What was she doing while all this was going on? Filming it? Joining in? While dressed as a nurse?'

Well.

The thought had crossed my mind.

'Why didn't you tell me?' I said. 'That's what I don't get, Cyd. Just tell me. What are we? Husband and wife? Or room mates?'

She laughed bitterly. 'I didn't tell you because I know how much you have on your plate,' she said. 'Because I know how hard it is for you right now. Because I thought I could deal with it. I didn't want to worry you. I thought I was doing a good thing.'

And I loved her. All of her. I had never loved her more than I did at that moment.

I loved the thin white scar just above her eyebrow, a reminder of a childhood accident with a baseball bat, kept like a secret under the black veil of hair. I loved her faraway brown eyes and her decency and her bravery. I loved the fact that she could keep love in her heart even after love had gone. And I loved the fact that she was not fucking another man. I may have laughed out loud. Did I really do that, or did I just smile? I don't know. But whatever I did, it was definitely a mistake.

She stopped and stared at me.

'You act as though it's good news, Harry,' she said. 'The father of my child is diagnosed with this terrible disease and you stand there acting as if you just won the Lottery.'

'No,' I said, and she started walking but I stopped her and I held her hands, wanting her to understand. 'It's just that – I love you, that's all.'

'You're happy,' she said. 'I can tell. Look at you. How can you be happy?'

My wife looked at me as if we had never met.

seventeen

I was at the production company when my phone began to vibrate. GRIMWOOD CALLING, it said. I stared at the name for a moment, and then I pressed IGNORE. I slid my phone back in my jeans. Not even feeling guilty. As far as I was concerned, I had done my bit.

I was in a holding area, drinking bad macchiato from a vending machine and waiting for my interview to start, feeling the sting of rejection before it had even happened.

The office was open plan, so everywhere I could see busy young people with their All Saints sweaters and cocaine hangovers, scuttling around importantly. Ten years ago I would have known their names. But ten years ago this lot were in school, and the busy boys and girls of my time had been shipped off to uncool careers outside Soho or to families in the suburbs.

A slip of a girl stood in front of me, giving me her professional PA smile.

'Harry . . . Sliver?' she said, squinting at a clipboard.

'Close,' I said, happy to put down the rotten coffee and stand up. 'It's Harry Silver, actually.'

And I've got a fucking BAFTA! And a glass earhole! And a pigeon! Or at least I did have until I smashed them all to bits.

She wasn't embarrassed. Who cared if it was Silver or Sliver? We both knew they were going to give the job to a twenty-one-year-old who would work for peanuts.

I followed her down corridors lined with posters of *PC Filth: An Unfair Cop*. I stared at the faces of all those RADA graduates trying to look well hard, and my mind went blank. There was the young female cop who used to be a lap dancer and the cop with the booze problem and the cop who got shot . . . what were they called again? And among those beautiful faces, only one shone out, the most beautiful of them all. Jim Mason looked down at me, looking glamorously tortured.

My phone began to vibrate and I ignored it. Because the PA had stopped outside an open door, where a thin woman in glasses was showing out a kid with uncombed hair and jeans hanging down the crack of his skinny little bum.

My rival.

'Fantastic to meet you, Jake,' the thin woman in glasses was saying. 'I loved your shorts.'

His shorts? I glanced dumbly at my rival's baggy jeans. And then the euro dropped. Oh, his *shorts*! His short *films*! I was still grinning inanely as the woman in glasses buttered up the departing Jake, watching me from a wary corner of her eye.

'And I loved your vision for *PC Filth: An Unfair Cop*, Jake. We will definitely be in touch.'

I should have just turned round and walked away. But I stood there, the shadow of my inane grin still playing meaninglessly around my mouth as the woman in glasses looked at me with slightly less warmth than she'd summoned for Jake and his impressive shorts, and she led me into her office, sneaking a quick glance at her watch. She settled herself behind a desk that was empty of everything apart from five BAFTAs and a BlackBerry.

'Sara,' she said. 'No H.'

I nodded. 'Harry,' I said. 'No job.'

She grimaced, as if in physical pain. Oh well.

I swallowed hard and looked at the posters for inspiration – PC Dobbs? PC Dibbs? What the fuck was Jim's character called? I lowered my eyes but had to instantly raise them again to peer up at Sara, for her chair was considerably higher than mine.

Ah, that old trick, designed to make me feel small. It was working.

'Okay, Larry,' she said. '*PC Filth: An Unfair Cop.* Series six.' She leaned forward, squinting behind the specs. 'Thoughts?'

'Well,' I said, and my phone began to vibrate. Why couldn't he just leave me alone? 'Clearly, the inciting incident has to be the shooting at the end of the last series.' The phone felt warm against my thigh. I took a breath. 'The tragic shooting of . . . PC . . . Tibbs?'

A flash of irritation behind those glasses. 'PC Dibbs,' she said. She laughed and it chilled me to the marrow. 'There is no PC Tibbs as yet.'

'Of course not,' I babbled, the first beads of sweat breaking out on my brow as the phone vibrated again. Could she hear it? Was it too late to take it out and turn it off? 'The major editorial question is . . .'

We smiled in perfect harmony, and it was a real smile from her this time.

'*Does he live?*' we said together. Then she nodded curtly. 'We are still in negotiations with the actor's agency,' she said. 'So nothing has been signed.'

'Kill him off,' I said. A bold move, I know. 'Then the entire series can be about the aftermath. The hunt for vengeance. The search for the killer. The impact of his death on the team. I am thinking – complete mayhem. Cross-dressing coppers! Back on the booze! Beating up hoodies in the cells!' I took a chance. 'DCI Rooney back with the wife but she doesn't understand how these mean streets can tear out a man's guts . . . and make a good cop go bad.'

'What about K-9?'

K-9? Of course! The police dog!

'I loved that episode, "A Bent Cop's Best Friend",' I said. Sara smiled.

Yes! Back of the net!

Then she looked thoughtful.

'I was thinking of bumping off the mutt,' she mused. 'A hit-and-run accident? Stopping a bullet as he throws himself in front of DCI Rooney?' She scrunched up her mouth. 'Too corny?'

'We could always get another dog,' I suggested. 'Son of K-9 . . . K-10?'

'Brilliant, darling,' she said.

I was on a roll.

Then a little red light began to wink on her BlackBerry. She picked it up and sighed. 'I have to take this,' she said. 'It's my nanny.' Hand over the BlackBerry, confiding in me. 'At least, she calls herself a nanny. She's more like a fucking lobotomised au pair.' She smiled thinly. 'Yes, Milena, what's the problem now?' She listened for a bit, tapping her fingers on her empty desk, staring at her BAFTAs. Then she held up a hand. 'What do you mean, Lukey refuses to eat his vegetables? You know the modus operandi, darling, when Lukey refuses to eat his fucking vegetables. Didn't we discuss this only yesterday? No, shut up, darling, and listen to me. You may learn something. When Lukey refuses to eat his vegetables then *we remove his privileges.* Threaten to take away his Wii Sports Resort and he will soon be necking the organic carrots, believe me.'

While she was chewing out the nanny I sneaked a look at my phone.

TEN MISSED CALLS, it told me.

Jesus Christ, it must be serious.

I licked my lips and slipped the phone back inside my jeans. Sara was talking to me and she was smiling but I wasn't hearing her. And I remembered my father on the last night of his life. Scared and shot full of morphine and eaten up by the cancer that was about to kill him.

And left to die alone.

We didn't mean to let him die alone, my mother and I. We had just come home to get a change of clothes and to shower and to catch our breath. And to get out of that hospital, and that cancer ward, for a few hours. And that is when he died, and I would regret not being there for the rest of my life.

Then she had stopped smiling.

And she was waiting.

'I said – what about WPC Chang?'

I opened my mouth and nothing came out. Ten missed calls? Even if I left now, would I even be in time? Was I going to let everyone I cared about die alone? Was that the kind of man I had become?

I looked up at the posters on the wall. WPC Chang? What one was she? Was she a new character or an old character? There was no obvious WPC Chang in the posters. And I felt the panic flying, as I rose to my feet.

'WPC Chang?' I said. 'What about her?'

Sara leaned back in her chair, looking up at me now. 'What about her?' she said. 'Is that the question? Well, obviously – what about her abortion in series three? Should she still be bearing the psychological scars?'

'Ah,' I said. 'Look, Sara – I really don't know, to be honest. In my experience – I mean, in real life rather than in *PC Filth: An Unfair Cop* – nobody ever gets over that kind of thing. Not really.' I looked up at the posters. I didn't want to be rude. I needed a job. But – ten missed calls! – I had to go. 'I only really started watching the show a few days ago, to tell you the truth. I may have missed WPC Chang's abortion.' I was heading towards the door, already getting out my phone. 'I could do this job. I know I could. I know you'll go for some kid who knows every episode inside out and will work for a pocketful of pistachio nuts.' I shook my head, and nodded at the awards on her desk. 'But I have two things that he doesn't have. A BAFTA and some grey hair.'

'Give him time,' she said.

I smiled sadly. She was hard but she was good. I could see that. I would have loved to work with her. But the world was not like that any more.

176

'I see you're a mother,' I said. 'So I hope you understand. Domestic emergency.'

At the death, she was surprisingly sympathetic. Before my very eyes, I saw something inside her melt.

'Lukey is seven,' she said, smiling as she nodded at the phone in my hand. 'How old is this one?'

I had to think about it for a second.

'Eighty-two,' I said.

I was back out on Old Compton Street, lunchtime Soho swirling all around as I desperately called Ken's number. It just kept ringing until it went to voicemail.

So I checked my phone and swore under my breath because the old man never left messages. I hailed a black cab and headed north to the Angel, wound tight with the anxiety and fury that you feel when your child is suddenly and unexpectedly out of sight, and you know with total certainty that the very worst is about to happen.

Singe Rana opened the door. Ken was sitting in front of the racing on Channel 4, a mug of tea by his side and today's *Racing Post* on his lap.

'Got a red-hot tip for you,' he said. 'Chinese Rocks in the three thirty at Goodwood tomorrow.'

I stared at him.

'A horse?' I said. 'You've been bombing me with calls because of . . . a horse?'

He frowned at me. 'Doing you a favour, mate,' he said. 'It's Chinese Rocks in the three thirty at Goodwood tomorrow and it's a dead cert.' He looked at Singe Rana as the old Gurkha eased himself into his favourite chair. 'What are the odds?'

The smooth golden face turned to me with quiet satisfaction. 'Twenty-five to one,' he said, and Ken cackled with triumph.

'Put everything you've got on it,' he advised. 'Bloke in the bookies gave us the nod. Didn't he, Singe?'

'You called me ten times in the middle of a job interview,'

I said, still trying to understand. 'Why didn't you pick up when I called back?'

'Probably a bit mutton,' he said.

'What?'

'Mutt and Jeff. Deaf.'

'Can you speak English?' I said. 'All those calls – about some stupid horse . . .'

He bristled at that. 'It's not some stupid horse, sunshine,' he said. 'It's Chinese Rocks in the three thirty at Goodwood. And if you don't get on it, then it's your loss.'

Then he shook his *Racing Post*, and he narrowed his eyes at me with exactly the same amused contempt that I sometimes saw on the face of my father, a look that said he knew exactly how this world worked, while I was still looking for the user's manual.

The cinema was half-empty on a wet Monday night. I shook my head and irascibly munched my popcorn. I couldn't believe it.

A new print of *Seven Samurai* and all it attracts is a few hard-core Kurosawa fans and a bunch of courting couples who could be necking to some rom-com corn? As the seven Samurai clashed with the bandits who were terrorising the villagers, I could see the glow of mobiles in the darkness. Unbelievable.

As I left the cinema, I wondered what Pat would have made of it. He would probably have said that it wasn't a patch on *The Magnificent Seven*, and I would have said that was a barmy position to take, as the Yul Brynner–Steve McQueen western was only a Hollywood remake of the Japanese original. And then Pat would have got a sly little smile and said, sure, but Kurosawa's film was conceived as an homage to John Ford in the first place.

But Pat wasn't there.

I stood outside the cinema, shivering in the night and feeling my stomach rumble. If I went home then I would have to rummage among sashimi and shellfish in the new fridge when all I really wanted was cheese on toast. So I walked across to the pizza place on the far side of Islington Green where I paused outside, held by a familiar face.

Peter was in the window of the pizza joint with a woman and two kids. No, three kids, because the woman had a new baby in her arms.

She looked like Gina's plain younger sister.

Tall, highlights, but without the glow that Gina had. I watched her soothing the baby with one hand as she ate a piece of garlic bread with the other. The two bigger children seemed very well behaved. They were eating their mini pizzas, their legs swinging above the floor. Their father was raising a bottle of Peroni beer to his lips. He stopped when he saw me, his mouth half-open, the bottle not quite there.

He turned back to his family. He took a swig.

And I stood there staring at him because I wanted him to know that I saw it all, and I wanted him to squirm.

Even now there was a part of me that felt Gina was under my protection. Ludicrous, I know. I kept on staring until the woman looked at me – the loon with his nose pressed up against the glass at Pizza Palace – and then I turned away.

I was still hungry, but I walked the length of Upper Street without finding anywhere to eat. There was every kind of food imaginable. Thai, Mexican, Chinese – you name it. But everywhere seemed to be full of families and couples. I walked all the way home with my stomach growling in protest, feeling like I should just walk into the next restaurant.

But it is tough when you are on your own.

'Don't take your coat off,' Cyd said.

She was in the ground-floor bathroom, wrapped up in a winter coat that I hadn't seen before. It had a fake-fur collar and it made her look like a woman in *Doctor Zhivago*. She had a torch in her hand and was shining it at the boiler. I realised that there was mist coming from my mouth every time I exhaled. The house was an icebox.

I peered over her shoulder. The boiler was as silent as a

corpse. In the panel at the bottom, there was a digital display with three red letters.

'What does "err" mean?' I asked.

She didn't look at me. There was a pause. 'It means error, Harry,' she said, making my name sound like a euphemism for 'big fat stupid fucking idiot'.

She switched off her torch and turned round, still not looking at me. She ran her hand through her hair and sighed.

'I'll get someone in the morning,' I said. 'Dig out Yellow Pages. Go on Google. Get it sorted.'

She brushed past me, and I thought of my father. If he was alive, I would have been on the phone to him already, and he would be happily digging out his toolbox.

My dad was what they call 'good around the house'. I was what they call 'crap around the house'.

I followed Cyd into the kitchen. I craved cheese on toast, but I knew this probably wasn't the perfect moment to feed my face.

'Can't we get someone now?' she said. She took a yellow beanie hat out of the pocket of her winter coat and pulled it over her ears. It sort of spoiled the *Doctor Zhivago* effect. 'I'm worried about the girls,' she said. 'They've had to go to bed with their socks on.'

'I'll try,' I said, and she nodded, somewhat unimpressed.

'I know it's late,' she said. 'But I don't care how much I have to pay.'

'Fine.'

Our eyes met for just a second before she looked away. I felt a shiver of resentment. Or perhaps it was just the cold. But it wasn't my fault that my dad was good with his hands and I was crap with my hands. It wasn't my fault that I had given my father's toolbox to Oxfam.

But I had seen the look in Cyd's eyes and it stabbed me with shame. It said, Could you please remind me one more time? What's the point of you, Harry? What exactly are you *for?*

*   *   *

180

There were footsteps on the stairs. Peggy was lugging a suitcase down. I took it from her and carried it down. Cyd was waiting for her. She went to her mother's arms and the pair of them embraced.

'Is it the right thing to do?' Peggy said. 'I don't want to get in the way.'

Cyd nodded. 'Stay with your dad. Whatever feels right. Be strong for him. Show him you love him. And stay positive. He's got great doctors. Liberty's a good nurse.' She squeezed her daughter. 'And he's got you.'

There was a car horn outside. A taxi had arrived. Peggy looked at me. She tried to smile but did not quite make it. I gave her a hug.

'Nothing bad ever happened to me before, Harry,' she said. 'I thought bad things had happened to me – but not really. This is the first time. My dad getting sick. It makes the world look sort of different. As though nothing is certain. Do you know what I mean?'

I nodded. I knew exactly what she meant. And I knew that moment finds us all.

But Cyd just stared at us, her face empty of all emotion, as if I was just pretending to know.

When I got back from the bookmaker's the next day a white van was parked outside our house. PLUMB CRAZY, it said on the side, with a mobile phone number that I had located just after midnight.

The front door was open and Joni came out with a battered Barbie in each hand. She grinned at me and walked round to the side of the house, where the giant cardboard box that had once contained the fridge stood by the re-cycling bins.

A small army of dolls was lined up inside the box.

I went into the house, immediately hearing the boiler and feeling the heat. Cyd was wearing a T-shirt and jeans. She was digging out a credit card for the plumber.

'Here, let me get it,' I said. 'Cash all right?'

He was one of those shrewd old Cockneys that remind me of my uncles. Left school at fourteen but had a PhD in life.

'Even better,' he said. 'Saves on the paperwork.'

Cyd watched me pull a wad of fifty-pound notes out of my pocket. Joni came into the house and raced up the stairs. I peeled off a few of the notes, including a generous tip. The plumber left, telling us that we would be cosy and warm for the rest of the winter. When he had gone, I offered Cyd a fistful of fifty-pound notes. She folded her arms and looked at me.

'It's not just about money, Harry,' she said.

'Jesus Christ,' I said. 'I can't win with you, can I?'

Joni came back down with a stuffed monkey and one of the Bratz dressed in ski wear. I held my tongue. Not in front of the children. I hated to argue in front of the children. Joni babbled happily to her toys. Then she looked at Cyd. 'Can I do dress-up? Is that all right? If I do dress-up?'

'That's fine,' Cyd said. 'Doing dress-up is fine.' When she had gone, Cyd said to me, 'Where did you get it, anyway?'

I was still holding the money. 'Do you want it or not?'

'Keep your money,' she said. 'I can make my own money.' She smiled at my giant wad of red notes. 'You probably won it on some stupid horse . . .' She looked at my face and began to laugh. 'My God, you really did, didn't you?'

'Chinese Rocks,' I said. 'Twenty-five to one. I put everything I had left on it. So I'm not completely useless after all, am I?'

'Is that your idea of a productive life, Harry? Betting on horses in the middle of the day with a bunch of men who smell of pubs and kebab shops?'

'Here,' I said, forcing the money into her hand. 'Stop treating me like a lodger who's behind on his rent.'

She threw it in my face. It fluttered to the floor between us. We stood there, staring at each other. And then, from the street, we heard the sound of the recycling lorry. With the front door open it sounded very close and very loud. You could hear the bottles breaking as they were tipped inside.

'Joni,' Cyd said, and then we were both out of the house and into the street.

Men in sleeveless yellow jackets. The green bins empty and scattered across the pavement, the wind whipping one black lid away. And the big cardboard box that had held the fridge already being chewed up inside the steel maw of the lorry, collapsing in on itself, being folded down to nothing.

And Cyd screamed now. *'Joni!'*

She was halfway across the street when we heard the voice. 'Mama?'

Joni stood in the doorway. She was dressed in her angel costume, which came with white dress, wings and halo. When we had bought it, we had added a star-shaped padded wand with handle and tinsel as an optional extra. It was a bit small for her now, and the handle of her wand was bent. She watched us, uncertain what was going on, or if she had been bad.

Cyd crossed the road quickly. She stopped when she reached me and slapped me just once, as hard as she could, across the side of my face.

'What's that for?' I called to her back.

But I knew what it was for.

eighteen

In the middle of the morning Marty and I sat in the Jolly Leper.

It was a traditional Soho boozer. Subdued lighting, exhausted sofas and a lone young barman who would not catch your eye even if the gaff was empty because he was going to be the next Robert Pattinson. Weak sunlight crept through windows that were stained by the cigarette smoke of the ages and advertisements for extinct beers. The Jolly Leper was a Soho institution. Francis Bacon had once spent forty-eight hours locked in the lavatory. We used to be in the Jolly Leper all the time. But it felt like it'd been quite a while.

'The good news is that they like our idea,' Marty said.

I leaned forward, all excited. 'What one? *Britain's Monkeys Got Talent? How Clean is Your Hamster Cage?*'

Marty shook his head. He waved at the distant barman, who folded his arms and looked away. 'The tattoo show. You know – *Whose Tattoo Are You?* The game show where you have to guess who the tattoo belongs to. The one with David Beckham as a guest.'

Ever the optimist. There was a bowl of sugar lumps on the table between us. Marty picked one up and tossed it into his mouth as if it was a peanut. I pinched his adorably chubby face and laughed.

'They really like it? Channel 4? And we have the green light?'

'Not Channel 4. Madeleine TV. Know who they are? Cable cowboys who have been doing bonzo business with repeats from the seventies, eighties and nineties.'

'Madeleine TV?'

'The idea is that you watch *Magpie* or *The Girlie Show* or *The Avengers* or *The Word* or *The Tube* or *Six Pissed Students in a Flat* and it makes you think of happier days – like Proust taking a bite of his Madeleine biscuit, and his childhood all coming back.' He reached for another sugar lump. 'And now they're ready to start making their own content.'

I leaned back, smiling at him. 'Proust, eh?' I looked across at the barman and raised my hand. He glanced up from the latest copy of *Heat*, reluctantly catching my eye.

'Champagne, I think,' I said.

'The bad news is they have their own ideas on production,' Marty said, getting it all out at once. 'So maybe not champagne.'

'Bad news?' I said. 'I didn't know there was any bad news. Who said anything about bad news?'

Marty took a breath. The barman went back to his magazine with an exasperated tut-tut-tut.

'They don't want you, Harry,' Marty said. 'They want Josh.'

'Josh? What Josh? Not the Josh from our old show who went to Oxford and ended up fetching coffee in Broadcasting House? Josh with the posh accent who chased up our mini-cabs and was even crap at that? Josh with the five A-Levels and three brain cells?'

'Yeah, that's the guy.'

I was on my feet and ready to storm out of the Jolly Leper. But even at that moment I could see that Marty was trying to do the decent thing. Few people in our business ever have the nerve or the decency to reject you to your face. He reached for the sugar bowl, hesitated and pushed it away.

'What's Josh got that I haven't got?'

Marty changed his mind, snatched up a sugar lump.

'He's young, Harry,' Marty said.

'Cheap, you mean.'

Marty shrugged.

'Same thing,' he said, his mouth full of sugar.

I stood outside the Jolly Leper, blinking in the daylight, suddenly disorientated. Soho was strange to me now.

When Marty and I were starting out, when we were first on radio, we were in these streets all the time. Working, eating, drinking. Looking at girls who were not interested. Dreaming of glory. The people who came out of the editing suites and production offices and screening rooms were known to us and we were known to them. Now everyone was ten, fifteen, twenty years younger and I didn't know a soul. It was more like another planet than another postcode.

And then there was Gina.

I saw her standing at the end of an aisle in one of those surprising little Soho supermarkets that suddenly appear between the sex shops and the clothes shops and the pizzeria.

She was holding a six-pack of Evian to her face. And she was crying.

I went inside and I said, 'Hey,' and I put my arm around her. She leaned into me, and it awakened something that I thought was long, long dead.

'Hey,' I said again, and I held her closer, smelling her hair. 'Hey, hey, hey. What's wrong?'

She shook her head, pushed her face into my jacket. 'Ah, everything,' she said, all full up with sadness.

I looked at her and then pulled her back to me. Her body pressed against me. Under her raincoat she was dressed for the gym. I realised that she was in incredible shape. Not for a woman of her age. For a woman of any age. There wasn't a twenty-year-old junior researcher in Soho that was a patch on Gina.

'It's all messed up, Harry,' she said, wiping at her face with her hands.

I tore open a packet of kitchen towels and ripped off a strip. A passing security guard glared at me as Gina dabbed her eyes.

'I'm going to pay for that,' I told him.

He nodded grimly. 'I know you are,' he said.

Gina slipped her arm around my waist, her head lolling sideways. I felt her breath on my neck. She said my name. Something stirred. Something definitely stirred. She looked up at me with sleepy blue eyes.

'You want to come up to my place?' she said.

'Okay.'

I paid for the kitchen towels and the Evian and we got out of there. We walked back to her place on Old Compton Street with our arms around each other. It felt good. I liked comforting her. I tried to remember why we had ever split up and it was beyond me. Something to do with the one thinking that the other one did not love quite enough, or in the same old way? Madness. And suddenly it was like the Soho I had known half a lifetime ago.

We climbed the stairs to her apartment. We said nothing. My mouth was dry with nerves. I did not know what was happening. Yet it was all curiously comforting.

But as soon as we were through the door a small woman with short red hair in a child-sized tracksuit was bouncing around in front of us.

'Where were you?' she demanded. 'I was worried about you.'

Gina shook her head and kicked off her shoes. She always observed the ways of old Japan. I took off my shoes too. The redhead put her hands on her hips and glared at me.

'I just needed some air,' Gina said, all exhausted. She drifted into the flat. I followed. There were Tatami mats on the floor. Framed calligraphy on the wall. The scent of jasmine in the air. She had done it up nice. I noticed the redhead was looking at me as if she wanted to rip out my throat.

'Is this him?' she said, taking half a threatening step towards me. 'Is this Peter?'

Gina laughed. 'God, no. This is Harry. You know? Pat's father?'

The redhead snorted. 'I thought it was Peter. I thought

you were giving him another chance.' She followed Gina into the flat. 'Giving the kiss of life to something that's already dead in the water. Knowing you.'

Gina faced her, looking pained. 'I'd love some tea, Siân.'

The redhead calmed down. Happy to be of service, she bustled off to the kitchen. I could hear her clanking about and wondered if she was going to make one for me. Gina collapsed into her only sofa.

'Pat didn't come home last night,' she said. 'It's happening more and more.'

My mouth was dry. What was wrong now?

'Boys will be boys,' I said.

'He's got a girl now,' she said. 'He wanted to bring the little slut round here for the night. I soon put a stop to that.'

'A girl? What's her name?'

'Elizabeth Montgomery,' Gina said, surprised, and offended when I began to smile. 'What? Do you know the little bitch?'

I remembered the way that Elizabeth Montgomery had looked at him when he was sent off against UTI. That sleepy, interested look. It felt completely right that they were together at last. He had loved her for so long.

'Why are you grinning like an idiot, Harry? You don't actually think this is good news, do you? Our son staying out all night with some Ramsay Mac slapper.'

'Why are you so nasty about her? She seems like a regular girl to me. Maybe she's had a bit more attention than is good for her. But that's because she's so pretty. Come on. You understand that, don't you?'

Gina waved me away.

'She'll dump him as soon as she finds out what a good, kind-hearted boy he is,' Gina said. 'That's what I object to, Harry, if you want to know the truth. She's the kind that likes being treated badly by some thick-necked yob with tattoos. And Pat is better than that. Better than her.'

I was appalled.

'How can you say that? Elizabeth Montgomery might be the best thing that ever happened to him.'

Gina laughed. 'You don't know much about young girls, do you, Harry?'

I couldn't argue with that, so I went out on the tiny balcony and looked down on Old Compton Street. From up here, it seemed unchanged.

I could see Ronnie Scott's and Patisserie Valerie, the Algerian Coffee Store and a flight of stairs that had been offering French lessons on the first floor for twenty years. I could have been fluent by now.

'They cut his hair,' Gina said. 'At school. Got him in the toilets and cut off all his beautiful hair.'

I was suddenly shaking. 'Who did?' I managed, gripping the railings as if I might fall. 'Cut his hair? When?'

'You know,' Gina said. 'The ones who don't like him. The rough boys. The first day he went back. After his suspension.'

I couldn't speak. I couldn't stop the shaking. This had gone on too long. This had to stop.

'I want him out of that school, Harry,' Gina was saying. 'You know he's talking about dropping out? He's talking about getting a job? What kind of future will he have if he quits school and gets some crappy little job?'

'I'll find him, okay?' I said. 'I'll find him and I'll bring him back.' I sat down beside her, and risked putting an arm around her shoulders. 'I understand why you're upset,' I said. 'But I will find him. And I will find them. And I am going to stop this thing, I promise. They are not going to hurt him any more, I swear to God.'

'It's not just Pat,' she said, and I took my arm away. Not just Pat? Then what?

As if I couldn't guess.

'Things haven't been going too good with that bastard Peter.' I said nothing. 'Turns out he was more married than he let on,' she said. 'Turns out his wife has not been recycled after all.'

'Wow,' I said. 'What were the odds of that?'

'You're such a cynic, aren't you, Harry? You old romantics are all so bitter and twisted. Because you're always being disappointed.'

189

'I saw the pair of them,' I said. 'Peter and his missus. With their kids.' A beat. 'You're much more beautiful than she is, Gina. I saw the woman. She's nothing special.'

I expected Gina to deny her beauty. That's what she always did in her twenties. Like all the beautiful ones, she got sick of people talking about it, as if the way she looked was the most interesting thing about her. But now she just laughed.

'Yeah, well. The Japanese have a saying – a man gets bored with a beautiful woman after three days but he gets used to a plain woman after three days.'

'They're a cruel race.'

'It probably loses something in the translation. And they are actually the kindest people in the world.'

She looked away. The barrier between us had briefly lifted. But now it had come down again. And I saw that Gina had not wrecked our lives. She had wrecked her own life. And I knew that I could never find it in my heart to hate her.

The redhead – Siân – brought the tea. She had even made a cup for me. Green, Japanese, healthy-looking tea. Luckily I wasn't expecting Brook Bond PG Tips and a custard cream. I perched on the edge of the sofa, giving Gina some space.

'I could stay, if you want me to,' Siân said.

Gina smiled and shook her head. 'It's okay.'

The redhead glanced at me quickly and looked away. She began backing towards the door, like a courtier leaving some regal presence. 'Call me later?'

Gina closed her eyes, nodded, and smiled. There was a click as Siân shut the door quietly behind her.

Gina sipped her tea. 'She's been great.' She looked at me meaningfully over the rim of her green tea. 'Really supportive.'

I smiled. 'She's gay, right? Siân is gay.'

Gina put down her tea. 'Not much gets past you, does it, Harry?'

I smiled. 'What are you saying to me, Gina? What are we talking about here?'

She looked at me. Mocking, defiant. Enjoying it.

'What do you think I'm saying, Harry? What do you think we're talking about? Have a wild guess.'

I laughed. 'You're not a lesbian, Gina,' I said. 'If that's what you're planning for the next experiment, the next adventure, the next quest for fulfilment, then I wouldn't bother.'

She mimed confusion. 'What's it got to do with you?'

'Nothing,' I said, standing up. 'But I'm more of a lesbian than you are, Gina. Trust me, you're not a lesbian.' I took a few steps to the door. It wasn't a very big flat after all. 'You're just tired of men,' I said.

Then I went to find my son.

A mile from the house where I grew up, there is a church on a hill.

And when I saw Pat sitting cross-legged by the grave, an almost-empty bottle of cider in one hand and a cigarette in the other, with Elizabeth Montgomery sitting opposite him, her legs stretched out, watching his face, I knew that I had been wrong all along to believe that my parents were not here.

I saw both my parents after they died, and it was a definite anti-climax. I wanted a big moment – some emotional final farewell – Katherine Jenkins singing 'Time to Say Goodbye' in the soundtrack of my mind – and it wasn't like that at all. I had the same reaction to both of the bodies. My father in the back room of the undertaker's on the suburban high street. My mum still at home in the bed she had shared with my father, and then slept in alone as his widow. And the feeling was one of anti-climax.

That is not he.

That is not she.

Whatever light had made my father the man that he was, and whatever light had made my mother the woman she was, it had gone out, or gone away. And while I could not say if it had gone to heaven or oblivion, I knew that it was gone. That was not my dad in the undertaker's back room. That was not my mum in the bedroom where she slept for

191

forty years. My parents were elsewhere, or they were nowhere at all.

And that is why I always resisted the hour's drive out to the grave they shared. Apart from the fact that I was always busy with my life, and apart from the fact that it was a drag battling through the commuters heading east on the M25. Apart from all that, I did not believe that my mother and father were actually resting in this bleakly picturesque graveyard, with the five-hundred-year-old church behind it and the yellow fields rolling away beyond.

And I was wrong.

They were here.

And their grandson, his long blond hair roughly shorn close to his head, was with them.

Elizabeth Montgomery looked up as I approached the grave.

I saw Pat take a drag on his cigarette, his eyes squinting as he exhaled and muttered, 'It's only my dad.'

Elizabeth Montgomery stood up, smoothing her skirt, and smiled. She had a great smile. And I thought, What a wonderful choice. If you are a boy and you are choosing a girl to go crazy about, then you couldn't do better than Elizabeth Montgomery. A girl who will come and smoke and drink cider with you at your grandparents' grave. How could you do better than a girl like that?

'Excuse me,' she said. 'The need to pee.'

I looked at Pat and then I looked at the grave. They had brought flowers, I realised with a pang of guilt.

'You certainly know how to show a girl a good time,' I said. 'Cider. A graveyard. And a packet of low-tar. Last of the big spenders.'

'Don't tell me you never hung out in graveyards,' he said, not looking at me.

I laughed, remembering lurking in this very graveyard with my best mate, looking down the sights of a .22 air rifle and running for home every time the sky got dark and we heard the rustle of leaves behind a gravestone.

Pat held out the bottle of cider.

'Go on then,' I said, and I took a swig.

'The thing about grandparents,' said my son, 'is that they love you in a different way. Parents – sorry – but they drive you up the wall. Because they are always on at you to be better. Smarter. Tougher. Nicer.' He looked at the gravestone. 'Grandparents just accept you the way you are. Grandparents are *happy* with you in a way that parents never are. Parents are always trying to make improvements – as if you are some derelict property that needs doing up. With grandparents it's unconditional love. That's how I remember it, anyway.' Pat glanced at the gravestone.

'That's how it was,' I said, and took another swig of the cider.

'They've been gone for quite a while,' Pat said.

For most of his life. 'I wish they'd known Joni,' I said. 'I regret that – them not knowing her.'

Pat laughed. 'They'd have eaten her up.'

I gave him back his bottle of cider. 'Yeah, she's an edible little thing.' I felt like hugging him, but I didn't. 'Your hair . . .'

He self-consciously ran his fingers through it. 'Don't worry about it,' he said.

'I'll complain to the headmaster.'

'Good luck with that.' He shook his head. 'They've done worse. They do worse every day. You just don't see it.'

Elizabeth Montgomery came back. She crouched down by Pat's side and kissed his face. He didn't move, just pinched out the remains of his cigarette and put it in his school blazer. The grave was very clean.

'Give you a ride back?' I asked them.

Elizabeth Montgomery looked at Pat, and he shook his head.

'We'll stay for a bit longer,' he said.

Elizabeth Montgomery held up a paper bag that said Gourmet Fare on the side. 'We've brought sandwiches,' she said. 'We were going to make a day of it.'

I looked at them uncertainly. 'You promise me you'll go back tonight? She's worried. Your mother's worried.'

Pat looked up at me. I was expecting some coruscating teenage sarcasm, but he nodded seriously. 'We're going back tonight, okay?'

Elizabeth Montgomery stood up and smiled at me. 'We're fine,' she said. 'We can get the train.'

'Okay.'

I looked down at the yellow fields. With that perfect harmony that made them seem more like a private world than a married couple, my parents had died on almost the same day. More than a decade had separated their deaths, but on the calendar it was only twenty-four hours apart. So when I saw the yellow fields of spring, they both came back at once. I should come to this place more often, I realised. If only to see the yellow fields.

I shook Elizabeth Montgomery's hand and gave my son a hard, fierce kiss on the top of his head. That was definitely the right way round to do it. I stuffed a few notes in the pocket of his school blazer. All done without asking his permission, and without giving him a chance to protest.

Then I walked back to my car, where I phoned his mother and told her that Pat was with his girlfriend, and with his grandparents, and that our boy was safe and sound.

nineteen

Oh yes, I thought, as I crawled out of bed, got dressed in the dark and drove to the hospital. I remember now.

With my parents gone for so many years, I had forgotten that in the end there is always the call that comes in the middle of the night.

But the scene at the hospital was so unchanged – the men standing outside in their pyjamas and dressing gowns, sucking down a shot of nicotine, the laughing nurses looking forward to the end of their night shift, the homeless man sleeping on a bench outside a shuttered shop in the deserted reception area – that it could have been the same stage set, populated by the same characters.

It all came back to me now.

Walking along the corridors with their same old night noises of equipment being moved and the sick moaning in their sleep, for one mad moment I felt that I was looking for the bed where my father lay dying. I found the nurses' station I was looking for and they directed me to a dark, crowded ward where the end bed had the curtains pulled around it. I stepped inside.

Singe Rana was sleeping, propped up in bed with his head falling forward. Ken sat by his bedside, rifling in a large box of Quality Street. Even at this hour, he was wearing his Sunday best. But then he always wore his Sunday best.

'Stroke,' Ken said. 'Know what one of them is, do you?'

I shook my head. 'Not really.'

I only really knew about cancer. My parents were from the generation that courted to *Casablanca*. Cigarette smoke and true love were inseparable in their minds. So it was always cancer that was big in our house.

'Not really or not at all?' he snapped, furiously unwrapping a Caramel Swirl.

I looked at Singe Rana's face. It was still smooth and youthful, but the beautiful golden colour seemed more burnished now, suddenly older, as though many years had passed in just one night.

'Not at all,' I admitted.

'The quack called it a pulmonary embolism,' Ken said, his mouth full of chocolate. 'Blood clot. Finds its way from the heart to the brain.'

He considered his box of Quality Street. Picked up a Coconut Éclair and threw it back. 'Sorry to call you in the middle of the night,' he said. 'Just thought you might want to know. Bit pointless, really.'

I shook my head. 'I want to know. I'm glad you called. And I am not big on the whole sleep thing right now.' We both looked at Singe Rana. 'What's going to happen to him?' I said.

'Too soon to tell.' Ken shrugged. 'Impaired functions, they told me. That's quack-speak for anything from a tingling sensation to coma, paralysis, death.'

'Jesus.'

'Yeah – they don't narrow it down much, do they?' He looked at his sleeping friend. 'If he gets through the first week or two, he'll be right as rain.'

He held out the Quality Street and I shook my head. But then he rattled the box at me and I took a Green Triangle. I remembered this one. Delicious hazelnut wrapped in milk chocolate, if I wasn't mistaken.

'We were at the dogs,' he said, his eyes not leaving Singe Rana's face. 'He was talking about Italy. He likes to talk about Italy more and more. He rattles on about Italy as if it was the best holiday of his life.' He chuckled. 'Oranges and lemons, he talks about. The fields and the girls and the wine. The mountains and the vineyards. I don't remember much of all that. But then he's a glass-half-full kind of bloke, old Singe Rana.'

Ken scratched his leg, the one he had lost, and I wondered if the story was true, I wondered if he could still feel it after all these years of living without it.

'What I remember is the cold,' he said. 'And the noise. And the mud. And the stink. It stunk, that mud in Italy. Bloody stunk, it did. Somebody said it stunk in exactly the same way that the Somme stunk in the first turnout. Something to do with the mud and shells and the rotting bodies.' He nodded. 'I remember that smell. And I remember the wounded lying in rows with the kind of wounds that they never show you in the films or on the news. Boys with their guts hanging out, calling for God or their mother to come and help. Men holding their intestines. Head wounds from 88-millimetre shells so bad that you could see bits of brain. This is on the living, mind. Limbs gone. Minds gone. Faces blown off. Bollocks shot off. Smashed bodies everywhere.' He looked up at me. 'Still wish you were there, do you?'

I felt a stab of anger.

'I never said that, did I?' I said.

'You don't have to. It's clear as day. I saw it in my Mick – the one that's in Australia.' A thin smile. 'Wishing he was there. This feeling that he – your lot – the sons – had missed something. Something big. Something important. A test. A challenge. The experience. I don't know what you call it, but you know what I mean. And I know you feel it too, even if you can't admit it. That wanting to be part of something bigger than yourself. This need to do something bigger and better and more important than buying a car that you've seen Jeremy Clarkson drive on *Top Gear*.'

'I thought Mick was your favourite,' I said.

'He is,' Ken said.

Then suddenly a family was there, bustling around the bed,

unloading presents. A tiny old lady, thin as a child, Singe Rana's wife, and two strapping middle-aged men and their wives, and assorted nippers from their teens to a babe in arms. And they all had that open-faced calm that I now thought of as Nepalese.

As if awakened from his dreams by the smell of Aloo Chop, Singe Rana stirred. He sleepily smiled at the sight of his family as they unloaded parcels of food. But they ignored Singe Rana and began offering it to Ken and me. Flat bread, curried vegetables, fried rice, milky tea and of course the spicy potato cakes. Ken brandished his box of Quality Street, trying to return the hospitality. They impatiently waved him away.

Over extensive protests, Ken gave up his chair to Singe Rana's wife, and then gently placed a hand on his friend's shoulder.

The two old men looked at each other but said nothing. He took his hand away. We left.

In the corridor, Ken removed a stiff cream-coloured envelope from his blazer. I assumed it was a Get Well card and that he would want to go back to give it to Singe Rana. Despite his unsentimental front, I suspected that Ken was the kind of man who would bring someone a Get Well card. He looked at the card for a moment as if he had forgotten it was there and then he slowly removed it from the envelope, as if he was going to announce the winner of some great prize.

It was a white card with discreet silver bells and roses and swirly gold writing.

'This is my invitation,' Ken said, as though he had never received one before, or as if it was so long ago that it was lost to memory.

He held the white card with swirly writing very gently and in both hands, like a thing of great delicacy and value.

'My invitation,' repeated Ken Grimwood. 'I was meant to go out there today. Or do I mean yesterday? My Tracey was going to take me. But I stayed here. Missed my lift.' He gestured towards his friend. 'Because of him in there.' A short laugh as he slipped his invitation back inside his jacket. 'My Tracey went mental.'

And loneliness too, I thought.

That's what old age is about, even more than the calls that come in the middle of the night. The kind of loneliness that comes when most of what you have loved has gone.

A crop-haired boy in a suit stopped us as we were going into the church.

'Bride or groom?' he said.

'Neither,' Ken said, and the boy rolled his eyes, as if he had heard that one already today.

'Bride's side,' I said, and the boy gave us both a white rose buttonhole, the little stem sheathed in silver paper.

We stepped inside. Light streamed through the stained-glass windows and lit up the women in their hats. It smelled of even more roses. There were children everywhere, running up and down the aisle, and their laughter echoed with the protests of their parents.

Ken was still holding his rose in both hands as if it was a tiny bouquet. I took it from him and put it into his blazer's buttonhole. Then we found a seat on the bride's side, towards the back and on the aisle, as if we were planning on making a quick escape. There were two young men waiting at the altar with a female vicar. Tracey was standing up in the front row, adjusting her hat.

'I don't know these people,' Ken muttered.

Then I saw his daughter spot him. She came down the aisle, holding her hat, her high heels clicking on the flagstones.

'Glad you made it, Dad,' she said, giving me a quick nod as she took her father's arm and gently lifted him to his feet.

Ken looked bewildered. 'You're the bride's granddad,' Tracey explained, her eyes scanning the entrance. 'You have to sit with us.'

He let her lead him to the front row as the organ began the wedding march. Then the bride was suddenly there in an explosion of white, with Ian clinging tearfully to her arm. The bride was pretty and pregnant, hovering between smiles and tears, and she looked more like her grandmother than anyone else in the front row. There was the same sweet, dark-eyed mischief about her that I remembered from the wedding pictures of Ken and his Dot. Or perhaps it was just because she was around the same age as her grandmother had been in those wedding pictures, and everything was still before her.

They started down the aisle and every eye followed them. I could tell which of the boys was the groom now. He smiled at the girl, turned his head to the ground and then looked at her again. Tracey began to smile and dab at her eyes. Although he was head and shoulders shorter than the rest of the front row, I could just about see Ken. And I watched him watching the bride, narrowing his eyes as he squinted at her face, as if she was a girl he knew from somewhere, but it was just out of reach.

The next time I saw him he had a glass of champagne in each hand and was staggering through the wedding reception to where I was talking to the vicar.

'Beautiful service,' he said, and attempted to kiss her full on the lips.

The vicar flinched and pulled away but somehow he kept going, eyes closed and lips pursed in readiness. I intercepted him before he fell and as he steadied himself a small crescent of champagne sloshed from one of the glasses and down the vicar's cassock.

Ken blinked at her from behind his glasses. 'Beautiful,' he said.

'Thank you so much,' the vicar smiled, and quickly slipped away. Ken watched her go, thoughtfully draining one of the champagne flutes. I gently removed the other one from his hand and downed it before it could do any more harm.

We were in a marquee in the grounds of a country house hotel. It felt like more than a fancy tent, as though it had stood for a thousand years instead of having been erected that morning. When the music began – a big blast of happy funk, 'Celebration' by Kool and the Gang – it seemed to bounce off ancient walls.

Ken headed for the dance floor.

I followed him, suddenly understanding why I had felt the need to stick around.

Tracey cut us off, looking concerned.

'Dad?' she said. 'Have you tried the canapés?'

But Ken kept going, gently bouncing off a waiter with a silver tray of Bellinis and on to the dance floor.

Tracey touched my arm. 'Don't let him spoil it for me,' she said.

He was the third person on the dance floor. Only the bride and her groom were out there before him, holding each other and swaying from side to side, the curious dance of people who had never really learned how to dance. They seemed glad to see Ken appear, if only as a distraction from their embarrassment.

Ken was smiling, doing a technically perfect twist – the ball of one foot stubbing out a cigarette while his hands moved as if drying himself after a shower – and I wondered what long-ago night out with his wife had lodged in his head. People began to clap and cheer. The bride broke away from her husband and reached out for her grandfather.

He looked at her face and his smile vanished.

'Dot,' I saw him mouth. 'My Dot . . .'

Then his good leg seemed to slip from under him and he was sitting down, still looking up at the girl in her wedding dress, staring at her face as if he remembered everything.

And there was laughter now, not the good kind, as he sat there on the dance floor, and all around the marquee I could see the blue-white glow of screens as people filmed him with their phones as he sat there on the ground. The bride and groom were laughing too, and Kool and the Gang were ordering everyone to have a real good time as I pushed my way through the crowd to get him.

And despite the ten-grand party and the designer duds and the river of cocktails, I could see them in all their modern ugliness now.

The hard-eyed women with the tattoos on their arms and legs not quite hidden by their dresses. The soft-bodied men with elaborate hair, as brittle as toffee apples from styling products, or shaved escaped-convict close to cover the old male pattern baldness. Some of the men were like children – tieless at a wedding, as though they had yet to master the knot. And the children dressed like adults – little girls in high heels, little boys in bow ties wielding mobile phones like blunt instruments, filming the old man on the floor.

All drunk, all overweight.

I shoved the last of them out of the way and bent down to lift Ken. Suddenly his daughter was there, her face in mine.

'Get him out of here,' she hissed.

In the shadow of the country house hotel, we sat by a swimming pool, the lights under the water making it shimmer blue and gold.

Music from the marquee drifted to us across the manicured grounds. I could hear that the DJ had moved from family favourites to club classics.

Some guests were coming out of the tent and drifting across to the hotel. Behind us were open French doors, and an almost deserted bar.

Ken groaned. 'It's killing me,' he said, and I helped him on to a sun lounger and watched him roll up his trouser leg until it was above his knee.

His prosthetic limb looked completely lifelike, yet totally inanimate. It seemed alive and dead at the same time. I watched him unclamp it and place it to one side with a relieved sigh. He began to massage the flesh above his knee. It was a mass of scars.

'You can get these new legs,' he said. 'Sports legs, they call them. Where you see all the joints and hydraulics showing.'

202

His fingers vigorously pressed his livid flesh. 'All right if you're a kid,' he said. 'Fancy a dip? I might just have a paddle.'

I helped Ken to the side of the pool. Me holding him as he took these grunting, steady hops. We took off our shoes and socks and dangled our three feet in the water.

'Lovely do,' he commented, staring towards the distant sound of 'Pump Up the Volume'. He gave me a sideways look. 'Remind me what you're sticking around for? You don't know these people. I don't know most of them myself.'

'Designated driver,' I said. 'Don't worry about me. And I know you, don't I?'

He produced his Rizlas and his tin of Old Holborn and rolled himself a cigarette. I was happy that there was no one to stop him. And I thought that these men should be allowed to smoke wherever they wanted to. If you free the world from tyranny, I thought, you should be allowed a roll-up. He smoked slowly, as more people came out of the tent and began drifting across the grass.

'Help me up, will you?' he said.

I got him up and we held on to each other, my arms around his waist, his arm around my shoulder. With his free hand he extinguished his roll-up and tossed it aside. We watched the wedding guests coming towards us. When they were coming up the slope to the pool, the old man began to shout.

'Shark!' he screamed. 'Help me! Shark! Shark! Oh God! Help! Shark!'

Somebody screamed. We stared at their appalled faces, the eyes wide with horror, and then I helped Ken back on the sun lounger, both of us rocking with laughter.

He was clamping his leg back on when Ian arrived. 'That wasn't funny when you did it when we were kids,' he said. 'It wasn't funny at Frinton, Clacton or Margate. And it's not funny now.'

And then there was Tracey.

'Do you know why he left?' she said.

Ken rolled down his trouser leg. 'Who?' he said, genuinely interested.

'Your son,' she said. 'Your precious Mick. Your favourite child. Do you know why he went away? Know why he moved to Australia, do you?'

Ken wasn't smiling now. 'A better life,' he said quietly. 'Sun. Barbecues. Penguins. A higher quality of life.'

Tracey laughed, shaking her head. 'To get away from you,' she said. 'He couldn't stand it any more. He left England to get away from you.'

After they'd gone back into the hotel, Ken smoked another roll-up in silence and then we made our way down to the car. It was nearly two now, and the wedding party was breaking up.

In front of the hotel, a crowd had gathered to see off the bride and groom.

We could hear them all cheering, and then the sound of tyres on gravel and the tin cans that had been tied to the bumpers, as the happy couple went off to start their new life.

'Let's get you home,' I said to Ken as he sagged against my car.

The old man was very tired.

'It's not true,' he said.

'We need to keep the noise down a bit,' I said, as I put the kettle on, and Ken began to noisily clear his throat. The sound of a dying seal. I glanced meaningfully at the ceiling, indicating my sleeping family.

Behind those glasses, his eyes followed mine.

'Things bad at home, are they?' he asked.

I could see how he could get exhausting after a lifetime or so.

'It's not that things are bad at home,' I said. 'But it's – what? – the middle of the night. My wife has to get up for work in the morning.' I turned back to the tea, milk and sugar. 'And I don't.'

He made himself comfortable at the kitchen table. 'That must be tough,' he said. 'When the missus is the breadwinner. That's not easy for her. Or you.'

I turned to look at him to see if he was taking the piss. His face was impassive. I went back to my boiling kettle.

'It's just temporary,' I muttered.

'Still,' he elaborated. 'Not like my day. More simple then.'

'You've had your day,' I said, and it sounded far more cruel than I had intended.

But it made him laugh.

'Poor you,' he said. 'You've got a wife that takes care of you. I only had to deal with Nazi Germany.'

'That's right,' I said. 'Poor me.'

I brought two cups of tea to the kitchen table. He was only here because he had declared all the way home that he was, 'Gasping.' He was always gasping, that old man.

Gasping for a cup of tea. Gasping for a cigarette. Gasping for air.

And I finally saw what it was in him that reminded me so much of my father. There were the obvious similarities – the war, the medals, the hard, damaged bodies that would carry their scars to the grave.

And there were equally obvious differences – my father was every inch a suburban dad, all for Home Counties politesse, tending his garden and not swearing in front of the children, while Ken Grimwood had never left the council estate, never left Nelson Mansions. But what they shared was this – a bottomless well of bitterness about how their country had treated the boys who came home.

We gave everything. Some of us never came back. And you bastards let us down.

My father hid it better than Ken Grimwood, but it was there just the same. Behind the net curtains and manicured lawn of my family's little pebble-dash semi – the modest house that demanded my dad work at three jobs just to scrape together the deposit – there was a man who was beyond anger.

And as I grew up, and the crop-haired blond lad became just another mousey, fallible adult, capable of cocking up his life, and the lives of all those around him, I could not hide from the fact that I was one of the many bastards who had let my father down.

'You have ruined my life,' he told me when I broke the news that my marriage to Gina was over.

'You've had your life,' I told him, wanting to hurt him as much as he hurt me.

There was ice in my father. He was a decent man, and a gentle man, and there were many good things about him. But there was that hard black ice, too, and I never saw it melt until my son was born. It wasn't until Pat came along that I ever really saw a look on his face that perhaps things could be good again after all.

'Good cup of tea,' Ken said, nodding approvingly.

I glanced at my watch. I still had to get him back to the Angel and then come home. I took a gulp of tea although it burned my mouth.

And then I saw the light in the garden.

More of a glow than a light. Out in the darkness, inside the Wendy House, a pinprick of light that burned bright red for a moment and then settled to a tiny smouldering ember.

'That little bastard,' I said, kicking back my chair as I got up.

Ken looked at me and then at the garden. He saw nothing.

'My son,' I said. 'He's in the Wendy House. He's smoking Mexican weed in the Wendy House.'

Ken tilted his head to one side. The Wendy House? Mexican weed?

I spluttered, speechless, and then realised that I couldn't be bothered.

'I'll kill him,' I said simply, and suddenly Ken sort of got it, holding up a hand as I headed for the garden door.

'They say a child needs your love most when he deserves it the least,' the old man told me.

I stared at him. 'Oh, is that what they say?'

He nodded. 'So I've heard.'

'Right,' I said. 'Like I'm going to take advice from a man who just got kicked out of his granddaughter's wedding.'

Ken Grimwood just smiled. 'Is it all right to smoke in here?' he asked.

'No,' I said, and I went into the garden.

I could smell that sickly sweet Mexican scent before I even reached the Wendy House. And I could see Pat inside, Gulliver-like, hunched up and far too big for the playhouse. I opened the door and went inside. Defiantly, he took a toke on his joint. That red glow again. And I knew that I was not going to kill him. Not tonight or ever. I loved him, you see.

'You don't need that,' I said.

He ran his hand across his shorn head, as if he could still not quite believe that his hair was gone. 'Maybe it's exactly what I need.'

But then he coughed, suddenly sickening, and inhaled deeply, trying to regain control. He stared at the soggy joint in his hand.

'Not so cute any more, am I?' he said.

'You'll always be cute to me,' I said.

He laughed. 'Rotten liar, aren't you?'

'Always,' I smiled.

He sighed and ran the red tip of the joint over his bare arm. I heard the fair, almost invisible hair on his arm sizzle and burn. I could smell it too. The burned hair on his arm. I held my breath. Then he took the joint away, and I breathed again.

'It's not your fault, Pat,' I said. 'None of it. This whole mess that's been going on for years.' He wasn't looking at me. 'None of it is your fault.'

He laughed shortly. 'I blame the parents,' he said.

'I wish,' I said, and he looked up at me as my voice got caught. 'I wish it could have been . . . more settled for you. When you were growing up. And now. I just wish that it could have all been a bit more settled.'

He shook his head furiously. 'You already told me,' he said. He did not want to talk about all that.

Then he looked at me. He looked at me at last.

'I didn't know where else to go,' he said.

'Then you come here,' I said. 'You come back to me. When there's nowhere else to go, you just come home. And you stay as long as you want. Okay?'

He thought about it.

'Okay.'

'Come inside,' I said, standing up.

'Okay,' he said again. I watched him throw his Mexican weed on the floor and stub it out. The sparks flew and died. We had to bend our heads to get out of the Wendy House.

We looked up at the house. It was in darkness apart from the light in the kitchen. All the houses were in darkness. I put my arm around my son's shoulder and I realised with a jolt that he was taller than me. When did that happen?

Then we walked back to the house, where the old man was waiting.

part three: *summer term — what are you waiting for?*

twenty

Then there was the day my wife came home too soon.

I was up in my room, editing a shooting script for *PC Filth: An Unfair Cop.* I had been back in gainful employment for a month, although it all felt a bit different now. Somehow this was more like the work my father had done. Because it wasn't a career any more. It was a job.

I was going over a scene that had been nagging at me all morning, when I heard the Food Glorious Food van down on the street. I looked at my watch and then turned back to the script.

In the scene I was stuck on, PC Filth had a violent career burglar down in the cells. He – PC Filth – was whistling, 'I'd Like to Teach the World to Sing' and doing a little jig around the cell. Police brutality seemed on the cards. It was a direct rip-off of Tarantino, but that wasn't what troubled me. It was the role reversal – giving the uniformed officer all the power and the catchy pop song, and having the bad guy squirm. As if the good would ultimately triumph and the bad would be punished.

And the thing that bothered me was – I knew that just wasn't true.

I put the script down and went to the window. The Food Glorious Food van was parked outside. That did not make sense. It was lunchtime. The van should be down in Canary Wharf. I watched Cyd get out of the driver's seat. She went to the back of the van and began taking out trays of food.

One of her girls was standing next to her. Not helping too much because she was crying. I went downstairs.

Cyd was coming through the front door with her trays. Mozzarella fingers. Gyoza dumplings. Sashimi. Chicken satay. Mini frittatas.

'What happened?' I said, standing to one side. Her girl was behind her, sniffing and sobbing over a sixty-piece oriental platter. I took it from her and carried it into the kitchen. The food was lined up on the surfaces where it had all been prepared earlier. Cyd was already coming back out.

'Turn on the TV,' she said.

I stared at her back. I hate it when people say that to me. *Turn on the TV*. It means that something is wrong. It means that everything is wrong. I turned on the TV and at first I could not understand what I was looking at.

The pictures were coming live from some shining glass tower. Men and women in suits were coming out, and they were all carrying boxes. Some of them were crying. Some of them were angry, shouting at the camera crews and the heavens. Someone threw a skinny latte in the face of a photographer. The camera closed in on one young buck with a champagne box in his arms containing a riding crop and a golf club. The wind whipped some papers from his box but he did not seem to notice, or care. There was a name on the side of the glass tower in big bold letters. The camera went in close. The name rang a distant bell.

Cyd was by my side.

'Don't they insure our fridge?' I said.

'Maybe not any more,' she said. 'That's where I was meant to be fixing lunch. And they've gone bust.'

'When?'

'About two hours ago.'

We watched the workers coming out of their shining glass tower.

'What does it mean?' I said.

'I don't know,' Cyd said. 'But I think this is just the start.'

'The start of what?'

'The start of everything changing,' she said. She almost laughed. 'I don't think they'll be needing sashimi for two hundred for a while. Maybe never again.'

Cyd's girl was hovering behind her. Cyd wrapped her arms around her and let her cry. I turned back to the TV, trying to put it together. The workers with their belongings in champagne boxes. The trays of unwanted party food in our home. I turned up the volume. Cyd's girl was crying so hard, I could hardly hear Robert Peston's incisive analysis.

'I'll call you, okay?' Cyd was telling her girl. 'When something happens.'

I perched on the edge of the sofa, wanting to understand. I heard the front door gently open and close, and a bit later the sound of my wife cursing our refrigerator.

It was not big enough today.

She was at the kitchen table staring out at the Wendy House. I put my hands on her shoulders and she rose to her feet, her eyes closed as she sank against me. I felt the full length of her pressing against me. I brushed my lips against her face and tasted the salt of sweat and tears.

Then she said three little words against my shoulder, making no attempt to pull away.

'You love it,' she said.

I looked at the top of her head. 'What?'

'It's the twenty-first century out there but it's 1958 in here,' she said, pulling away now, pushing her hair from her face. '*And you love it,*' she repeated, looking me in the eye now. 'For me, today is a bloody disaster. For you, today is when the natural order gets restored.'

We were standing apart now. 'Don't say that,' I said. 'Don't think that.'

She laughed. 'Why not?'

'Because it's not true.' I still thought I could win her round. 'You sit down,' I said. 'I'll make us some tea. The kids will not be home for hours. I'll do my Barry White voice. You'll laugh and think I'm nice.'

'The big provider,' she said. 'The great protector. The mighty breadwinner. *You love it.*'

I shook my head. I held out my arms and, after thinking about it for a moment, she came back to me.

My phone began to vibrate. It was in the pocket of my jeans, and it gently throbbed between the tops of our thighs. I ignored it. But the phone kept pulsing away, and in the end we could not ignore it. Cyd pulled away with a laugh of derision.

'Attend to your career, big shot,' she said, and she turned to face a kitchen covered with a mountain range of canapés.

And a few minutes later, on my way out I passed Cyd, staring into the back of the Food Glorious Food van. It was empty now. We did not speak.

And the funny thing is, that phone call had nothing to do with my career – not unless my true vocation, my life's calling, my once and forever full-time job is being a father.

The front office at Ramsay Mac were calling. They knew that Pat was back living at home and they were phoning to ask why he had not been in school for the past few days. I almost laughed out loud.

The boy was fifteen.

So how would I know?

Pat sat at the dining table in the old man's overheated living room, puffing thoughtfully at a cigarette as he read the *Racing Post*.

My son glanced up at me for a moment when I came in, and then ducked his head down. I could see his long blond hair poking over the top of a front page that said KING GEORGE SPECIAL – AS GOOD AS HE'S EVER BEEN.

Pat studied the *Racing Post* with the same lip-chewing focus that he had once brought to Edward de Bono's Lateral Thinking. Singe Rana sat opposite him, a bookmaker's biro in his hand and his eyes fixed on nothing, figuring. Ken and I watched them from the other side of the room.

'He helps me,' Ken Grimwood told me. 'Your boy. He helps me a lot.'

I looked at him and sighed. 'You mean – doing a bit of shopping? Running errands? That kind of thing?'

'With me bets,' Ken said. 'Looking at form.' He raised his voice with a chuckle. 'We've had a few winners, haven't we, Pat?'

A nod of the wheat-coloured mop.

'He's meant to be in school,' I said. 'He's bunking off.'

Ken reached for his tin of Old Holborn, and the flat was silent apart from the sound of that metal box being opened. Then I made a move to get my son but the old man touched my arm.

'Can you blame him?' Ken said softly. 'We know why he's bunking off, don't we?' The old man produced his packet of Rizlas. 'Wouldn't you?'

I look a breath. 'I protected him when he was little,' I said. 'Then one day I couldn't.'

I watched Ken constructing his roll-up. It looked exactly the same as the tiny spliff of Mexican weed that Pat had smoked in the Wendy House.

'What do you want to do about it?' Ken said.

I looked at him. 'Really?'

He nodded once.

'I want to hurt them,' I said. 'Especially – the leader. The big one. William Fly. I want to hurt him the way he's hurt us. The way he's hurt Pat.'

The old man laughed in my face.

'A nice professional person like you?' he said. 'And you want to hurt someone?'

He struck a match and the smell of new tobacco joined the smell of old tobacco that always filled that flat. Pat turned the pages and big green headlines jumped out of the *Racing Post*. PRICEWISE. TRADING POST. TIPS BOX. TALKING POINT. COME RACING.

And I looked at Singe Rana and I remembered something that he had said about Italy. How the women smiled at him but the men could not look in his face.

Ken coughed by my side. That old death rattle cough that

I had heard before, as familiar to me as a track from Sinatra's *Songs for Swingin' Lovers*.

I looked at the old man and he smiled.

'Me too,' he said. 'I want to hurt them too.'

twenty-one

I had hated him for years.

I had told myself that it was because of the way he had treated my wife when she was his wife.

And I had told myself that it was because he had been a haphazard parent to Peggy, breezing in and out of her life as the mood took him.

But I saw now that my abiding loathing for Jim Mason was not quite so noble.

Because most of all I had hated him for loving her when her world was uncomplicated, unbroken and new. For loving her first, and for being loved by her in return – that's why I hated his guts.

Because she had loved him in a complete world. She was trying again with me. That's all. Trying again. She had always been trying again with me. I knew that now.

But as I watched his face in close-up on the monitor, I was shocked to discover that the old hatred just wasn't there any more. It would have been good to think that I was all grown-up now, and beyond sexual jealousy and romantic envy. But I suspected it was just that I no longer cared so much. And that felt like the saddest thing in the world.

'Are you watching this, Harry?' the director said to me.

I leaned closer. We were in the show's sound stage, an aircraft hangar of a building containing all the sets we would need for a series. But it all fell away – the cameras, the lights, the hovering make-up girls and continuity editors and the carpenters and the sparks – and all I saw was the monitor before me.

Jim was playing DCI Steele. He was in an Irish bar – we would dub on the Pogues' 'Rainy Night in Soho' later – and depressed after discovering his ex-wife was going out with a rich lawyer.

The scene didn't require him to do much – just sit there drinking whisky – iced tea – and looking suicidal.

But he was shaking.

The hand that held the pretend whisky was visibly trembling, and it seemed to transmit anxiety to every part of his body.

The director bridled with irritation.

'What's with the Method Actor crap?' he said.

I said nothing. The camera went in close and I had never seen such panic in a pair of eyes.

'I know he's supposed to be a recovering alcoholic who's about to fall off the wagon,' the director said. 'But this Stanislavski crap – being in the moment – it's too much, isn't it?'

Jim had not told them about the Parkinson's. They thought the trembling hand on the iced tea was Jim trying to be Brando.

And I wondered how long that could last.

'Shoot it,' I said, and I looked at that handsome face I had loathed for so long. 'He's good.'

We sat in the hotel bar and I watched Jim sip his beer. His hand was steady now. He smacked his lips and deliberately placed his beer on the coaster, smiling at me. He had a beautiful smile.

'It's not all the time,' he said. 'The shakes. Unwanted excitation of muscle, as my doctor calls it. They come and go. Today was the first time that I got it on set.'

I sighed. 'But it's only week three,' I said. 'You've got to tell them sooner or later.'

'Isn't that your job?'

'Probably. I guess. What about your agent?'

'She's not talking. Because as soon as it's news, my stock plummets. The bastards will write me out, I know they will. Who wants an actor who doesn't know if he'll make it to the Christmas special?' He looked at his strong, steady hands. 'The way I see it, I'm only really screwed when it gets to my speech.' Some hardness crept into him, and I had seen it before, in the early days when the wounds from his marriage to Cyd were still fresh. 'Parkinson's doesn't make you stupid. Mental faculties are not affected,' he said, and I could tell he was quoting his doctor again. He held his beer. 'They just seem to be affected because you can't control the muscles of speech.'

Over his shoulder I saw a middle-aged man and his daughter enter the bar. She was wearing a summer dress. He was in a suit jacket and jeans.

And then the man leaned into the girl and I knew it wasn't his daughter.

The man had to be around my age, although he was fighting it. With the jeans, the store-bought tan and of course with the girl.

And the girl was Elizabeth Montgomery.

'Don't they have drugs?' I asked Jim, tearing my eyes from her. 'They must have drugs.'

Jim grinned. 'Yeah, they have Benztropine, Benzhexol, all that good stuff to reduce muscle spasms. But it's a degenerative disease. They control symptoms. They're not a cure.'

There were no tables. A waiter escorted Elizabeth Montgomery and the man to seats at the bar. The man picked up a cocktail menu and squinted at it. With an embarrassed little smirk, he took out some frameless reading glasses.

Elizabeth Montgomery got up, kissed him on the cheek and left the bar.

I looked at the man and I wondered if he had a room here. And I wondered if there was a wife and kids waiting at the end of some gravel drive. And I wondered how he had met Elizabeth Montgomery, and how it worked.

219

When she came out of the rest room I was waiting for her. She didn't look remotely surprised to see me. Maybe she had clocked me when they came in. Or perhaps she was just a very cool customer, that Elizabeth Montgomery.

'Helping you with your homework, is he?'

She laughed.

There was one of those little mirrors in her hand. She glanced at it and then back at me.

'I don't need anyone to help me with my homework,' she said, and the mirror went into the small bag she was carrying. She didn't look as though she was planning to spend the night here. Or maybe they had checked in already. Or maybe it was all still undecided, and he would make his play after a few £15 cocktails. I felt sick to my stomach.

'He's too old for you,' I said. 'And what about Pat?'

Presumably she had thought about Pat already.

Still, I felt I had to ask.

'Maybe Pat's too young for me,' she said, and started back to the bar, her high heels click-clacking on the marble of the hotel lobby. I wanted to stop her but I knew I could not touch her. But she stopped just outside the bar. 'Look,' she said, 'I love Pat.'

'Yeah, looks like it. Drinking cocktails with Granddad.'

'Nick's thirty-five,' she said.

'Is that what he told you? And the rest,' I said. 'What did he tell you about his wife? Let me guess – she doesn't understand him but they stay together for the sake of the kids.'

'Isn't that what everyone does?'

'Very funny. Where did you meet him? In a chat room? They always lie about their age. He's grooming you.'

She smiled as if she was older than I would ever be. 'Unfortunately I am way beyond the grooming stage, Harry.' She looked into the bar. Her decrepit old lover was still squinting at the price of Mohitos through his reading glasses.

And I saw that she wanted me to understand.

'Pat is the most lovable boy I have ever met,' she said. 'He's sweet and gentle and all those things. But I am seventeen years

220

old and I am just not ready for all that big love stuff. Maybe I never will be. Maybe when I'm old. Twenty-five or something.'

'Don't do this to him,' I said, although I knew it was a ridiculous thing to say. The hotel maid was probably placing his-and-her chocolates on their pillows even as we spoke.

'Don't you get it?' Elizabeth Montgomery said. 'Pat's just too serious.'

She went back to the bar. I followed a few seconds later, reeling from a world where they could dump you for caring too much.

Jim had ordered another round of beers. He pushed one towards me.

'Keep an eye on Peggy for me, will you, Harry?' he said. 'Whatever happens. Keep an eye on her.'

I held his gaze. 'Always,' I said.

Then he had a conspiratorial smile on his handsome face.

'I hated you for so long,' he confessed.

They had pushed the furniture back to give them space.

The old man had two battered old leather pads on his hands, these scarred old mitts that were flat on one side and with a sort of glove on the other, and they made a sound like something cracking when he slapped them together.

Pat faced him, his long thin arms hanging by his side, his hand inside the huge brown boxing gloves that said, *Lonsdale – London – sixteen ounce.* They looked beyond old. They looked fossilised.

'This is stupid,' I said, and they ignored me. This wasn't what I had in mind at all. I am not sure what I had in mind. But not this wax on, wax off *Karate Kid* bullshit. This could get him killed.

Ken held up the pads either side of his head and shuffled forward.

'Double jab,' he said, and the boy tentatively poked his right hand at one of the pads. 'Southpaw, see?' Ken said to me. 'Leads with his right because he's left-handed. Double

jab,' he said, and again Pat struck the pads with the force of
a medium-sized butterfly. 'Good,' Ken said, but it sounded
like lavish praise to me. 'Keep that left tucked up. Elbow in.
The hand protects your chin and the arm protects your ribs.
Nice and neat. Not like a statue. Not just standing there
waiting to be clumped. Movement, movement. On the balls
of your feet. Dance, Pat, dance!'

Then he began coughing and had to sit down.

I sat down beside him.

'You want to see him dead?' I said.

Ken finished coughing and said, 'Do you?'

With rising panic, I watched Pat help Ken up from the
sofa – not easy in those big gloves – and they took up their
positions.

For a dying man with one leg, Ken was remarkably nimble
on his feet. I glanced at the photo of the young boxer on the
mantelpiece. Kid Loco, Ken had called himself. Almost thirty
fights when he was in the forces. Undefeated. Never knocked
down. He had told me, without pride or self-pity, that he
would have turned professional if he had not lost a leg at
Monte Cassino.

And now he shuffled forwards, backwards and sideways,
calling out combinations that Pat followed with gentle
obedience.

'Double jab – right cross – left hook,' Ken said, and Pat
meekly went through the motions.

'Look,' I said. 'He's not Kid Loco, okay? And he's not his
grandfather.'

'Typical modern parent,' Ken sighed. 'Wants to wrap the
kid in cotton wool.'

'Better cotton wool than a coffin,' I said.

'Dad,' Pat said quietly, and I looked at him. With the
thumb of his glove, he pushed back his hair, longer than it
had ever been. 'I want to, all right?'

But the violence wasn't in him. The spite. The malice. The
urge to hurt – it just wasn't there. It was one of the reasons
I loved him.

222

'All right,' I said.

'Double jab,' Ken said, and Pat hit the pad twice, slightly harder this time. 'Always the double jab. Like this.'

Ken threw out his left and the speed amazed me. It was as if he was catching a pair of flies. 'Everything comes off that double jab,' he said. 'Bam-bam, in their face. The rest follows.'

When we were driving home, I told him about Elizabeth Montgomery. I had to tell him, didn't I? Maybe not. But she would have told him. Or let him find out.

'I saw your friend,' I said, my eyes fixed on the road, although I felt his head snap towards me. 'I saw Elizabeth Montgomery.'

He was watching and waiting. He was thinking that maybe it wouldn't be so bad after all.

'She wasn't alone,' I said.

A beat. 'The guy from UTI?' he said, his voice very low. 'The one with the car?'

'Somebody else. Somebody older. Almost as old as me.'

Once that could have been his cue for a crack. *But, Dad – nobody's as old as you.* Not tonight. He said nothing.

'Sorry,' I said. 'Look, there are so many great women in the world, Pat. I know –'

'I don't want to talk about it,' he said. 'Okay?'

I nodded, my eyes on the road. 'Okay, kiddo.'

'And stop calling me kiddo,' he said.

When I looked at him he was staring at his hands with something like wonder, his fingertips lightly brushing the knuckles, scuffed raw and bloody from the missing layer of skin.

We slept differently at the start.

Before marriage, before Joni – at the start of our ten years – we wrapped ourselves up in each other, and we found that we fit. Face to face. Knee to knee. Mouth to mouth. You name it. We fit together. In those first nights I woke up with her limbs curled around me, and it was the best thing in the world.

But somewhere along the line – after the wedding photographs had started to gather dust, after the baby came along and the nights were split and sleep was suddenly like gold dust – we found that we both just slept better with our backs pressed together.

Still touching – always touching – from the soles of her feet to the delicate wings of her shoulder blades. And touching in the other way – the strokes and the pats just before sleeping or waking that said the same unsayable thing.

I am still me.

You are still you.

We are still here.

Nothing has changed.

But now our sleep seemed to have reached a third and final act. Now our backs turned to each other, but without touching, as if some barrier had built that neither of us could breach.

It was like sleeping in a single bed.

It was like sleeping alone.

'Do you ever feel that you are too old to start again?' Cyd said in the darkness, not turning towards me, her voice so soft and low she could have been talking to herself. I heard her sigh. 'To go through all that business – meeting someone, and seeing if it works, and wondering if what you feel is enough to live with all the baggage they bring? You ever feel like that, Harry?'

I lifted my head. I wanted to put my arm around her. Or just lightly touch her to send the old message. It is still me. But there was that barrier, you see, and I could not cross it.

'Cyd,' I said. 'Are we breaking up?'

'I feel that way sometimes,' she said, answering her question and not mine. 'Just too old and tired to try starting again.' I felt her pull her legs up and hug them. I wanted to hold her then, but I didn't. 'But then sometimes I feel too young to settle for what we've got,' she said. Then she laughed. 'It's a bit of a bugger,' she said, an American dedicated to keeping alive those old English aphorisms.

224

After that she said nothing.

And I must have slept for a bit because I saw my parents in a dream, in the living room of the house where I grew up and where they grew old, and it seemed so real, and so shockingly normal. As though everything was as it had been. But when I awoke with a start it was still dark with not even the first sign of morning showing at the bedroom windows. And my parents were long gone.

And as I lay there I believed that I could actually hear our children sleeping. The three of them. The boy. The two girls. All of them sleeping in their rooms, the sound of their breathing soft and, even in the night, like ribbons of solid air.

And I knew it was the only thing holding our home together.

The car stopped outside the twenty-four-hour supermarket.

'Can I have champagne?' Peggy said from the back seat. 'Just one glass of champagne? If I promise not to run amok? Or become an alcoholic?'

In the passenger seat, her mother turned to look at her.

'One glass,' she said. 'Then bed.'

Peggy clapped her hands. We had been to see an end-of-term production of *Guys and Dolls*. Peggy had stolen the show in the Jean Simmons role – the buttoned-up Bible-basher who lets her hair down when she falls for a charismatic bad boy.

Not all those kids were going to be stars of stage and screen. But when I watched my daughter – and I never thought of her as my stepdaughter, we had been together too long for that – when I watched her singing, 'If I Were a Bell' and 'I've Never Been in Love Before' and 'A Woman In Love', I believed that she might. And it wasn't just parental pride. I had known her since she was five years old, and she had always made life look easy.

Cyd stayed in the car as Peggy and I went inside the supermarket. 'And some bread and milk, Harry,' my wife called. 'Not just champagne, okay?'

225

'Can it be rosé?' Peggy asked me.

I laughed. 'It can be whatever colour you want.'

'You get the boring stuff,' she said. 'I'll get the champagne.'

I grabbed a basket and went off to find the boring stuff. I heard the bell on the door go, and the low rumble of laughter. I looked up, but I could see nothing. More laughter. I grabbed a loaf of Hovis, found the refrigerator and threw in a couple of pints. Then I went looking for my daughter.

She was by the wine shelves and the two boys were on either side of her. She was holding a bottle of champagne but she was not smiling now. Spud Face was holding a six-pack of beer and cackling as William Fly leaned his bluebeard face in close, whispering in her ear. My daughter averted her face, her eyes closed, but rooted to the spot.

'What's happening here?' I said. 'What are you doing to her?'

The three of them looked at me.

'Just talking, Daddy,' William Fly said, and Spud Face got a rise out of that.

I took Peggy by the arm.

'Let's go,' I said, and we paid and we left.

'What's wrong?' Cyd said when we were in the car.

Peggy shook her head.

'Nothing,' I said.

We went home and we drank our champagne. And I put on the original soundtrack of *Guys and Dolls* and we smiled at Marlon Brando getting to sing the best song in the production, 'Luck Be a Lady', when his co-star was Frank Sinatra. So that was good, getting a smile before bedtime.

But when the two of them had gone upstairs and I was certain that they were sleeping, I went out and got in my car and drove to the fireworks factory on the City Road.

Nobody stopped me as I walked through the gates. I shook my head. It was lucky there wasn't a gang of hardened sparkler thieves working in the area.

I found them in the warehouse, surrounded by the dusty

226

boxes of roman candles, Catherine wheels, bangers, rockets and jumping jacks. Singe Rana watched the old man and the boy as they went through the routines again and again and again.

'Don't stick your elbow out when you throw those punches,' Ken said. 'Tuck up neat. Nice and neat. Double up on that jab. Faster. Snappier. Where's the snap? Chin down. And don't be a statue. Up on the balls of your feet. Dance, Pat, dance!'

And my son danced. A different kind of dancing to his sister.

The old man held up the pads and called out combinations and the boy did exactly what he was told. And when they had a break, the pair of them soaked in sweat, I took the old man to one side.

'Is he ready?' I said.

Ken looked at me as if there was something that I still did not quite understand.

'Nobody is ever ready,' the old man told me.

Pat stood patiently, his gloves still on, clumsily cradling a bottle of water, lifting his face with his eyes closed tight as Singe Rana wiped away the sweat with a grubby towel.

'Bit soon to be back at work,' I said, nodding at the elderly Gurkha. 'He was in hospital five minutes ago.'

Ken looked at me as if I never ceased to surprise.

'What would you prefer him to do?' the old man asked me. 'Crawl away and die?'

twenty-two

I sat in the car park across from the bar.

Beyond a red velvet rope at the end of a tatty strip of red carpet, a forty-year-old skinhead in a Crombie stood guard next to a girl with a clipboard, the pair of them trying to pretend that it was Hollywood not Holloway.

And as drunks reeled in and out, I thought about moving away. I thought that maybe we could start again. All of us. Clean slates. New house. New school.

Australia sounded nice.

And as I saw them coming out of the bar, I knew it was too late for all that. Not enough time. And too much already on our slates. You get to a point when you know – this is it.

The skinhead in a Crombie lifted the rope so that William Fly and Spud Face could make their messy exit. There was a stray supermarket trolley parked in the road and Spud Face reclined in it as William Fly wheeled him across the street towards me.

I sank down in the car. William Fly launched the trolley containing Spud Face across the near-empty car park. He was a big strong boy. It spun around a few times and tipped over. When they had laughed about that for a while, William Fly scraped up his friend and they had a little chat. I looked at the bar across the street. The skinhead in a Crombie was looking down at the girl with the clipboard, his huge face shining with lust. And when I looked back, Spud Face was staggering out of the far side of the car park, heading towards the market that leads to the main drag.

And William Fly was weaving his way towards me, his car keys jingle-jangling in his hand.

He had a nice car. Its lights blinked an orangey welcome. He leaned against it, trying to decide if he wanted to be sick or not before he drove home. And when he looked up, I was standing there.

No recognition. Not a flicker. How quickly they forget. But his eyes lit up with malice.

'Who you looking at, faggot?' he slurred, turning to face me, even drunker than he looked.

'What did he ever do to you?' I said. My voice came out very soft. There was a group of girls falling out of the bar across the street, and I did not want any attention. But he still didn't get it. 'My son, you rotten bastard,' I said.

He squinted at me. Then he laughed, truly amused. 'Ah,' he said. 'Sick Note's daddy. Of course.' Then he was in my face, so fast that I almost fell backwards. I could smell the Red Bull and vodka on his breath. 'And?' he said, and I was afraid for the first time. But I needed to know.

'Why Pat?' I said, and something changed when I said his name out loud. It seemed to take something away from the youth in front of me. He took a step back and snickered.

'Just a bit of a laugh,' William Fly told me, looking at me sideways, as if I might see the funny side.

I shook my head and sighed. 'Somehow I knew you were going to say that,' I said. '*Just a bit of a laugh, innit?* It's the, *I was just obeying orders* of our time. You pathetic, overgrown piece of crap.'

Then he was suddenly tired of me.

'What you going to do about it, old man?' the big ugly bastard said. 'Give me a good hiding?'

He shrugged the stiffness out of his shoulders. I think he was planning to stick one on me and go home. Just that — a straight right to the chin and maybe a kick in the head when I was down. Then mirror-signal-manoeuvre all the way home, driving with the due care that only a drunken driver can muster.

'Not me,' I said. 'My son.'

He stared at me for a moment. And he didn't stop laughing until Singe Rana stepped out of the shadows with the blade in his hand.

William Fly and I both stared at the knife. It was an impressive sight. The kukri's curved blade seemed to fatten and bend in the moonlight. I realised I had stopped breathing. For a long time there was no sound at all apart from the distant boom-boom of the music in the bar and the much closer sound of William Fly wetting his Diesel jeans.

'He's got a sword,' William Fly said.

'He's got a kukri, you ignorant ape,' I said. 'It's better than a sword.'

After a while I realised that Singe Rana was looking at me. It was time to go.

William Fly tore his eyes from the kukri and looked at me with pure hatred.

'What's this?' he said. 'Dad's Army?'

'Exactly,' I said.

We walked him over to my car. I opened the boot and gestured for William Fly to get inside.

'You have got to be fucking shitting me,' he said, and I saw him look around and think about making a break for it. And now I stepped into his space, and now I was breathing in his face, my heart pounding, and wondering if we were all going to jail.

'Do I look like I'm joking?' I said. 'Do I look like I'm just having a bit of a laugh?'

He looked at the kukri and got into the boot. I had cleared everything out but it was still a tight fit.

'My dad is going to sue the pair of you,' said William Fly, curling up like a six-foot foetus. 'I have my human rights, you fuckers.'

Somehow that made it all a lot easier. The threat of legal action, the mention of human rights – that was the world this brute came from. Where everything you do unto others is forgiven by just being a bit of a laugh, and everything that might be done unto you is protected by your human rights. I slammed down the boot as hard as I could.

'It's not far,' I said, slapping it twice. Then Singe Rana seemed to slowly deflate in front of my eyes, and I put my arm around him as he sagged against the car.

'Just a sit down,' he said, through short gasps of breath. 'Then I am well.'

I sat him in the passenger seat, leaving the door open so he could get some air. The kukri had been slipped inside a worn leather scabbard and was hidden now under his nylon anorak. We could hear some metallic rattling in the boot, like a washing machine with a full load, and some coins left in a pair of jeans.

Singe Rana raised his smooth face and considered the supermarket car park as if it was one of the great sights of London.

He took a small paper-wrapped parcel from his anorak. Before he had unwrapped it I could smell the Aloo Chop. They smelled of ginger and onions. He offered me the spicy potato cakes and I took one.

'At the end of the war we had a choice,' he said. 'Gurkha troops could join the Indian army, the Pakistani army, or remain with the British.' He selected a potato cake and broke off a small piece. 'We stayed with the British and they sent us to Malaya. Rebels make trouble.' He chewed for a bit and waited until his mouth was empty before continuing. He had impeccable manners. 'There was a lottery for some of us to go to Britain. I was fortunate enough to be among those selected.' He glanced towards the sound coming from the boot. Under his calm brown eyes, the noise suddenly stopped. 'We saw Whipsnade Zoo, the Ford Motor works and Buckingham Palace, although we were not permitted inside. Then we went back to Malaya to hunt rebels.' He chewed thoughtfully for a while. 'In the end we got back to Nepal in 1956. Then Hong Kong. Then Britain . . .' He began to wrap the remainder of his Aloo Chop. It was time to go.

They were waiting for us just inside the gates of the fireworks factory.

Pat was in tracksuit bottoms and a school vest. Ken had a towel around his neck, and he was smoothing Pat's bare arms with long, slow strokes. I guessed that he was trying to relax his muscles, but it looked like something else. It looked like a gesture of love.

I popped the boot, and William Fly sat up like something unspeakable rising from its grave.

'Remember what I told you,' Ken said. 'Double up on that jab. Dance. And don't be a statue.'

Pat nodded, lifting his fists to his face as William Fly got out of the boot, looking around the fireworks factory, and then at Pat.

And then he smiled.

'Let's be having you,' Ken barked, and we all jumped.

William Fly swaggered towards Pat, stiff from the boot and still rat-faced from the bar.

My son met him halfway, Ken with one of his arms around Pat's shoulders, still smoothing his muscles with the other.

Singe Rana and I stood either side of William Fly, as if we were his seconds.

'Rules,' Ken said.

William Fly guffawed with contempt. 'Rules, old man?' he said. 'There are no rules.'

Ken's eyes got very small behind his glasses. 'There have to be rules,' he said. He patted Pat's belly, and then William Fly's. 'Everything above here is all right. No gouging, no weapons, no kicking.'

William Fly took a step back and aimed a winkle picker at Pat's groin. I pulled him back by the scruff of his neck.

'You kick him in his wedding tackle,' Ken promised, nodding at Singe Rana, 'and this man here will cut yours off. Got it?'

William Fly laughed, shook his head. Although they were around the same height, Fly's bulk made it seem as if he towered over Pat. The difference between them was the gap between a man and a boy. I have no doubt that Fly thought he would kill him.

Then Pat nodded. 'Let's just do it, shall we?'

They stepped apart. Above them the dirty neon of the factory's sign shone down like a dying moon. Then they came together.

William Fly rushed in, fists flailing, wanting to get it over with quick, and thinking he would, but Pat snapped his head back with a stiff jab. It was as if he hardly did anything – just stuck out his right southpaw lead and let William Fly's weight and movement do the rest as he walked straight into it.

Pat's fist came out again and again, the way he had been shown, as if he was catching flies. Jab, jab, jab. Every time his fist came out, William Fly's head snapped back. I saw the shock in Fly's eyes. I saw the first black spot of blood on his upper lip.

Pat bounced around in front of him, up on the balls of his feet, his guard high, his chin tucked into his shoulder. William Fly, flat-footed and bloody, took a step back. He touched the wet spot on his upper lip and cursed.

'It's a sideways sport and you're standing face on,' Ken shouted at Pat, his hands nervously tugging the ends of the towel around his neck.

Pat adjusted his stance, turning his body so that he was at a slanted angle to the larger boy. There was nothing for William Fly to hit.

He took half a step forward and Pat's fist snapped out, blacking an eye.

Then William Fly rushed him.

He took another light jab flush in the face, but this time he kept coming, his meaty arms wrapping themselves around Pat's neck. He tried to throw him over his hip but Pat stayed on his feet.

They waltzed around the factory forecourt, grunting and sweating, William Fly's hold unbreakable around Pat's neck, but unable to get him down.

I looked at Ken, wanting him to do something. But he just watched the boys, and he did nothing.

I went to his side. 'What's happening?' I said.

'Grappling,' the old man said. 'We didn't do grappling.'

'What do you mean, you didn't do grappling?' I said.

Pat went down. One brute movement and William Fly swung him from his feet to his back. One move. And then Fly was on top of him, straddling him, his knees on Pat's arms, the tattoo of his fists pummelling Pat's face.

It went on. Nobody said a thing. Not the boys. Not the men. I looked at Ken. He was staring at the ground, still tugging at his ridiculous towel.

'Enough,' I said, and took a step towards them but Singe Rana was there first, his arms wrapped around William Fly's shoulders, pulling him away.

Pat lay there for a moment and then sat up, blinking as if he had just awoken from a dream. He touched his head. I had thought there would be nothing left of his beautiful face. But somehow he just looked a bit bedraggled.

Ken helped him up. 'It's over,' he said, and Pat stood uncertainly on the legs of a newborn deer. 'It's over now, son.'

Singe Rana still had hold of William Fly but lightly now, and my heart fell away when I saw that he was not going to be punished any more.

'Shake hands, you two,' Ken said, but his authority seemed to have melted away, and William Fly just laughed and stuck up two fingers. Singe Rana let go of him.

'Shake hands?' William Fly said. 'Shake hands? Who are you? The Marquess of effing Queensbury? I'll shake his scrawny neck.'

But he made no move towards Pat.

And then suddenly William Fly realised that he was free to go. The gates of the factory were open. There was nothing and nobody stopping him.

Pat was standing unsupported, although his legs were still jelly, and now I could see that there was a small deep cut under one eye from a ring. His eye seemed to swell and discolour as I watched it. The beating was just starting to show.

Ken looked at me.

'You should give the boy a lift,' he said, and it took me a dumbfounded moment to understand that he was talking about William Fly.

'What?' Fly said. 'In his boot?' He dabbed at his bloodied nose, and patted his pockets for a mobile phone. 'I'm going to call my dad.'

Then he was gone.

Singe Rana took out his parcel of Aloo Chop. I watched Ken slap Pat once on the back and turn away. There was a thermos flask and a copy of the *Racing Post* by a kit bag. The old man began packing his things away. It was over. And I looked at my son, swaying in the breeze, his face looking more battered and swollen with every passing second, and then at the old man.

'That's it?' I said with disbelief. 'That's our revenge?'

'That's it,' he said, putting his belongings away. 'And I never promised you revenge.'

'It went very well,' I said. 'Don't you think it went really fucking well?'

Finally he looked at me.

'You don't get it, do you?' he said. He glanced over at Pat, who had decided to sit down for a while. The boy was holding a spicy potato cake, but seemed to have no idea what to do with it. 'It's not about winning,' Ken said.

'Don't tell me,' I said. 'It's the taking part that counts.'

'No,' the old man said. 'It's the standing up for yourself that counts.' He zipped up his kit bag. 'Being a man. It's the being a man that counts.'

I felt like laughing in his face. Because I felt like I had been hearing this stuff all my life. *Walk tall. Be hard. Be a man, little boy.* And this is where the philosophy of my fathers had got us – to a beating in the forecourt of a fireworks factory.

'Can we go home now?' Pat asked.

*   *   *

Cyd got up when she heard us.

We were in the bathroom, Pat sitting on the edge of the bath as I swabbed at the blood under his swollen eye. The cut from the ring was deep and neat.

Cyd stood in the doorway, fastening her dressing gown, staring at Pat's face without expression.

'I'll do it,' she said, and I let her.

She said nothing as she cleaned him up. First she got off the caked blood, and then she dabbed at the cuts with TCP.

The sound of crying from down the hall.

Joni, calling out in her sleep.

'I've got it,' I said, and before Cyd had a chance to reply I went down to Joni's bedroom. She was sitting up, rubbing her eyes. I sat on the bed and took her in my arms.

'An asteroid,' she sobbed. 'An asteroid is going to hit our planet.'

Her body was so warm. I touched her forehead, checking for fever.

'No, it's okay,' I said. 'An asteroid's not going to hit our planet.'

She was suddenly furious.

'An asteroid wiped out the dinosaurs,' my daughter insisted. 'Rulers of Earth for a hundred and sixty million . . .' a pause to choke down a sob '. . . years. Dead. Gone. In seven days. Wiped out by a giant asteroid.'

She simmered down. I patted her back, kissed the top of her head. She got back under her duvet.

'That's the dinosaurs,' I said. 'That's not us, Joni.'

'But the average gap,' she said, although she was fading fast. 'Average gap between giant asteroids striking Earth.'

'Average gap?' I said, not following.

'Every hundred million years,' she said, taking a deep breath and as she let it out, she seemed to slide deeper into sleep. 'A giant . . . asteroid . . . hits Earth . . . every hundred million . . . years . . .' I patted her head as she buried it into the pillow. 'Dinosaurs . . . sixty-five million years ago . . . so . . .'

She yawned.

I completed the math for her, stroking her hair.

'So that means we're due for another asteroid in thirty-five million years,' I said. 'Little darling, let's worry about it in the morning.'

When I was sure that she was sleeping, I went back to the bathroom. Pat's eye seemed to be closing by the second and yet somehow he looked a bit better now that Cyd had removed the dried blood. Or maybe it was just being cared for that made him look a bit better. As though he was safe now.

'All right?' she said.

'All right,' he said.

When she had finished, the floor of the bathroom was covered with white towels that were stained a strange rusty brown. Then she made him open his mouth and inspected his teeth.

Then she smiled. A private smile, something between the pair of them.

'You'll live,' she said.

But she told him to go down to the freezer, find a pack of frozen peas and hold it against his eye for as long as he could stand.

'Okay,' Pat said. 'Thanks, Cyd.'

He left us.

'That poor kid,' she said. 'What did you do to him now?'

I reached for her as she brushed past me. I said her name, softly because I did not want to wake Joni, but she just kept going. I watched her enter the darkness of our bedroom.

'Sorry, Harry,' she said. 'I'm just too tired for you now.'

After a few moments I followed her. I got undressed and slipped under the covers, our bodies not touching, a few inches and several light years apart. I lay there for a long time without sleep coming. I did not turn on the light.

And I must have slept at some point, because I woke up to the sounds of them leaving.

The bags being lugged downstairs, the diesel engine of the taxi in the street, and the excited chatter of Joni deciding what books she would take.

237

I got out of bed and went to the window. Cyd was watching the driver hefting a suitcase into the cab. I came downstairs and found Joni kneeling beside another suitcase, and stuffing a tattered copy of Jacqueline Wilson's *Sleepovers* into her pink rucksack.

'We're going on holiday,' my daughter told me, her eyes shining. 'We're going to have a bit of a break.'

Cyd came inside and looked at me.

'Peggy's going to stay on with her dad for a while,' she said. 'I think it will be good for both of them.'

I shook my head and held out my hands.

'I hope Pat's all right,' she said. 'That cut is the worst of it.'

She reached for the suitcase but I picked it up. Not because I wanted to help her but because I wanted to stop her.

'Where are you going?' I wanted to know.

'And I hope your friend doesn't suffer too much,' she said. 'The old gentleman.'

'He's not my friend,' I said. 'He's my father's friend.'

'I think he's your friend, too,' Cyd said.

I shook my head. 'When are you coming back?'

'I don't know. I just need to catch my breath. I need to see where I am. Do you ever feel that way, Harry? I feel that way all the time.'

She reached for the suitcase but I held it away from her. Our daughter stood in the doorway, her pink rucksack turned towards us, looking at the cab.

'Don't stop loving me,' I said to my wife.

'I'm trying,' she said. 'It's just a bit harder than it used to be, okay?'

I nodded. And when she reached for the suitcase for a third time, I let her have it. Then I picked up my daughter and I kissed her although she squirmed in my arms because kissing was gross. I put her down and she ran laughing to the cab. And I felt that if I lost her then it would be the end of my world.

I followed them to the kerb and I told our daughter to

mind her fingers as I closed the door. Then I watched them go. The taxi's brake lights flashed red twice in farewell as they reached the end of our road, and then they were gone.

I looked up at the sky, checking for asteroids, and then I went back inside the house, closing the door quietly because my son was still sleeping upstairs. He had no school today.

He had no school on any day.

twenty-three

We stopped at the top of the stone steps and the stadium laid spread out before us.

The expanse of green like a secret garden in the heart of the city. The track of wet sand. The six traps waiting, open. The old men in flat caps and the young men in trainers. Everybody smoking, coughing, studying form, then looking up to watch the greyhounds being walked by their handlers.

Pat sucked on his cigarette and narrowed his eyes.

He was wearing his school uniform but it looked like something a pirate had plundered from a dead midshipman. Buttons missing or dangling by a thread on his Ramsay MacDonald blazer. The Ramsay Mac tie rakishly tucked inside his shirt, like a David Niven cravat. The top two buttons undone on his white shirt. Bunking off had turned into a way of life. I knew he wouldn't go back.

'You'll stop one day,' I said, looking at him with his cigarette. 'Right? The smoking thing. It can't go on forever.'

He nodded, toking hard. 'When I'm thirty,' he said, and I could tell he honestly believed that he would never be thirty, not in a million years. 'Don't worry. I want to live.' Then his face lit up. 'There they are!' he said.

The old men had parked themselves down by the winning post. As we approached, they raised their ancient faces. Ken from the *Racing Post*, Singe Rana from the programme.

'Going to miss this old place,' Ken said, and we all looked

at the condemned dog track. 'Online poker. Internet bookies. E-casinos. What a load of old bollocks.'

They were tearing Badham Cross dog track down. This was the last BAGS meeting ever, but even free admission had not tempted many punters through the gates. Only the young men with no jobs to go to and the old men who had nowhere else to go. And the boy who should have been in school.

They stood in the first sunlight of summer, watching the dogs.

'That one,' Ken said, getting out his tin of Old Holborn. 'Number six. He smells the blood.'

We watched the greyhounds approach, as sleek as panthers. The dog in black-and-white stripes with the red number six had his nose in the air, his eyes black and gleaming. He was a very light brown, the colour of a beach at the end of the day.

Ken coughed as he rolled his snout. 'Don't tell me that mutt's been training with some tin bunny,' he said to Singe Rana, who just shrugged at him. 'Look at him,' Ken insisted. 'He's had more live rabbit than you've had Aloo Chop, sunshine.' Ken looked at Pat. 'He's already had a couple of winners, the jammy git.' Then back at his thoughtful friend. 'When's your lucky streak going to end?'

Singe Rana didn't look up from his *Racing Post*. 'It is not a lucky streak,' he said. 'It's an era.'

Ken licked the Rizla on his roll-up as the dogs came past us, heading for the traps. 'Only Boy,' he sighed, and it took me a moment to realise he was talking about number six.

Pat studied form. 'Only Boy is a long shot,' he said doubtfully. 'Beaten every time in thirteen starts.' He nodded at the red numbers flickering on the tote betting board. 'The smart money's all on Vigorous Fella.'

'But Only Boy smells the blood,' Ken insisted.

He drew deeply on his roll-up and then embarked on a coughing fit. When it had stopped he blinked at us from behind his glasses, his eyes wet from the effort. 'You can't stop them when they smell the blood,' he pointed out, taking one last suck on his snout before he tossed it away. It tumbled down the old stone steps, sparks flying. 'Get on it,' he whispered to me.

I nodded. Pat and I went down the steps to the rails where the line of bookies were waiting, and he put our bet on: £25. First place or nothing.

'A pony to win on Only Boy for the young scholar,' the bookie said, and his assistant wrote it down. 'Good luck, son.'

The noise was rising when we came back. It was that giddy, fleeting moment when everyone in the place still believed, when everyone still had a chance. The dogs were in the traps.

The metal rabbit came rattling by on its ludicrous run.

Pat offered Ken a cigarette and he shook his head. The old man smiled at the boy. The pair of them looked back at the traps. The dogs came bursting out with a metal clack and then there was the pounding of their paws on the sand, and the sound of their panting. Their tongues hung out like strange pink lizards and the cries of the men and the boys drowned out the metal clatter of the rabbit.

Only Boy had come out of the traps as if he was late for dinner. Vigorous Fella hung on to his tail but he was always falling away and by the final bend Only Boy was a length ahead. Pat and Ken jumped up and down, clinging on to each other, and in the final straight Singe Rana just smiled and shook his head with disbelief.

'He smells the blood!' Ken shouted. 'He smells the blood! I told you!'

Only Boy came past the finish line and Ken turned away, his fists full of Pat's Ramsay Mac blazer, his face shining with triumph.

Then some cloud seemed to pass across his eye and as all around us the men threw away their losing tickets, I watched the life seem to just seep out of him. Pat was still laughing, and Singe Rana slapping him on the back, the pair of them

242

staring at the track where the greyhounds had reached the rabbit. It was still now, and the dogs were bashing their muzzled mouths against it.

But I saw Ken Grimwood reach for the breath that did not come, and I saw his hands fall away from my son's school blazer, and I caught him as he fell.

Much later I read about the Victoria Cross he had won at Monte Cassino. For some reason – a lack of imagination on my part – it had never before crossed my mind to find out how he had won it, just as I had never wanted to talk to my father until the day that it was too late to ever talk to him again.

And so I discovered that on Valentine's Day 1944 Ken Grimwood had single-handedly attacked an enemy machine-gun post in the rubble of the bombed monastery. Despite suffering from multiple wounds in his legs, and with all his comrades dead or wounded, he had used his Bren gun and hand grenades to kill the crew. Then he directed fire at enemy positions until he was relieved by New Zealand troops. He had done these things when he was just a few years older than my teenage son.

He had taken the lives of men, and he had saved the lives of other men. He had come very close to dying for the freedom of generations yet unborn – and he would have laughed in my face if you had put it like that. Then he would have told you that he fought for his friends, and that he fought for his survival. That's what he would have told you, and it would have been true, but it would not have been the entire story.

You would not have looked twice or even once at this old man if you had seen him standing at a bus stop. But he had lived a life that mattered, a life of weight and importance. And that was strange.

Because when I held him in my arms on the day they closed down the old dog track, and I smelled the Old Holborn and Old Spice on him for the very last time, it felt like he weighed nothing at all.

*   *   *

After midnight, Pat and I stood at the vending machine sipping scalding-hot hospital tea that we did not want.

I looked at my son and I remembered taking him to see my father just before the end. Was he four or five years old? He must have been five because he had started school. But it had been a mistake.

They had worshipped each other, my son and my father, and because of some misplaced sentiment on my part I thought that they should have a chance to say goodbye. But Pat was too young and my father was too sick. It was brutal for both of them.

'Ten years ago you were full of questions,' I said, moving the plastic cup from one hand to the other to prevent third-degree burns. 'What happens when we die? Do we really go to heaven or is it just an endless sleep? If God really exists, then why does he allow all this suffering?' I nodded, both hands burning. 'That's what you asked me after we came to see your granddad. All the big stuff. All the big questions.'

He laughed. 'I remember,' he said.

But I wonder if he really did. Sometimes what we think we can remember are just stories that we have been told by our parents.

'You grow out of all that, I guess,' he said.

'Asking the big questions?' I said.

My son shook his head, and blew on his tea. 'Expecting any answers,' he said.

We went back to the ward.

We sat either side of his bed, watching him sleep.

There was light coming from somewhere, that hospital night-light that is as unavoidable as moonshine, and I could see his face inside the oxygen mask that was clamped over his mouth, and I could see where the straps pressed into the flesh of his cheeks.

He was in the High Dependency Unit with eleven other men, and we could hear them moaning and moving in their

244

sleep, and sometimes the sharp electric buzz of the metal box that called for help, and then the voices of the nurses – soothing, reassuring, endlessly practical – as they did what they could.

'He hasn't got long, has he?' Pat said.

'It only ends one way,' I said. 'You know that. People talk about bravery when someone's fighting illness.' I shook my head. 'In the end, that's meaningless. A life just narrows down to a point of pain, and bravery doesn't come into it.'

Pat almost smiled. 'If it was just about bravery,' he said, 'then he would get out of that bed and walk out of here tonight.'

I watched my son watching the old man's face, and I thought I knew what he was thinking. Even with the oxygen, the air being pumped into those exhausted lungs was not enough. Ken's chest rose and fell in that restless sleep, the breath wheezed and strained. Not enough air. Never enough air ever again. It was like watching someone drown.

Nothing anyone can do, I thought bitterly. I had called his children, and left messages on their machines. Singe Rana had gone home and would be back in the morning. All anyone could do now was to sit and wait for the end.

A nice Chinese doctor gave us a reassuring rap about making him comfortable. But that just meant pumping him with enough opiates to kill the pain. Until the pain killed him. Already his face had the ghostly pallor of morphine.

Ken moaned in his sleep. Pat reached out and held the old man's hands. Ken twisted and settled, and the moaning stopped. Pat continued to hold his hands. It seemed to soothe the dying old man.

The boy held the old man's hand. 'I'll stay with you,' he said.

And so I was wrong.

There was still something that could be done.

The night moved slowly. I must have slept for a while because his voice jolted me awake. The fog had cleared for a moment, that fog that comes in with the morphine and smothers the pain but also smothers everything else. Above the oxygen mask his eyes were shining with tears and fear. The terror of it, I thought. Knowing the ending is here in this bed in this room and there is nowhere to go.

Pat was staring at him, wide-eyed and alert. The boy had not slept. He leaned forward as the old man's words came out on a trickle of breath. Their hands clawed at each other.

'This is not me,' the old man told us.

I stood in the hospital car park and I shivered in the dark as I watched the day creeping in. A smear of white over the East End, and then the birds starting up as a halo of light appeared above the rooftops, then the flat red glare of sunrise. It wasn't so cold. I felt my body relax, and I realised I was tired and needed to sleep. I leaned against the hospital doors and closed my eyes. I snapped awake when a woman said my name.

'Harry?' she said. 'Thanks for being here.'

Tracey and Ian. I looked at Ken Grimwood's grown-up children and I tried to see him in them. Ian had those gimlet eyes, like little blue lasers, but his face and his body and his manner were just too soft to resemble his father. I could see more of Ken in Tracey – not so much the broad forehead, or the sharp razor-cut of a mouth – but the unforgiving, implacable hardness in her. It was there even now, even after they had been crying all night long.

'My son's in with him,' I said. 'Your dad seems to like him being there.'

Tracey nodded briskly, as if the family were taking over now, and the old man would like that even more.

'It hasn't always been easy,' Tracey said. 'In fact, it's never been easy. My father can be a very difficult old man,' she said, and her words got clogged up on the bitter truth of it.

Ian had started to cry again. I didn't look at him.

'But you can always make up for lost time,' she told me. 'It's never too late, is it?'

I nodded and I watched them go through the hospital doors to see their dying father.

'Isn't it lovely to think so?' I said.

Pat came out after a while.

I knew he could talk to the two adults. He could handle it. He was gracious enough, smart enough, sensitive enough. He would tell them what kind of a night their father had had. He would be able to accept their stuttered thanks. Then he would know when it was time to go. I knew he could do all of that and I wasn't worried.

I was proud of him. Proud of the man he was growing into.

I watched him light a cigarette and suck on it hungrily, struggling to keep my eyes open. It was full summer daylight now, and getting brighter by the moment.

'I might go in,' he said after a while, and at first I thought he meant go back into the hospital. 'To school,' he said. 'To Ramsay Mac. I might just go in today.'

I shook my head, suddenly completely awake.

'You don't have to,' I said. 'It's nearly the end of term. You missed all your exams.'

A flash of something in those blue eyes.

'Maybe I didn't miss them,' he said. 'Maybe I strolled in and knocked off my exams, and they were all a piece of cake, and I'll do better than all of those thickos.'

I brightened. 'Is that what happened, Pat?'

'Maybe,' he said. 'Who cares? Exams mean nothing. They don't get you to stay in school so you can find a better job. They get you to stay in school because it keeps the unemployment figures down.' Then he nodded, deciding something. 'But I want to go in today. When they are all there. All of them. Every single one of them.'

'Nobody at Ramsay Mac cares if you show up or not,' I said, feeling uneasy. I felt that he was free of Ramsay Mac now, and that we should put it all behind us.

I did not want him to go to school.

'But I want to,' he said, reading my mind, and exhaling two trails of smoke from his nostrils. He crushed the cigarette under his scuffed school shoes and kicked it into the gutter. 'I just think it's something I should do,' he said.

So we went for some breakfast and then I drove him to Ramsay Mac for the very last time.

Out in the playing fields they were erecting some kind of marquee. This big white Bedouin tent for the last day of term, for all the prize-giving and the back-slapping and the speeches. I thought it likely that we would probably skip all that.

The bell was tolling for the start of lessons as we pulled up outside the gates. But the exams were over, and the holidays were coming, and the Ramsay Mac regime was even more lax than normal.

And so they were all outside the school gates.

All of them. The regular kids, who just wanted to get through it all in one piece, and the rest of them.

William Fly. Spud Face. The assorted snickering thugs and butterfly-tormentors that attach themselves to the likes of Fly and his spud-faced henchman.

And Elizabeth Montgomery, more beautiful than ever, almost a woman now, and an engagement ring the size of a Ramada Inn flashing on the third finger of her left hand.

They were all there. The one my son had loved, and the ones who had made his life a misery, and all the bit players in their ragged blue blazers.

They watched him get out of the car and approach the gates.

Then their eyes turned to William Fly, and they saw him as he looked away from Pat's face, and stared at the ground.

Pat walked to the gates of Ramsay Mac and William Fly stepped aside. The boys who followed him did the same. Elizabeth Montgomery did not move. She just scratched her ear, the fat diamond ring flashing in the end-of-term sunlight.

Then William Fly nodded at Pat, almost deferential, dipping his broken nose.

But Pat walked past them all, his long hair shining, his blue eyes staring ahead, as if none of them were even there.

My son walked into school.

And they all left him alone.

twenty-four

False alarm. No need to panic.

Gina wasn't a lesbian after all.

The new guy was in her kitchen making us tea. He was wearing a silky vest and snug shorts and his hard, hairless body was almost hysterically male. His skin jutted with carefully nurtured muscles that had been pumped and pampered and fed with protein. He looked like a condom stuffed with walnuts. I was more of a lesbian than he was. We smiled at him as he placed a tray before us, and then withdrew to the kitchen for more domestic chores.

'Wow, Gina,' I said. 'He's got muscles in places where I don't think I have places. Where did you find him?'

She sat cross-legged on her sofa, pouring milk for the pair of us. She knew how I liked it. She didn't need to ask. She was wearing tracksuit bottoms and a T-shirt. Hair pulled back so you could see that fabulous face in all its slightly goofy beauty. No make-up, skin still glistening from her early morning exercise – whatever that might have been.

'He works at the same gym as Siân,' she said, fussing over our cups. One sugar for me, none for her. Just a dash of milk for both of us. 'We struck up a conversation when he helped me with my glutes.'

'Very romantic.'

I sipped my tea, ever so slightly disappointed that Gina had not stuck with being a lesbian. There would have been something strangely reassuring about a woman who goes off men after breaking up with you. Turning your ex-wife into a lesbian – you could take it as a backhanded compliment.

'Siân was just so possessive,' she said, reading my mind. 'The sexual jealousy – my God! Worse than a bloody man.' She sighed. 'Shall we go outside?'

We went out to the balcony. Four floors below us Soho was caught between night and day. There were still hollow-eyed revellers sipping one last espresso in Bar Italia and going for breakfast in Patisserie Valerie, but the security grilles were coming down all along Old Compton Street.

'I want it to be better, Harry,' Gina said to me, and when she looked at me, the years fell away. All the dead ends and disappointments and distractions – working in Tokyo and a small army of Mr Rights and Mr Right Nows and her short-lived career as a lesbian – none of it mattered as much as what we had once been together. Because I knew exactly what she meant.

'I want it to be better too,' I said honestly. 'For you. And for Pat.'

'I wanted to talk to him,' she said. 'Before he left. Before he went back to you. I wanted to tell him – I don't know. That I loved him. That I had always loved him. But it didn't happen. Somehow I never got the chance. He just packed his stuff and left. He was here and then he was gone.'

She glanced back at her apartment, as if seeking evidence that he had really lived here for a while. But there was nothing.

'We wait for these big moments,' I said. 'When everything will be settled and revealed. And most of the time, they don't happen. People just go.'

'But when he was living with me,' she said, 'it was like we were two strangers. He wasn't that little boy any more. That blond moppet who wouldn't put down his light sabre. He was this . . . teenager. And I didn't recognise him.'

'That happens,' I said. 'They grow up. And it's true – you don't recognise them. You struggle to find the connection between this great big scowling lump and that sweet little kid with the light sabre. But he's still the same boy.'

251

Did I really believe that? I knew that I loved him now because I had loved him then. But it was different for Gina. She had missed so much. I knew she wanted to make up for all the lost time. She was ready – now she had worked out where she wanted to live, and who she wanted to sleep with, and now she was done with all the endless searching for the core of herself. But while she was preparing herself, while she was getting ready, our boy had grown up.

And it was hard to love a stranger. For both of them.

'What's he like, Harry?' she said, and I felt the time piling up between us. She looked like a kid today – what with the sun shining on her toned skin, and all the good sex with the new guy, and her hair pulled back. But Gina was not a kid any more, and there were unknowable years between us.

'He likes football but he's not that good at it,' I said. 'He likes lateral thinking. And he likes racing.'

She looked interested. Gina the health nut. Gina the queen of the cardiovascular workout. I think she imagined they might bond over their deltoid thrusts. 'Racing?' she said. 'Field and track? Working out, you mean?'

'Horse racing,' I said. 'And dog racing. Greyhounds. That kind of racing.'

She frowned. She disapproved. She wanted him to be someone that he would never be.

'And cigarettes,' I said. 'He enjoys a Marlboro Light at every opportunity, although I imagine someone will get him to stop one day. But it won't be you or me. It will be a woman. Or it will be a child. And he will stop for them. Because he loves them.'

'I want us to do things together that he enjoys,' Gina said grimly. 'But what am I meant to do? Buy him a packet of fags and take him to a betting shop?'

'Yeah, that would work,' I said. 'They're not that hard to please, Gina,' I said. 'Kids – they don't want much. They just want your time. They just want your attention. Someone said to me, "They need your love most when they deserve it

252

the least." He was talking about that difficult age, I guess. When they suddenly look like strangers.'

Mr Universe strolled on to the balcony. He was swigging an orange protein drink out of a plastic beaker. He looked like he could crack nuts between those biceps. I was very impressed.

'Not now,' Gina said sharply, waving him away.

'Girls have just started,' I said. 'I think he may have lost his virginity with Elizabeth Montgomery. She dumped him, but I think he still likes her.' I shrugged. 'I know what you mean when you say you don't recognise him any more. It's true. Something changes when they become teenagers, and you struggle to see your kid in there. The sweetness. The innocence. But it's still there, if you look hard enough.' I looked at my watch. It was time to move on. 'He's a beautiful boy, Gina. He places great stock in kindness. Get beyond the surly surface, all the mood swings and the Marlboro Lights, and smoking Mexican weed in the Wendy House and all the stuff that he is already growing out of, and he is just a beautiful boy who is growing into a good man.' I looked at her and I could just about see the girl I had loved. 'It's like the old song,' I said. 'To know him is to love him. The problem is – you don't know him, do you?'

She flared up at that and, funnily enough, at that moment I could see him in her.

When he was four years old and his mother had walked out and it was clear she wasn't coming back by teatime, he had looked at his lovely face in the rear-view mirror of my car. *Who do I look like?* he asked me.

And the truth was he looked like both of us, although the taken-for-granted beauty had nothing to do with me. That dirty blond hair, those stabbing blue eyes, the sweep of the jawline – he was a good-looking boy and he got all that from his mother. But what had she done for him lately? Being a parent is a daily slog, or it is nothing. Fish fingers, Cyd had told me. Fish fingers and name-tags and nit combs. And she was right. That's what being a parent is made of.

'He's as much my son as he is your son,' Gina said, and we both knew that, somewhere in the unrecoverable past, that had stopped being true.

She turned towards the kitchen, where Mr Universe was waiting.

'We made a good kid, Gina,' I said. 'We really did.'

It was the best I could do.

Pat would be there when he woke.

Night and day had lost their meaning, and Ken would wake when the morphine was wearing off. He would twist with the incoming tide of pain, and try to sit up, and that's when he would need the oxygen mask over his face, and then some water on his lips, and then the mask again.

A glass of water sat on one side of the bed but it never needed to be refilled. So an intravenous drip stood on the other side of his bed, hooked to a vein in his left arm.

The waiting exhausted me. It exhausted his children. Even his oldest friend, Singe Rana, would slip away when it was near midnight and the ward was bedding down. For the hours piled upon the hours, and there was nothing to do but sit by his side and watch him sleep. Well-meaning gifts sat by his bedside, fruit and flowers and copies of the *Racing Post*. All unopened, and all unneeded now.

The total isolation of death. The loneliness of the dying man. That is what I had noticed about my father's death. We loved him but, in the end, we left him and he died alone. Because we were tired. Because it was late. Because there was nothing we could do. We loved him and yet he was on his own.

But when Ken awoke in the dead of night, flinching with the pain that was never far away now, his mind numbed by the opiates but not so much he did not know, he was never alone.

Because the boy never left his side.

You never knew what would be waiting for you at the hospital.

Sometimes I hoped that I would get there and it would all be over, and the thought made me fill with shame.

Because our every instinct is to cling to life, even when life has narrowed to a world of pain. And I could not stand seeing him in that place, endlessly and senselessly tested, coming out of the fog of drugs when all that was waiting for him was more suffering.

Enough, I thought, as I left Pat with him one night and went home to my empty house. Hasn't he suffered enough?

But when I went back in the morning, Ken was sitting up in bed, his eyes shining with life, his face covered in shaving cream. In his striped pyjamas he looked like Father Christmas having a bit of a lie-in, and I laughed in that place for the first time. He had rallied. And I knew that could happen too.

'I want to get spruced up,' Ken said.

He talked the language of my father. *Getting spruced up.* Meaning – to make oneself smart, to become presentable to the world, to have a shave even though there is something growing inside me that will kill me very soon. *Getting spruced up.* When did getting spruced up go out of fashion?

There was a silver dish full of steaming water by his bed. Pat was holding a cut-throat razor. He approached the bed, the blade glinting in the hospital lights. The old man raised a hand.

'Do you shave yet, son?' Ken asked him, pressing back against the pillow.

'Every Sunday,' Pat said. 'Well, more like every other Sunday.'

'Then better let your dad do it,' the old man said. They both looked at me.

'If you don't mind,' Ken said, and I quickly shook my head. 'Try not to cut me bleeding throat,' he suggested.

'You don't stop moaning, do you?' I said, taking the razor. 'You really are a grumpy old man.'

'I've got a lot to be grumpy about,' he said, and the shaving foam on his face split in a big grin.

I dipped the razor in the water and began to scrape the stubble from his face. It was surprisingly tough, like the stumps

255

of crops left in a field after harvest, but the skin beneath was smooth. He cleared his throat and lifted his chest as he released a wheezing breath. I could hear the blocked lungs struggling for another breath.

'Keep still,' I said quietly, wondering if that was even possible, but he did not move again. Then I felt the curtain around his bed pull back and when I looked up my wife was standing there.

'Please,' she said. 'Carry on.'

She was holding a covered tray of food. I could smell sausages and batter. Ken opened his eyes, smiled and closed them again.

'Hello, love,' he said, and he sort of sighed with contentment. I think it was all of it. Feeling the stubble scraped from his face, the sight of a woman bringing the gift of food. And he liked getting spruced up.

And my wife watched me shave the old man.

She stood there, one hand holding the tray of food, the other resting on Pat's shoulder, and she watched me and the old man with those wide-set brown eyes. I looked up at her once. She half-smiled, and nodded, so I carried on. I did not look at her again, but I could feel her watching me. And it sounds stupid after ten years and marriage and children and all the rest of it. But as she watched me shaving the old man, I sort of felt that she was starting to really like me.

And when I had finished shaving Ken, and the silver bowl was full of foamy water and his face was clean and pink and smooth, and his throat had not been cut from ear to ear, then Cyd unwrapped the small tray of food, and it was really special.

These little Yorkshire puddings with half a pork sausage inside each one and a curly smear of English mustard on the top.

'Toad-in-the-hole,' Ken said. 'Little ones. Never seen that before. Lovely.'

And we all admired the food that she had made, even though we all knew that he would never eat it.

256

She did not stay very long. And when it was time for her to go, she hugged the old man and kissed him on his freshly shaved cheek.

'Smooth as a baby's bottom,' Ken chuckled, and I looked away because I knew that the pair of them would never see each other again.

When I looked back she was hugging Pat.

She had this special way of hugging him, and it had not changed in ten years. A short, fierce hug and then suddenly letting him go. They nodded at each other, and something seemed to pass unspoken between them.

Then she looked at me with half a smile and slipped out of the curtain. I followed her. She banged through the ward's swing doors, wanting to get out of there, but I caught up with her in the corridor.

'Hey,' I said, lightly touching her arm, and she turned round and placed her mouth on mine.

I staggered backwards, still kissing her, and knocked against a double-parked IV drip.

She kept on kissing me and so I kissed her back. And even as I heard the amused laughter from the nurses' station down the corridor, my head reeled with dumbfounded wonder at the way our mouths fit so perfectly. A mouth that is a perfect fit for your mouth. That's not such an easy thing to find, if you ask me.

'It's the proximity of death,' I gasped, coming up for air. 'It makes us want to cling to life. It always –'

'Don't talk,' she said. 'Don't try to say anything smart, Harry. Not right now, okay?'

'Okay.'

'And don't do your Barry White voice.'

'I wasn't even going to do my Barry White voice,' I said, a bit offended.

And she kissed me some more, but saner kissing now, less feverish, less desperate, and when a nurse walked past and said, laughing, 'Oh, get a room, you two,' Cyd took a step away from me.

I stood there looking at her.

'Are you coming home?' I said, touching her arm. She let me do that. 'Are you? Come home. Come home, okay?'

She looked at the ground. 'I'll see you, okay?' she said.

'Is Joni all right?' I said. 'She's not worried about an asteroid hitting Earth?'

'She hasn't mentioned the asteroid,' she said. 'I think she's more concerned about global warming. Climate change, that's the big fear now. And the Weeping Angels from *Doctor Who*.'

'Those bastards,' I said, with feeling.

'The asteroid – she's over the asteroid.' Cyd took a breath. 'But she misses you.'

'And I miss her,' I said. 'And I miss you. And whatever problems there are, we can work them out. Because I'm lost without you.' I shook my head. 'And I will always be lost without you.'

It was true. It would always be true. So I reached for her. I thought maybe one more go at the kissing could win her round.

But she backed off, arms folding protectively.

'I'm going now,' she said.

I nodded. I could read the signs. With her arms folded, I could see there was no more kissing to be done right now.

And nothing else to say.

'All right,' I said, and then I felt the panic as she turned away. She was really leaving. But this time I did not follow her.

'See you then,' I said, just for something to say, but she did not turn around. She just raised her left hand in farewell, and the way she held it there for a moment longer than strictly necessary made it seem as though the gesture meant something more. *I hear you, I love you, but I am going now.* That is what I saw in her gesture, although I could have been kidding myself.

But I noticed that on the third finger of her left hand, Cyd still wore her wedding band.

And that had to mean something, didn't it?

The way she walked away, the way she waved goodbye

without turning round – it was straight from the end of *Cabaret*, one of my wife's favourite films, when Sally Bowles leaves the man she has loved and goes back to her life. Except that old Sally Bowles wasn't wearing a wedding ring when she walked away.

And in my experience, a ring makes all the difference when you are trying to walk away.

The ring, and the children.

twenty-five

I wandered the empty house.

There were traces of the family we had been, archaeological clues to a previous lifetime. A pink scooter in the hall that Joni had grown out of. A paperback called *Love Sucks* that Peggy had finished with on the garden table, a sensitive vampire boy looking mean, moody and undead on the front cover. And, everywhere, the traces of my wife.

Her winter clothes. Her CDs by Enya and Macy Gray, original cast versions of *Oklahoma!* and *West Side Story* and *Singin' in the Rain.* Old copies of *Grazia* and *Red.* The books of films she had loved. *Chocolat* and *The English Patient* and *The Unbearable Lightness of Being.* And especially in the kitchen — her workplace, her domain – things that she had bought because she needed them, or because she thought they were nice. All these jolting moments that brought the reality of her home to me in a way that I had never felt when she was still here.

I found a T-shirt in the bottom of the laundry basket and I buried my face in it. It said Juicy on the front and it was threadbare and comfortable. And I could smell her on it and it made me reel with the longing for her. I missed my wife. I missed my daughter. I wanted my family back.

And the old question from years ago gnawed at me now, as I wondered if Pat and I were still a family. Did we qualify? If there was just the two of us, then could we still call ourselves a family? Or was that just a bit too grand for our two-man band?

I wanted to believe that we were still a family. But I don't think you are a family if there are just the two of you left.

I think that you want to be, you really do.

But if I am honest, I think you are just trying.

Pat was sleeping when I got to the hospital.

It was the middle of the day, and the ward was full of the clanking of the lunch trolley, and the smell of inedible food, but Pat lay slumped in his chair with his head lolling forward, totally exhausted.

I looked at Ken. I could hear his breathing snagging deep inside his chest, but he looked better. Perhaps it was the shave, but he looked more like himself.

Pat stirred and opened his eyes.

'Come home for a bit,' I told him. 'Get your head down in your own bed. Have a kip.'

Have a kip. That was another one. The language of my father's generation. Soon it would be gone forever. Pat stood up and stretched, looking at Ken.

'Just a smoke,' he said, and so we left the cancer ward because my boy was gasping for a cigarette. Outside the glass doors, Pat blinked in the first sunlight he had seen for a while.

'He had a good night,' Pat said, lighting up. 'I only had to use the mask once. One of the nurses told me that it sometimes gets better before the end.' He squinted at me through a haze of smoke. 'Do you think that's true?'

I shrugged. 'I don't know. It goes up and down, I guess. He might be better than he was a while ago. But it's always getting worse.'

'He said his wife was there,' Pat said. 'Dot?'

'Yes,' I said. 'Dot.'

'That freaked me out. He was so certain she was there. What's all that about? Is that some kind of hallucination because of the drugs? Or is it something else?'

I thought about it.

'I would like to think it's something else,' I said.

261

We said nothing for a while, thinking about the dreams of the dead, and when Pat had finished his cigarette, we went back inside.

There was a middle-aged man sitting in the chair that Pat had occupied for days, watching Ken's sleeping face. He stood up when we came into the room, and he wiped his eyes with the back of his hand. Short, muscular, tanned. I knew who he was before he opened his mouth.

'Mick Grimwood,' he said, and he shook our hands, and from his accent you would never have guessed that he had grown up in this city, and in this country.

'From Melbourne,' I said. 'Your dad talked about you a lot.'

We all looked at the old man.

The weight had fallen off him. I saw that now. Mick's face was a mirror image of Ken as a younger man, and with him at the bedside I saw how much weight his father had lost.

'Does he have a passport?' Mick said.

I was stunned. 'A passport?'

I thought of when I had looked through the drawers of his home, and when I had seen the ransacked contents of those drawers strewn across the floor of the tiny flat.

Had I seen a passport among the remains of a lifetime?

I could not remember.

'I don't know, Mick,' I said. Pat and I exchanged a look. The guy was clearly out of his mind with jet lag and grief. I wanted to be gentle with him. 'But he's really sick,' I said. 'Your dad is really sick.'

He lifted his chin with impatience, and suddenly he was every inch his father's son.

'I know how sick he is,' he said, 'and that's why I want to know if he's got a passport.' Ken stirred in his sleep and his son's hands clenched and unclenched with frustration. 'I told him to always keep his passport up to date. I bloody told him, I did.'

'He's better,' Pat blurted, and I tried to silence him with something in my eyes, the way I always used to. It didn't work any more. 'But he is though,' my boy insisted. 'A little bit better. You said so yourself.'

I wanted to stop this madness.

'Mick,' I said. 'You really think he's up to making a trip?'

'This would be one way,' Mick said.

And then I finally got it.

Ken going to Australia at last.

Not to live.

But to die.

The police were raiding the flats.

Blue lights swirled on the four sides of Nelson Mansions and gave the proceedings a jolly, festive air. Children rode their bikes up and down their walkways, shouting with delight at being up way past their bedtime. Residents came out to watch officers in Kevlar stab-proof vests streaming up the stairs. Some were already on the top floor, shouting orders to open up. They were directly above Ken's flat. They had come for the Old Lads.

In the courtyard there were three cop cars and one van, all with their disco lights twirling, all parked where they felt like parking. I got out of the car and Tyson came up to me, thoughtfully sniffing my leg, as if remembering the good times. His thick leather lead with silver spikes was trailing on the ground. I patted him on the head and looked up at the flats where the cops had started to swing a battering ram.

'Let's look for it and go,' I told Pat.

He followed me up to Ken's flat, with Tyson trailing behind. More people were coming out of their homes. I had never seen such a feeling of community at Nelson Mansions. Perhaps it was always like this for police raids. Above us we could hear a door caving in. Screams, shouts, curses. And a ripple of polite applause from the spectators on their walkways. And cheering, as though justice was being done at last. I slipped the unfamiliar key in the lock.

I searched the living room. Pat and Tyson took the bedroom. It was not a big flat but it felt like Ken had never thrown away a piece of paper in his life. My fingers tore through offers of home delivery sushi, double-glazing solutions, pizzas he would never eat, cleaners he would never employ, limousine services he would never need. Bills for gas, water, electricity. A stack of postcards from Australia, curling with age, from a time when people still sent postcards. And then a photo of Dot. And then a tattered envelope – a strange colour somewhere between blue and green – the colour of the sea.

CERTIFICATE OF SERVICE if said on the front and his name, and rank, and number. And inside it was stuffed with yellowing paper. The actual Certificate of Service. My eyes ran over it, catching on details. Where born – village – *Deptford*. Where born – county – *Kent*. Trade brought up to – *Metal machinist*. Period volunteered for – *for the period of the present emergency*. Marks, wounds and scars – *scars on knees*. Wife – *Dorothy Maud Lillian GRIMWOOD*.

A square piece of blue paper fell to the floor and I picked it up. Buckingham Palace, it said. *Admit one to witness Investiture.* Signed by the Lord Chamberlain. Dot's ticket to see Ken meet the King.

Pat appeared in the bedroom doorway. 'Got it,' he said, waving a passport. Tyson bobbed excitedly at his feet, sensing the mood. Blue lights danced across the walls. The sounds of violence seemed to be directly above our heads.

'Let's get out of here,' I said, and the dog bounded ahead of us.

They were taking the Old Lads down. We stopped at the end of the walkway and watched them go. Those giant hard-boiled-egg heads lowered with defeat and loathing. Hands behind their backs, the fight knocked out of them. The cops in their Kevlar vests keen to be on their way.

'You go,' I told Pat. 'Get in the car and lock all the doors. I'll only be a minute.'

He looked at me for a moment and then started down, the dog panting at his feet. In the courtyard the back doors of the van were open. One of the Old Lads banged his enormous

264

shaven head hard against the roof as he was stuffed inside. The spectators laughed appreciatively.

I ran up one flight. The walkway was empty. A ribbon of blue police tape fluttered across the smashed door. DO NOT CROSS, it said, and I slipped under it and went inside.

Flat screen TVs lined the hall. Consoles for video games. Rubbish sacks full of handbags and gladrags with designer labels. Fancy phones and poncy palm-held devices. I opened a door and it was the bathroom. The tub was full of more shiny black rubbish bags. I opened one of them. It was full of credit cards. The place was a treasure trove of stolen goods, an Aladdin's cave of bent gear.

I looked over my shoulder. Through the open door I could see the blue lights had gone. Doors were being closed. Voices were fading. The children were being packed off to bed.

I went deeper into the flat.

It became more jumbled back here. Treasure shaded into junk, or at least items that were not easily disposed of. A wallet that contained nothing but the photo of a smiling child. A big gold Rolex watch where the second hand moved at a stuttering gait, marking it as a fake. And on top of a dustbin overflowing with plastic handbags and watches with rubber straps and an outmoded video player the size of a suitcase, I saw the box I was looking for.

Claret, edged with gold.

Small enough to hold in one hand.

I picked it up. I pressed the clasp and it opened. On the top half of the box there was ancient white silk and in small black letters it said, *By Appointment*, above the lion and the unicorn. Below that there was a name and address: *J.R. Gaunt & Son, Ltd, 60 Conduit Street, London.*

And in the bottom part of the box, held by a crimson ribbon and resting on dusty-looking purple velvet, there was the Victoria Cross.

For Valour, I read. I closed the box and turned away.

The cop grabbed me by the throat and sent me flying backwards.

I went over a stack of Blu-Ray DVD players and smashed the back of my head on a home cinema unit. The cop took a fistful of my shirt and pulled me to my feet. He put his face in mine and kept it there as he opened the box. I could feel that Kevlar vest like a brick wall between us. And I saw that he was around my age. He stared at the medal for quite a while and then back at me.

'This belong to you?' he said.

I shook my head. 'To a friend,' I said.

'Let's discuss it at the station.'

Then the door to the bedroom flew open and an old woman with a baseball bat came out screaming.

She swung at the policeman's head and he just about got out of the way. The bat shattered the screen of monster TV. Still screaming blue murder, she lifted the bat to swing again.

The mother of the Old Lads. They loved their old mum.

Then I got out of there as fast as I could, the medal in my pocket, leaving the cop in his stab-proof vest and the old woman with the baseball bat, grappling with each other among that useless luxury.

We sat in the half-darkness of the ward at night, the curtains pulled round the bed, and Mick's voice was soft so as not to disturb the men who were sleeping. Ken was propped up in bed, his hands crossed on his chest. His breathing sounded like the wind.

'You drive out of Melbourne for sixty miles,' Mick said. 'At San Remo Bridge you cross to Phillip Island.'

'That's the fish-and-chip place,' Ken said.

Mick nodded. 'Big fishing fleet at San Remo, Dad. They'll do you the best fish and chips in the world there.'

Ken nodded, satisfied. Mick continued.

'On Phillip Island, the penguins only come out after it starts getting dark. Avoiding predators. But then as soon as it's dark they come bombing out of the sea, masses of them, more penguins than you can believe, Dad, out of the sea and across the beach and into the dunes, into their burrows.

Thousands of them, Dad. Thousands of penguins coming out of the sea and parading across Summerland Beach every night of the year.'

Ken laughed at the thought of it, and then the laughter turned to a cough. I nodded to Pat and we slipped out while Mick helped his father with the oxygen mask. He was getting pretty good at it now. When we were on the other side of the curtains, Pat looked at me, reluctant to leave.

'He's all right,' I said. 'He's got his son now.'

twenty-six

I drove them to the airport.

The old man in the passenger seat, immaculate in his blazer, shirt and tie, although the clothes seemed to hang on him now. But his breathing was good and even today, and his face clean-shaven. The smell of Old Spice filled the car. He was all spruced up.

Now and again he would tap the tin of Old Holborn in his blazer pocket but he made no attempt to light up. I told myself that he was waiting until he got on the plane.

Mick dozed in the back seat, still jet-lagged from coming the other way. Pat and Singe Rana sat on either side of him, the pair of them craning their necks as we got closer to the airport, and the planes started to fill the sky.

Qantas had put on a lovely spread for him. Oxygen tank. Wheelchair. A pretty young woman with Melbourne in her voice and sunshine in her hair. Ken waved it all away, although he was frail now, and moved very slowly, that old rolling sailor's gait long gone, and he could only walk with one arm entwined very tightly in the arm of his son.

The family were waiting for us at the check-in desk. Ian and Tracey, wreathed in smiles. Their partners, and assorted children and grandchildren, scratching their navel rings and staring blankly at their mobile phones, wanting to be somewhere else, anywhere else. A baby was thrust into Ken's arms. He admired it for a moment and then handed it back.

'Dad,' said Tracey, throwing her arms around her father. 'Oh, Dad!'

Ken gently pulled himself away, looking at his bent boarding card.

'I almost forgot,' he said, reaching into the pocket that contained his Old Holborn. He took out the small claret box. We all watched him open it, take one brief final look at his Victoria Cross, and close it again. Then he gave it to Pat.

'Thank you,' said the boy, and he held the old man's medal with tender care, as if it was a bird's nest with eggs in it.

Tracey stared at my son as though she wanted his heart and liver. When she spoke her voice was trembling with rage.

'You silly old man,' she said. 'Do you have any idea of the value of that thing?'

Ken smiled at her. He didn't say, *'Do you?'* But that's what his look said.

She was speechless. Just for a moment. 'You can buy a *house* with what that would fetch at auction,' she said, and she glared at Pat, and for a second I thought she might try to wrestle him to the ground.

'But I'll never sell it,' Pat said, and he slipped it inside his own blazer pocket.

Ken shook his head, as if it did not matter what he did with it.

He just wanted him to have it.

'Come on,' Tracey said to her gormless tribe. 'We're going home.' She looked back at her father. 'And I hope you get savaged by a rabid penguin, you silly old git.'

Ken chuckled as they walked away.

We walked them to international departures where we could see the long queues of people being processed. Still holding on to Mick, Ken looked down at his boarding card, running his thumb and forefinger across it, although it didn't really need straightening any more. Singe Rana took out a paper-wrapped parcel and gave it to Ken. I could smell the cayenne pepper and turmeric spice of the Nepalese potato cakes.

'Aloo Chop,' Ken nodded. 'Just the job.'

269

He did not shake hands with his friend. He did not shake hands with any of us. We stood around awkwardly for a moment or two, not knowing quite what to do or say, listening to the security and immigration guards barking their bored commands in the background, and then Ken moved it along with three little words.

'Time to go,' he said.

And so they went.

We watched them for a while as their queue snaked forward. And we saw Mick helping his father with the laborious rigmarole of modern travel, helping the old man to remove his shoes and belt and watch. Then Ken went through the metal detector and set if off. A young man frowned at him sternly as he fished the tin of Old Holborn from Ken Grimwood's blazer. Ken went through again, standing unaided now, his hands in the air as if surrendering. And after that we could not see them any more. But the three of us lingered at the airport, Pat and Singe Rana and me, because without talking about it, there was really nowhere we would rather be.

Two hours later, we were up on the observation deck, the entire airport spread before us beyond the great glass walls. Pat turned to me with a grin.

'Look,' he said. 'It's him.'

A white plane with a red tail was taxiing towards us. As it headed for the runway I could read the words on the side. *Qantas – Spirit of Australia*, it said. There was a slash of white on the red tail, and when it got closer it revealed itself as the silhouette of a kangaroo that was as sleek as a greyhound.

The plane turned, moving parallel to the observation deck for a minute, no more, as it pushed out to join the other planes that were lining up for the runway. And I saw him.

In a window seat, with his son beside him. Mick turned and said something to his father and the old man seemed to be belatedly buckling up his seat belt.

I called his name, knowing it was stupid, knowing he would never hear me.

And then I found myself walking by the glass wall of the

observation deck, keeping up with the plane at first, and then seeing it pulling away from me, and starting to run. Just before I lost him he turned and looked out of his window.

He did not see me. But I saw the late afternoon sun catch his glasses, and turn them into golden orbs. He was smiling.

Then just before the plane was gone from my view, when I had reached the end of the glass wall of the observation deck and could follow it no further, I saw the old man lean back and take a breath.

It was not the kind of breath that I had seen him take all those nights at the hospital – shallow, grasping, desperate. No, it was nothing like that. It was a breath that suggested that he had all the time in the world. I saw him take that breath, and I saw him let it go, his head tilting slightly towards the window, the sun still catching his glasses, the faint smile on his lips.

I said his name one last time, my hands pressed against the glass.

And I watched him go.

I was at my desk when the fireworks began.

A long, slow crack of the sky, like summer lightning. I looked up at the window of my little room and then I turned back to the script. There was something wrong with it.

There should not have been anything to complain about, but I was struggling with *PC Filth: An Unfair Cop.* The money was good, and the ratings were buoyant, and there was no heavy lifting involved. But it made my heart feel like it was made of lead – all these alcoholic cops struggling with their ex-wives and their alienated children.

Was there no officer at the station who could have just the one glass of Australian Shiraz and then go home to bed with his wife? Was there not one uniformed or plainclothes policeman in the Western world who could just sink a few beers and then go home in time to read his kid a story at bedtime? Could a cop get divorced without becoming an alcoholic? Why was it so difficult to hold on to ordinary goodness?

The summer lightning again.

The long slow splitting of sky, followed by an eruption of stars. I heard voices in the street. People were coming out of their houses to look. I went to the window.

And I saw the sky ablaze with exploding light. Rockets that soared with a melodramatic *pheeeeew* and then ignited into a storm of falling colours. Trails of fire that seemed to launch with blistering speed, but then in slow motion collapse in beautiful dying lights. High above the City Road, the fireworks filled the summer sky.

Then I looked down when I heard the diesel rumble of the black cab outside our house, and I saw their shadows in the night. Doors slamming, suitcases being removed, the fare being paid. And the voice of my daughter asking something, and the voice of her mother as she replied. And high above us, the fireworks continued to go off like all the stars in the heavens coming to life for one brief shining perfect moment.

I ran down the stairs as fast as I could and I reached the ground floor just as Joni appeared in the doorway. We stood there staring at each other.

My daughter grinned uncertainly and I realised that she had lost her vampire smile. One of her two front teeth had come all the way through, and the other one was almost there. She was growing up.

'Hello, gorgeous,' I said.

'Have you seen them?' Joni said excitedly. 'All the colours? Up in the sky?'

I nodded, lifting my eyes to what Singe Rana had unleashed on his tea break.

'It's incredible,' I said.

I took her hand and we went to meet my wife as we heard her footsteps at our front gate. Then Cyd was standing before me, putting down her suitcases.

She gave me half a smile.

Maybe a bit more than half.

I took her in my arms and I loved her face, just loved it, and I knew that I would love it always, and I would watch

272

it get older over the years and I would never love it less than I did tonight.

Our mouths lightly touched.

They were still a perfect fit.

She rested her forehead against mine.

'What took you so long?' I asked her.

Cyd gently sighed. 'The Finchley Road was a bitch,' she said.

Then our daughter was squirming between us, taking our hands, tugging us towards the door where the sky outside was still exploding with lights, and I could feel her really pulling us with all her strength, as if impatient to show us the wonders of the world.

twenty-seven

On the last day of term I stood in the empty playground looking out at the playing fields of Ramsay Mac.

The marquee was still standing but as I started towards it, one bone-white wall billowed like a sail and fell gently to the grass. A few workmen appeared where the wall had just been, and I saw the stage, the lectern, and the row upon row of white chairs, all empty but for the few that Pat stretched across at the back.

He saw me coming and raised a hand in salute.

My foot kicked something and I saw that there was games equipment scattered all over the playground. Netballs, foot-balls, cricket bats. And esoteric stuff. A discus, shot putt and a couple of javelins. More equipment spilled out of a shed at the edge of the playground, its door hanging off its hinges. I idly dribbled a football ahead of me, reflecting that you never really lose those silky skills, and I picked it up as I reached the marquee.

I sat down in the row ahead of Pat and we watched the workmen dismantling the stage, their voices soft in the haze of the late afternoon. They spoke in a language I did not recog-nise. Another wall came down and we could see the fields, the chalky markings of the running track, and the goalposts beyond.

'Coming back in September?' I asked.

'I don't know yet,' he said. 'September's a long way away.'

I inwardly chuckled at that.

'Best days of your life,' I said, and I watched my son's slow smile spread across his face. He reached out and took the football from me, clutching it to his stomach like a hot-water bottle.

There was some female laughter from the playground and we turned to look at a group of girls tossing a netball at each other. They all had their Ramsay Mac ties worn around their foreheads like bandanas. I thought that I recognised one of them, but I wasn't sure.

'Elizabeth Montgomery?' I said, and the name still had that old power.

But Pat smiled gently.

'I talked to her,' he said. 'When they were giving out the prizes and making the speeches, some of us were at the back of the fields having a smoke. And I talked to her then.' He looked at me briefly. 'She told me about that guy. The one you saw her with at the hotel. She said she liked it that he could understand a wine menu. But she didn't like it that he needed reading glasses.'

'Women, eh?' I said. 'There's just no pleasing them.'

We stared at Elizabeth Montgomery and her friends. School was over for all of them, but they lingered on, mucking about with the pilfered sports equipment, reluctant to leave this place and join the grown-ups.

As the marquee continued to fall on every side, a pair of brown eyes flashed towards us. Elizabeth Montgomery's black hair swished in the summer sun.

'I might talk to her again,' Pat said, hugging the ball in his arms, and glancing at me as if he was breaking some prior arrangement.

'Go ahead,' I said. 'Don't let me stop you.'

I was not here to pick him up or anything. I was just checking that he was all right. But I should have known. He was going to be fine.

'Because that's the big secret, isn't it?' he said. 'There's no secret language that you have to learn. There's no secret language of girls. You can say anything you want.'

I got up to go. I felt like I was getting in his way. The walls of the marquee had all come down and the workmen had started to stack the chairs. In the playground Elizabeth Montgomery was chasing one of her friends with a netball. She looked up at Pat and then laughed as she looked away, hurling the netball at her shrieking friend.

Pat cuddled his football.

'You fancy a game?' he said.

'You're kidding me,' I said. 'Go and get your girl.'

'We've got time for one last game,' he said. 'Come on.'

So we stepped out of the dismantled marquee and on to the football field of Ramsay Mac. Pat looked at me and smiled. Then he turned away, facing the nearest goal, and booting the ball as high as he could. We ran off, both crying out as we collided, and as I looked up at the sky the ball seemed to eclipse the sun for a moment, and then start to come down.

And we went after it, skidding and sliding across the grass in our unsuitable shoes, holding on to each other and pushing each other away, laughing and protesting, our eyes to the heavens, and waiting to see where it would fall.